D1519283

All rights reserved

The characters and events portrayed in this book are fictitious. Any similarity to real persons, living or dead, is coincidental and not intended by the author.

No part of this book may be reproduced, or stored in a retrieval system, or transmitted in any form or by any means, electronic, mechanical, photocopying, recording, or otherwise, without express written permission of the publisher.

ISBN: 9798426025486

Printed in the United States of America

FOR CLAN O'REILLY

CONTENTS

MARA O'REILLY

PART ~ ONE ~ 2042

MARA O'REILLY

ONE ~ THE SCOURGE

❖ ❖ ❖

They considered us The Scourge of the Earth; it was a name we had earned through our own actions. At one point, we had been conquerors, the highest achievers in world history. But history had been scrubbed of this flawed way of thinking. We were now known for our true nature—we were the Oppressors, the Colonists, the Unwanted. We were no longer brave explorers, now we were invaders. Imperialists. Unwelcome. Those who dominated without consideration or care. We were evil, and we had caused more damage than good.

The world, it seemed, would have been better off without us. At least, that was the message they shared as nations earnestly worked toward correcting our dominion by eradicating us. Our place in history, having once been documented and recorded by our own people, was being re-written; a revisionist retelling which lifted the veil of our accomplishments and exposed them for what they truly were—evil, arrogant, and aggressive.

For many years, it was a common belief that we were The Scourge that must be excised from the world like a cancerous tumor. The fewer there were of us, the safer the world would become. There had been a time when thousands of our own kind had shared this sentiment, and willfully chosen suicide. Many believed that death was the only way we could ever make amends or atone for our Crimes Against Humanity. To them, ours was not a debt of monetary value, but a debt which could only be paid in blood.

But we were still here, after countless murders and suicides throughout those dark years. Despite all efforts to purge us from the nation, despite open discrimination and bigotry, despite endless persecution, we had not been exterminated. For many, our refusal to disappear was yet another example of why we were unforgivable and still dangerous. Our mere existence was a disgrace; it was a bitter slap in the face to everyone whose family members had once historically experienced tragedy or suffered at the hands of our own ancestors. To them, our complete and utter extermination was the only acceptable solution.

Still, we endured. And as we could not be entirely destroyed, we must be dealt with. They needed to reconcile that we were still part of this nation, and genocide would not be a viable option. Reparations, as much as possible, needed to be made, and our place within this new world must be clearly defined. The only way we could ever truly atone for the acts of our ancestors was to surrender entirely—to live humble lives, submissive and compliant, dutiful, and obedient. We must be silent as much as possible, eyes downcast, meek in both action and deed. We had an obligation to honor the new ways, to take ownership of all that our kind had once done to the world, and denounce it. Attrition was our only salvation. Shame was our only redemption.

This was what it meant to be The Scourge. Evildoers. Devils. We were Unworthy; polluted and tainted by bad blood and genetics, cursed with an inescapable legacy. This was who we were, and it was imperative we remember that it was only by the grace of our betters we were not all executed on sight like many of our fellow countrymen had advocated for. Being allowed to live was an honor and a gift. We would do well to never forget this, or our place.

Even this was not enough to appease many of our countrymen. They might never have been satisfied, but they promoted another method of restitution that we should pay to show we were authentically contrite. We must also abstain from bearing more children, to stop the perpetuation of our seed. Choosing not to reproduce was what was best for the world. If we were truly apologetic, we agreed with this policy; it wasn't law, but it was the only socially acceptable solution. Ensuring our evil bloodline was permanently stricken from the world was the only thing we should be proud of.

We were never to confuse our personal desire to reproduce with our global responsibilities to abstain. They had taught us this important lesson from our very first years; it was as ingrained as knowing why sterilization and abstinence were necessary for our society, and why we must always remember to prioritize our communities over our own selfishness.

I was part of The Scourge.

My destiny was likely to be spent in solitude. My best contributions could only be achieved if I did the most honorable thing which could be asked of someone of my lineage: I must forfeit procreation in order to let my evil genes die out. It was the only way I could achieve worthiness, and the only means I had to earn my place within society.

As I was not a parent, I could not speculate as to how great of a sacrifice this was. However, I resented that the choice was not entirely mine to make, and I often contemplated how we could consider ourselves free when they had denied so many freedoms either through law or social pressures. It was likely my poisoned blood that planted such thoughts within my brain, always making me more contrarian and silently rebellious than not, always questioning everything, never learning my place. A Good Person wouldn't resist doing what was expected of them. A Good Person would embrace what should be done for the betterment of our world. A Good Person would accept one's place without question and comply as commanded.

It was all further evidence that I was of a corrupt bloodline, and the world was right to demand I did not reproduce. It was always better to rid the planet of poisoned, toxic seed lest it fester, grow, and spread like a noxious weed. Because, as we were all taught, an invasive species could obliterate that which was Good and Necessary for our own nourishment and well-being if left on its own.

As I was the last of my bloodline, I sometimes struggled with these thoughts. Not so much about having children—they had thoroughly conditioned me not to waste time entertaining such notions—but rather what it meant to live a life without purpose. What would my purpose be, without reproduction, without a family? How could I have a life well-lived without love or connection? How did one even justify being alive if fulfillment did not come through family, friends, or a chosen field of education or employment?

And so, with no genuine sense of purpose or a meaningful existence, I stumbled through my days, living in perpetual limbo, waiting for my life to begin.

TWO ~ A ROUTINE EXISTENCE

◆ ◆ ◆

The morning of Week 31 in the Year of Our Lord, 2042, the sun was shining. It was expected to be a hot day, with temperatures in the 80s. Any summer day in the Pacific Northwest was beautiful, but on the West Coast, the skies were seldom clear enough to hit such highs. I was glad to have the day to myself.

My timestamp said it was almost 9 in the morning. This was a normal time to rise for me as I worked the swing-shift and usually did not start work until 4 p.m. They assigned my job based on my test scores; I had been working in our community library since I was a teenager. It was the only job I'd ever held. Being of The Scourge, I was typically expected to work in the back and to conduct my work with as little public interaction as possible. Given the hostility I received—not to mention the judgmental comments—I preferred this. I tried to do my primary responsibilities first and waited to return books to the shelves until after the library closed so I did not have to go into the public areas or see anyone. Sometimes this required me to work later than my required hours, and though I did not receive additional compensation for the extra time, it was well worth it for the solitude this system enabled me. They did not want to see any of The Scourge any more than I imagined most of The Scourge wanted to be seen.

But today was not a workday. Today was one of my four days off per month, and I intended to do what I usually did: shopping, cooking, reading, and resting. It had been a tiresome week, and all I longed for was to be alone.

After showering, I walked to the local market set aside for my kind. I made my purchases for the week and then took the long way back so I could walk along the trail by the lake.

Upon returning home, I made an easy lunch of bread and cheese and settled onto the patio with a library book. I was not expecting too much from it, but it was one that had been on the list for 'must-reads' of the summer. It was a short list.

The book was predictable, and an easy read. I never had to consult the dictionary. I was entertained, and not left with any uncomfortable new ideas or unsettling feelings. Everything about it was exactly as it should have been. The author was from an appropriate background, the word count was within contemporary range, and there was nothing offensive or unacceptable within its pages. The story was as unassuming as its author.

And so I passed the day.

THREE ~ AN EVENING
AT THE LIBRARY

◆ ◆ ◆

It was now the start of Week 32 in the Year of Our Lord, 2042. I was informed that there was a new shipment of books waiting for me in the back room. The head librarian, referring to me as M1 again instead of Margaret, told me I needed to sort through both shipments. She stated that one crate had been donated by a private donor delivered earlier by the Services For The Deceased, and the second was from the Primary Library Services—it would be the same shipment sent to every library throughout the nation. They issued almost all of our books through the Primary Library Services, as were the bulk of our deliveries. The Primary Library Services worked collectively with the publishing industry, who worked collectively with the nation's editors, literary agents, and authors, all of whom worked collectively with the Government Oversight Committee to ensure non-offensive and suitable content for everyone. There would be nothing remarkable contained in their shipment.

Books donated by private donors were always interesting though, and I often wondered about the people who loved to read and were no longer among us. It was standard for the books of the deceased to be donated to their local library branch, but sometimes the families kept physical books as they were frequently rare and difficult to find. Since the Primary Library Services became the main printers and distributors of printed materials, countless titles were out of print—even titles that had not yet been banned. It was just another means of controlling information without taking an aggressive stance; one couldn't read questionable things if they were inaccessible. It was a subtle power play by the government, and less likely to raise dissent than blatant outlawing.

Many of the books donated ended up being decades old, and often were considered too aged to grace the library shelves. Despite this, we still received donations regularly. It was part of my job to sort through such collections, though usually it was less than a handful per night. I once read that only about ten percent of citizens actually owned any books made from paper anymore, and obviously that ten percent weren't dying every day.

I worked first with the returned books, scanning them all back into the system and stacking them on metal trays to be transported back onto the shelves once the library closed. After this, I began adding the newest additions sent from the Primary Library Services into our system. This occupied my time for several hours and carried me through until the head librarian had vacated the premises and the building was locked. As usual, she did not acknowledge me before she left. Unless she had information directly pertaining to my work duties, she never wasted precious breath on me. Although she had known me for almost half of my life and had been my only employer since I was old enough to work, she merely tolerated me because she had to. Occasionally, when prompted, I would hear her make some sort of semi-compassionate statement about the 'poor orphaned Scourge' she was obligated to employ, but her comments were usually said with a hint of bitterness and only made to evoke the sympathies of whomever she was speaking to.

I did my best not to waste a moment of thought on her. I hated that she always made a point of calling me M1—a ridiculous way to categorize the two Scourges who were employed at the same location for the breadth of one summer who both had names which began with the letter M, and yet she had persisted in calling me by the abbreviation long after M2 had been repositioned in another library branch. I hated that she always told the visitors from the Primary Library Services when they made their annual visits I was an orphan—the offspring of not just one, but two Scourges, one whom had drowned while working on a fishing boat, and the other who had Taken Her Own Life shortly afterward. I hated that she paraded me out in front of them during such reviews and allowed them to walk around me, assessing and judging me, even sometimes touching me. I hated that she always instructed me to keep my eyes downcast, to remember my place, to remember that I was only employed and paid because of her good performance evaluations sent on my behalf.

Putting my thoughts of her aside, and grateful for the merciful silence that now filled the library, I went from section to section, checking the locks on all the windows and doors, walking slowly and quietly between the high bookshelves, running my hands along the familiar and beloved spines as I did every night. There was peace to be found within the hallowed halls of a library; a solitude of silence between the author and reader, both lovers of words and thus one another. There was no other place on earth I preferred to be than among the voices lining the walls of the library, and there were none whom I loved or respected more than those who gave us the gifts of travel, adventure, and new experiences through artfully chosen words. Here, I was never alone. Here, I was always among friends.

FOUR ~ CONTRABAND

◆ ◆ ◆

Once I had done my nightly security check and ensured the building was empty, I made my way to the back room. Aside from myself, only the delivery persons used the room. They delivered their shipments through the rolling metal door at the back of the building. As this usually occurred mid-day before I arrived, I seldom encountered them. I knew there were several who worked for the local community through the Services For The Deceased, and there were others who did the deliveries for the Primary Library Services, but I did not know any of them. Given that most were Scourges, we would not have engaged in conversation anyhow. They did not encourage us to interact with others, even our own kind.

I sat on the floor and began sorting through the boxes of books. Many were familiar copies found by the dozens within our own library system, and with little thought, I began piles based on the last name of their respective authors.

It was at the bottom of the third box that I made the first discovery. It was not just a rare find; it was an obsolete book— a relic of yesteryear, one that was thought to have been entirely destroyed over a decade ago. The author was a Scourge. The author was the creator of several books deemed so controversial that to have one of them in one's possession was too dangerous to consider.

I put the book down, my hand recoiling as if burned. My heart was beating wildly, and I looked furtively around the room as if someone were watching me. This felt exactly like a test. Was I being tested? Did they do that? Did they try to trip up Scourges just to see what they were truly capable of?

I was panicking and not thinking rationally. It was just a book.

I was alone.

Still, I looked around the room once more before finally reaching down to pick up the book again.

It was old. The pages were yellowed, the scent of its age familiar even if its contents weren't.

I flipped the book over, staring at the faded photograph of the mustached man. He didn't look like a demon writer attempting to usher in the end of the world with his anti-government writing. He didn't look like a Scourge. He looked exactly like countless men everywhere. His eyes betrayed him, however. He was corrupted. He was polluted. He and his kind had almost caused the end of the world. His words probably contributed to that.

This was contraband. This book was undoubtedly filled with untruths and such evils that I was probably committing the gravest of sins merely for holding it.

It wasn't even a thick book—a mere hundred pages, maybe a bit more. I stared into the eyes of the monster who had written the words contained within, trying to see any glimpse of evil I could. I could see nothing; he was just a man. His eyes, though they did not seem overly kind, seemed very thoughtful and intelligent. He was thin; he did not appear to have the build of a monster. Indeed, I could see nothing about his external appearance that showed he was a Scourge—but then, I knew from looking in the mirror that little was required in order to show the world that one was from bad seed. He was Scourge by genetics alone; his words must have been more than enough to verify the extreme danger he posed to our society, and that was why he had been blacklisted by the Primary Library Services. He had brought it upon himself.

FIVE ~ CHOICES

◆ ◆ ◆

I knew it was wrong, but I could not stop myself from opening the first page. It was a hardbound edition, and there was a synopsis of the story on the inside flap. The back flap held the same photograph of the author and a brief description of who he was. Born, 1903, died 1950. The book had been published in 1949, a mere year before his death. I knew his name. I knew I was holding one of the two most significant books he wrote within his brief lifetime. I knew his name well enough that its mere utterance could find me imprisoned or simply Disappeared. They could punish me and make me an Example for what I had already done.

I should have just put the book down. I should have immediately pushed the emergency switch and waited for government officials to arrive and take possession of the contraband. Still, I hesitated.

But I also recognized it would not just be myself that would suffer the consequences for such an action. Government officials would seek out the family whose deceased member had owned the books. They would investigate, interrogate, and likely seize all the assets of the entire family, never believing they were ignorant of their Loved One's possessions. They would say they knew what they had found when they boxed up the contents of the bookshelves and then donated them. The family members would all pay a price.

The person who had delivered the boxes would also likely be interrogated and punished. He had transported the illegal contraband. Even if he had not viewed the contents of the boxes, they would say he should have, and should have reported the findings in transit to the library. He would be punished—probably even worse than the family because he was likely a Scourge, and there were no second chances given to those who were Scourges.

Knowing these consequences, and knowing my life was already forfeit if I called the authorities now, I set the book aside—carefully concealing it beneath another, a permitted one—and continued going through the boxes.

There were more. Many more. Names of Scourge authors from the 19th and 20th centuries, book titles I had only read about or heard about as a matter of whispered debate, filled with quotes and concepts that were only ever found spray-painted below freeways or inside of tunnels. They were all here—the great authors of past centuries, the old, dead men of yesteryear —Scourge of the Earth not only by their genetics, but because of their corrupted, polluted, toxic minds.

I could barely breathe, so great was my fear of being caught.

I knew there were not any cameras in the back room—extra funding was seldom used to ensure the public safety of areas used by Scourge. Nonetheless, I was terrified I was being watched, studied, and allowed to do as I would with the materials left for me to find.

Even still, I took the books and placed every single one of them back into a box, and then closed the box, taping it shut once it was filled. There had been approximately thirty titles, almost all hardbound editions. Once done, I set the box near the back door where I usually left at the end of my shift.

Then, my heart still beating too quickly, I completed my usual task of returning books to shelves, finally ending my shift just after midnight, my thoughts entirely preoccupied by my discovery.

SIX ~ CONSEQUENCES

◆ ◆ ◆

I left through the back door, holding the box in my arms, and waited for the familiar click as the door latched, locking me out for the rest of the night with no means of re-entering. Whether or not I wanted to, I could no longer return the books to the building or call the authorities. I was now committed to both my theft and its consequences.

I hurried home, opting to walk the alleyways instead of the major streets as I usually did, sticking to the shadows and avoiding known CCTV locations. My shoes were soft-soled, and I walked with a deftness to my step, all but holding my breath as I moved through the night, grateful there were never many citizens out during these late hours.

I climbed the wooden stairs that led to my balcony, careful to avoid the parts prone to creaking. I did not have any close neighbors near my entrance, although the entire building was overflowing with Scourges. It was a building that should have been condemned, and would have been, had it not been used to house The Scourge.

Once inside, I set the box on my small breakfast table in the kitchen, then walked through the dark until I got to the living room lamp. It was a sparsely furnished space of a mere 580 square feet. I did not require a larger dwelling unit as a single person, nor did I qualify for more. My living area included one chair, a sofa, and a basic wooden end table holding a small iron lamp and a cream shade covering the bulb. There was a bathroom and a small bedroom with a twin bed and closet just off of the living room area. A singular window in the kitchen above the sink overlooked the back patio and stairs. The bathroom also held a small rectangular window. I took a few moments and closed the curtain in the kitchen and then closed the door to the bathroom so both windows were obscured from view. Only then did I take the box into the living room and, settling onto my small sofa, opened the box to explore its contents in greater detail.

Taking them out one by one, I reviewed my find. Tolstoy. Rand. Orwell. Bradbury. Twain. Huxley. Freud. Jung. Nietzsche. Fitzgerald. Steinbeck. Hemingway. All Evil. All contraband.

I found I was holding my breath, too in awe to even remember to breathe. My hands shook as I laid them all out across the floor.

They looked well worn, mostly. Most had paper covers—something remarkable to find, considering their age and what they must have been through. It was an awesome thing, such books surviving, being hidden away somewhere, and concealed for all these years. It was almost unfathomable.

One by one, I held each book, read through its synopsis, and thumbed through the pages. I studied the photographs and the blurbs about their authors enclosed on the back flap of the books, looking carefully at each of their faces for evidence of their Pollution. I found nothing. I found no deformities—no fanged teeth, no protruding horns, no clawed fingers. None of them struck me as particularly evil in appearance, but surely they must have been. They had spread terrible ideas in their time; they were Enemies of the State and all that was Good for our world.

Having met no one truly evil, it was difficult to see how such Devils had been so corrupt that the very words they uttered had to be outlawed so no one was harmed by them. How could mere words present such a powerful threat? What ideas, what values, what beliefs could these authors have shared?

SEVEN ~ CROSSING LINES

❖ ❖ ❖

I did not wake until almost noon.

I had stayed up, drinking in all the details of each contraband item, exploring pages, and reading passages that had been notated and underlined with soft, faded pencil marks. The books had been well cared for and treasured. Given their ownership would have meant severe consequences, I expected nothing less.

I wondered about the person who had owned them, and how their Loved Ones could have not known or noticed either the names of the authors or the books themselves when they boxed them up to be sent to the library. It seemed impossible they could have overlooked such details, but grief could have accounted for it. I doubt they would have made such a potentially deadly mistake on purpose.

By mid-afternoon, I had used a kitchen butter knife to pry away boards along the living room wall to create a hiding space. They had looked like any other book resting on a bookshelf when I was done, but I knew if anyone were to ever glimpse their titles or names, it would have been known exactly what they were. Not that there was much room for concern there—no one had been in my unit in many years. Even still, I was extremely cautious as I tucked them away, careful to reattach the boards with no noticeable damage or fresh markings on the aged wood before moving the chair in front of it.

After I was satisfied, I finished getting ready for work, showering, and putting on a fresh smock over my black clothes. Before heading out, I looked at myself in the mirror, pulled my hair into a bun and clip, and examined my eyes. I looked for signs of evil—something to betray what I had done, something different than usual to verify that I was as disturbed and criminal as everyone believed me to be. Now that I had committed such grave sins and kept such brazen secrets, surely I must have changed in some external way. But I looked exactly as I always did—small and plain, with the only remarkable characteristic about me being my absolute lack of outstanding features.

I had nothing physically to show I was of The Scourge. Some of us had been born howling, screeching to the world, the proof of our evilness on display from our very first breath. Some of us had spent every single moment of our lives being toxic and polluted, prone to aggression and violence. But if anything, I was the absence of excess; I was quiet and entirely non-confrontational. I abhorred loud, boisterous, and obnoxious personalities. I believed myself to be kind, courteous, and compassionate. There was no 'quiet rage' hidden below the surface as we were always reminded The Scourge were known for. I had never been violent, or cruel.

And yet I could not recall a single time I had ever looked into a mirror and not understood I was evil. I knew every time I looked at my reflection I was not only a genetic monster, but that I was inherently evil—an ancestor of the Devils who had almost destroyed the world. Only by the grace of my betters was I allowed to exist, allowed to perform work duties, contribute, and allowed to have as many freedoms as I did. The world did not owe me anything. My fellow countrymen could have left me in the woods to die—and many believed I should have been, just as they believed all Scourges ought to be. I owed my community everything.

And yet here I was, hiding stolen books created by my evil ancestors instead of reporting my discovery as I should have done. I knew I had already crossed the most important line, and proven to everyone that I was just as terrible and poisonous as they believed me to be.

I also knew I was going to read every single one of the books I had hidden away.

Because, really, if I were going to be labeled as evil, if I was already of bad blood and polluted, then why wouldn't I do exactly what they expected of me? I was already guilty; my thoughts and intentions had made me so. If I were discovered with the books at this point, they would assume I had already read every one of them, and I would be punished accordingly. I was guilty simply by having them in my possession, of having made that fateful decision to take them from the library in the first place.

Knowing this, it seemed fairly clear that I was already damned for my actions. So why wouldn't I follow through?

I was going to embrace my tainted bloodline and genetics and absorb the words left behind by my ancestors. Knowing that someone else had been brave enough to keep such books hidden away somewhere for all of these years almost made my own risk obligatory. Such books were banned for a reason. I wanted to know what those reasons were, and why someone had felt they were worth risking their own life to protect and preserve.

EIGHT ~ AN UNEXPECTED SURPRISE

◆ ◆ ◆

The following workweek passed without incident. The head librarian paid no more or less attention to me than usual, and there were no further drop-offs of books by the Services For The Deceased. I was cautious, at first, having felt significant paranoia that I had been set-up with the box of books, and monitored afterward. Although I had convinced myself that if I were discovered that I would be convicted regardless of having read the books or not, I had still been terrified of being caught all week, and had not even dared open the panel to read any of my illegal findings since that first night.

It was only after finishing my week of work as I prepared to return home that I decided there was no point in having the books at home if I would not read them. So I would read them —in order of shortest to longest—to absorb their contents as quickly as possible. My day off would be the following day, so I could spend it reading.

At the end of my shift, I put on my wool jacket, shut off the lights, and opened the back door to exit. The door moved something that had been resting on the other side of it. I stuck my head through the opening and saw a small rectangle wrapped in brown paper. It appeared to be a book. A solitary book left there during my shift, as I was the only one who used this door.

I stepped out, letting the door close quietly behind me, and listened as it locked. Then, looking around and seeing nothing out of the ordinary, I bent and picked up the package. It was hardbound, but the brown paper it was wrapped in was thick enough it was impossible to see through. I cautiously looked around once more, debating whether to open it right then or just take it home first. At least if I took it home before opening it I could always say I had found it in our donations but couldn't put it inside because the door had closed. I would have plausible deniability.

I stood there, weighing my options, carefully looking down the poorly lit alleyway. Although I could see no one, I felt as though I were being observed—or possibly tested. Paranoia won out in the end, and I put the book against my mid-section underneath my coat, tying it closed and then walking with my arms folded to secure the book tightly against me. So far, they could not find me guilty of doing anything beyond protecting a book from the elements by taking it home rather than leaving it outside. So far, if questioned, I could plead ignorance.

I did not know why, but I was certain someone knew I had taken the other books, that they had delivered the books knowing their contents, and that this was another offering.

My walk home was brisk and quiet. I saw no one.

Once safely home and locked into my small domain with the curtain drawn, I turned on the lamp in the living room and unwrapped the book with shaking hands.

It was a book of poetry, published in the 1900s, by one of the Scourge poets: Emily Dickinson.

I opened the front cover of the book and noticed a piece of paper nestled between the well-worn pages. The pages were faded, and the book had that familiar—beloved—smell. Opening the book to the page marked, I read what someone had clearly meant for me to read.

NINE ~ I DIED FOR BEAUTY

◆ ◆ ◆

I died for beauty - but was scarce

I died for beauty - but was scarce
Adjusted in the tomb,
When one who died for truth was lain
In an adjoining room.

He questioned softly why I failed?
"For beauty," I replied.
"And I for truth, -the two are one;
We brethren are," he said.

And so, as kinsmen met a night,
We talked between the rooms,
Until the moss had reached our lips,
And covered up our names.

~Emily Dickinson

TEN ~ PARANOIA

◆ ◆ ◆

That night I could not sleep. I knew, upon reading the poem, that someone had watched me take the box of books home. They had then planted the book by the poet, Emily Dickinson, expecting that I would take that home as well. I could not say that it was threatening to me—other than it being extremely unsettling to know that someone out there had been watching me and knew what I now held in my possession.

Examination of the contents of the poem led me to believe someone was trying to reach out and establish communication. It was dangerous, and it could have been a set-up. I was right to be cautious, and it was healthy to have a sensible level of paranoia. But it seemed the person was trying to share that they were like-minded—an almost guaranteed Scourge—and they meant no harm. The poem said, "We are the same; we are kindred spirits." And while I questioned how well a stranger could profess to 'knowing' me, how could that possibly be anything other than non-threatening?

I did not like being observed without my knowledge, and I found it very troublesome that I had noticed nothing out of the ordinary. My mind went back over the last few weeks, searching for anything unusual, but I could recall nothing. I lived an uneventful, predictable existence. I did not travel; I did not interact with anyone outside of the weekly trips to the market or the occasional conversation through work. I seldom spoke with other Scourges, and like most, did not have any close friends or family. I did not know anyone in the building I lived in, and because my staircase was its own entrance to my unit, I seldom crossed paths with other tenants. I was virtually invisible— as I was supposed to be, given my lowly standing within the community. To think someone had noticed me enough to take such a chance was extremely concerning.

My paranoia of being set-up only intensified as I considered these factors.

Sleep was slow to come.

ELEVEN ~ A PLEASANT SURPRISE

◆ ◆ ◆

I did not shop the next day. I stayed home, stayed inside, and devoured the books. I took them out, one by one, careful to put the wooden plank back in place so they were well-concealed. I thumbed through the pages, looking at publication years, their Table of Contents, or any other bits I could digest without delving into the chapters. For many of them, it was more information about their stories and personal lives than I had ever learned on my own. Our library system had purged virtually every known Scourge from our inventories and means of storing information.

Only one known Scourge remained in unquestionable good standing—someone so revered that even Time itself paid homage to his work—William Shakespeare. A few others remained—purely for educational purposes and their contribution to philosophy and literature—such as the works of Socrates, Plato, Dante, and Homer. But nothing from the 18th, 19th, 20th, or 21st century remained, to the best of my knowledge. These were the centuries where Oppression reigned through Colonialism and Imperialism, and those who were now The Scourge of the Earth had once dominated the world, creating misery and violence for all.

The taboo books were magical. They suspended time and took me to a world I'd never experienced. Their existence submerged me in danger, and yet it was all I could do to contain my emotions, to keep my heart from bursting, and hold my body still lest I dance gleefully around the room. I felt triumphant, exuberant, privileged.

If I were to die, at least I had lived enough to experience this much.

In a quarter of a century, I had never felt happiness. I had never known such pure, sweet joy. I had never had anything of value to call my own. Now, unbelievably, I held in my possession a collection of priceless books, all deemed dangerous and evil by our government, and outlawed accordingly.

I weighed the possibility of being found out, of being branded a domestic terrorist, of being sent away to the places one could only speculate about in fearful whispers, but I did not care.

What was my life worth if such treasures were not worth the risk of death to preserve and protect?

And so I reached a point where I made the conscious choice to absorb all knowledge, no matter the source, and extract from it what I believed for myself to be the truth. Never again would I so readily accept the messages funneled down through the Primary Library Services from our government officials. Never again would I accept anything at face value.

TWELVE ~ METAMORPHOSIS

◆ ◆ ◆

It was difficult, walking back to work at the beginning of my workweek. I felt a changed person. I thought it impossible to conceal how much my mind and perception of the world had changed in a mere forty-eight hours. I was certain I had a joy to my step—and there was no place for joy to be on display, least of all by someone such as myself.

As I walked, I took the time to casually look around. I don't know what—or who—I was expecting to see, but I had half-expected someone standing in the shadows quietly watching me as I made my way to the library. But I saw no one, and nothing seemed different except me.

Once there, work passed slowly. I longed to return home, to pull my covers up high and read and read and read until I could no longer keep my eyes open.

Instead, I kept to myself, sorted books, nodded silently when the head librarian issued orders, and carried on as usual.

The day passed without event, and shortly after midnight, I shut off the lights and left out the back door. I was, I found, more than a little disappointed that there was not another package waiting for me. But I walked home with a light step, knowing my time was my own and I would make good use of it.

I felt, once, as I rounded a fence at the end of the block, that someone was out there. I couldn't see anyone, but I had a powerful compulsion to turn around. Trusting my instincts, I thought perhaps it was the one who had left the book. But when I finally gave in to the urge and stopped to look around, I neither heard nor saw anything except the faint hum of the streetlight.

THIRTEEN ~ A NEW UNDERSTANDING

◆ ◆ ◆

The rain was pouring down when I awoke, and it did not let up. I walked the distance between home and work using my worn umbrella with the crooked spokes and tried to shield my backside from the downpour. Once inside, I attempted to pull my wild hair back into its tight bun, but there was little to be done about the frizz. I kept my eyes downcast, but could feel the irritation cascading off of the head librarian as she pursed her lips in disdain. Would that I could, I would purchase a new, higher-quality umbrella, a raincoat, or better yet, suitable transportation. But I must make do with what I had, and for that reason alone, I was glad to have a mostly functional umbrella for such days when I knew so many others did not.

She followed me into the back room, telling me to be sure to hang my wool coat so it would dry out or it would make the whole library smell like wet dog, and I didn't want that, now did I? Of course not, I muttered, Yes ma'am, I will.

From there, she told me the Services for the Deceased were running behind because of the inclement weather, and would not be arriving until later in the evening—possibly not until the library itself was closed. Until then, she said, I could focus on the latest books delivered by the Primary Library Services, and tidying up the shelves.

After she left, I went about my business, unpacking the newest books, chuckling to myself as I read through the titles. They were almost identical to countless other books on the shelves already:

timeless love stories of men and women who were dedicated first and primarily to ensuring Good Citizenry and advancing the correct political and social ideologies of our time. There were tales of heroic Community Organizers who fought on behalf of the National Equality Administration, ensuring that the values of our communities were never compromised or lost to those who would see us devolve into the savage, evil world we had once known. In addition, there were books on parenting, gardening, health and wellness, and other such topics—books that were already lining the library walls, many written by known contemporary authors, and if one were to look too closely, almost verbatim from text to text.

I knew now, having seen so many unique prints, that while each contemporary novel was inclusive and focused on diversity of characters, that there was very little originality of thought or theme. The authors and messaging were virtually interchangeable. The stories had all been told; the endings were all exactly as they should be. There were no more questions to be asked which did not already have the answers provided and printed.

FOURTEEN ~ AN UNEXPECTED DEVELOPMENT

◆ ◆ ◆

The library closed its doors to the community at 6 in the evening. The head librarian left directly after. As it was, I typically only had to spend two hours during my shift in the company of others. It was something for which I was always exceptionally grateful.

Just after 7, there was a pounding on the back door. It was unexpected enough that I jumped, but then I remembered the late delivery by the Services For The Deceased.

Unlocking the door, I gave it a push, half expecting the worker to have his hands full with at least one box. Instead, a man stood there—clearly a Scourge. He easily stood a head taller than myself. His eyes looked directly into mine with no hesitation, no humility, no effort to avert his gaze.

He smiled.

Flustered, I said nothing.

"I have more books for you," he said.

I was certain I looked surprised at his choice of words—and likely guilty.

He motioned to the door frame, indicating I should step back so he could enter. The rain was still pounding down, but he was under the awning. I moved aside, though, and looked beyond him toward the tall black van as if to verify his work connection.

He stepped through the door frame, brushing past me, smelling strangely exotic with unfamiliar scents. I was rarely close enough to anyone to breathe in their essence, to smell the scent of their soap, to take in any fragrances.

I let the door close behind me, standing just inside, only turning to face him.

He stared at me for a long moment, and I felt my face flush with heat.

"You're smaller than I thought you were."

I said nothing.

"Well, then! I guess I should go grab the books!"

He clapped his hands together, rubbed them briskly, and then walked past me once more. I turned, holding the door open for him as he stepped down from the porch and back into the rain. I watched as he opened the back doors of the van, revealing a multitude of boxes. Shifting through them, he extracted one small box, held it against his hip, and then shut both doors once more.

"The rest go to other libraries," he said, giving me a wink.

Who was this man? How was he so jovial? He was obviously of a bad bloodline—he was Scourge and polluted, same as me. He was so content, all but whistling as he moved back toward me. How could it be that he spoke so freely?

Once more, he walked past me, moving the small box to his front side as he made his way back into the building. He set it down on the table and turned to face me.

"You're here alone, yeah?" he asked.

I nodded. The door shut behind me, a loud click filling the air.

"You speak, right?" His tone was teasing, his smile lazily falling across his face like a happy puppy.

"Of course," I muttered, feeling the heat rise to my cheeks once more.

"I'm Ben," he said, and stuck out his hand.

I stared down at it. I knew what was expected—it was a handshake. But Scourges didn't shake hands. Scourges didn't intentionally touch anyone.

"Oh, boy, do we have our work cut out for us," he laughed, letting his hand drop to his side.

Turning away from me, he opened the box.

"Most of these are already titles that are on your shelves— probably by the dozen, and not worth doing anything with except burning. But I can't show up empty-handed, now can I? Have to give something to the PLS. Pretty peculiar if I notified your boss that I'd be running late and then not leave any books, huh? So most of these are for the library. But I did bring one book in particular that made me think of you."

He sorted through the box, retrieving one from the bottom, and then took a step closer, offering it to me.

Taking it from him, I looked at the title: Jane Eyre, by Charlotte Bronte.

"I really think you'll like this one. I don't think you have any of the Bronte sisters yet. What did you think about the book of poetry?" he queried.

So it was him. I had guessed—assumed—but the confirmation was good to have. His reckless, cavalier nature was another matter entirely, however, and it did not make me feel more secure about the contents of what he knew I had in my possession. Recklessness was how Scourges ended up Gone.

"Did you like the poem I marked?" he continued. He leaned his long frame against the table, talking comfortably as if we were old friends.

I nodded, still overwhelmed and more than a fair bit afraid

that this might all just be a trap waiting to be sprung. I felt panic rising; a need to escape before my criminal actions were revealed.

"Ok," he continued. "I can see this has been a bit much for your first meet with me. No worries; that happens from time to time. I'll let you get back to work. We won't likely meet again through here; I have a schedule and every time I need to make introductions, I have to come up with reasons the deliveries are delayed. So I can't do it very often, and I have to plan my deliveries carefully. And it's not usually a good idea to meet at our homes, but in your case, it's fairly isolated, so I think it might be ok. I can drop off books there, at least once it's dark. I can put them behind the bush directly underneath your stairs. I won't be able to do it regularly, but you should check nightly, just in case. I trust you found a decent place to stash them inside?"

He looked deep into my eyes, searching for answers. I nodded once again.

"Ok, well that's good at least. You'll have enough to tide you over for a while. I cover the entire region, and deliver to about a dozen libraries, so I'm usually only here once a week or every ten days. But my lodgings are here—only a few blocks from yours. Do you know the cemetery?"

The cemetery: a run-down parcel of land from the days when the Deceased were buried in the ground.

"Yes," I said, trying to clear my throat so my voice wasn't a mere whisper.

"Ok, well here's what we'll do: You carry on, enjoy your new books. Check the bush every night after work. When there's a new book there, you'll know I'm back in town. We can plan on meeting at the cemetery at 2 a.m. That will give you time to get off work at midnight, walk home, eat or whatever, and you won't be rushed. The next time you go to the market, take the long way so you can pass the cemetery. Look for the large oak tree toward the back. There's an Angel of Mercy statue next to it. I'll meet you there, and we can talk some more."

He looked at me, his eyebrows raised.

I met his gaze with a false, but hopefully convincing, confidence, letting him know I understood and agreed to all he was telling me.

"We can spend a bit of time together and you can ask your questions, get more comfortable talking."

With that, he pushed himself away from the table and stood to his full height once more. I looked up at him, and probably, to both of our surprise, smiled.

He smiled back at me, giving me a wink, and then stuck out his hand once more.

This time, I didn't hesitate, and felt his warm hand close around mine.

"OK! I'll get out of here," he said, dropping my hand and walking toward the door.

He pushed it open, turning to look at me.

"Until I return, then." And with that, he walked back toward the van, opened the driver's door, and disappeared inside.

I stood there watching until he left, holding the door wide, listening to the rain as it hit the metal awning.

For reasons I could not explain or define, I felt something completely unfamiliar stirring deep within myself. I didn't understand what it was, but later I would come to realize it had been the faintest glimmer of something known as Hope. It was a silent prayer for something better, something different, something I could never have imagined. It was the mere possibility of a life different from the one I had been given or expected I would live. To someone who had nothing, it was everything. I could not wait to see him again. I could not wait to read the book he had intentionally picked out for me. It felt, in that moment, that everything was not only possible, but that anything could actually happen.

FITEEN ~ CLARITY

◆ ◆ ◆

My eyes were opened that week, finally, at long last. Never had I imagined such a world could exist, or that I would have access to it. A lowly person, such as I, being gifted with the most beautiful, lovingly written tale of heartache and woe I was certain had ever been put to print—it was more than I could process.

My life could have been that of Jane Eyre's, and hers mine. She found happiness, and yes, even love, after many years of heartache. It was the tale of a lonely, plain girl, and I would not be truthful if I did not say that I found my existence mirrored in hers. I could only pray and dream of such a happy ending, but I did find myself relating to her far more than I could have ever imagined, and in her world, I found a quiet optimism as I prayed for all to work out in the end.

It made me wonder about so many things that I had never considered or contemplated. I wondered if love was possible, no matter our station in this world. I wondered if such love could truly yield the security, hope, and fulfillment that our beloved Jane Eyre found at long last. It filled me with hope—not merely for myself, but for the world entire—for how could everything be as terrible as it seemed if such redemption and love could be found?

And I thought of the man who had bequeathed this book to me, and how he had known that the parallels would resonate as profoundly as they did.

I did not know how he knew I would take home the box of books when presented with it, or how he would know a book like Jane Eyre would touch my soul, but I felt an incredible depth of heartfelt gratitude for his having made the effort. My entire existence had opened up, and for the first time in my life, I felt the pull of my inner-being toward another. Along with this, there was an excitement—a sense of anticipation—though for what, I could not say.

It was all I could do to make it through my workweek.

Every night I would walk home and check the bush below the stairs, and every night I would feel a pang of disappointment to find nothing.

I filled my spare time reading through the books I had in my possession, taking breaks from time to time to read the poetry contained within the book by Emily Dickinson.

The days blended together. The monotony of work was only alleviated by the adventures and new experiences I embraced with each story I stepped into during the long nights.

I did not understand why such glorious books had been banned and destroyed. I did not see the poison of evil men in their words—I saw heroism, survival, adventure, love, faith, and hope. I saw nothing toxic about the writing or the authors—I saw the beauty of words captured on pages capable of transporting readers into worlds unknown. The books were a magical portal, showcasing both historical periods of time and entirely new worlds contrived solely through the imagination of the author. They were magical creations of pretend characters, stories of humanity at its best and worst, and wonderful images of all that the world could contain—all told through the eyes of someone who felt compelled to share their thoughts and ideas by putting words to page. In all my life, I had never dreamed of such wonders.

All I longed for now was someone with whom I could discuss such topics—and I desperately awaited the return of the man who had opened a gateway to the world for me.

SIXTEEN ~ WAITING TO MEET

◆ ◆ ◆

Twelve long days later, at the end of the 35th Week of the year, there was finally a brown-wrapped package waiting for me in the bush below the stairs. I eagerly took it up to my unit, locked the door behind me, and turned on the light in the living room. I followed my usual protocols to ensure complete privacy, and then double-checked the lock on the door before settling down on the sofa. Only then did I unwrap the book.

Anthem, by Ayn Rand. It would be the second book by her now in my possession, with the first being Atlas Shrugged. Given that I was reading in order of length, I did not expect to read Atlas Shrugged soon. But Anthem appeared to be a much smaller book.

I wished I could access the database and see the word counts for all the books I had received, but I knew that would never happen for several reasons. First, the database only held current titles—they had purged all the books of yesteryear created by Scourges from the system. It was impossible to even find titles, or authors. Second, any information regarding them had been wiped from the internet as well, and both the PLS database and the internet were heavily monitored by the official Oversight Department. It was impossible to learn anything about the books or authors. And finally, because they monitored the information, even trying to search such books or authors—whether through the internet or the Primary Library Services system—would undoubtedly result in an official visit from government agents, and that was not something I was prepared to risk.

This was an unfortunate drawback to broadening one's base of knowledge. I knew that in decades past that such information would have freely existed on the internet, and that each of these authors would have had their professional contributions known to the world. Their lives would have been well-documented, and all the societal issues relevant during their years that may have been discussed within their books would have been common knowledge for the taking. But all of that was lost now; those who did not want such poisonous ideas and messages to be spread anymore had intentionally snuffed their entire existence out, thus obliterating any truth they may have written within their pages.

After spending some time looking over the book, I placed it in the wall with all the others and got ready to go to the cemetery. The timestamp read just after 1 a.m. when I left. I locked my darkened little unit, crept silently down the stairs, and then made my way through the alley toward the cemetery.

It was only a fifteen-minute walk, and as it was August, the weather was mild. I did not care for walking through the cemetery in the middle of the night, navigating my way through headstones and trying to move quietly without tripping over anything, but I had taken the time to chart a path earlier in the week, so I wasn't walking completely blind.

Using the Angel of Mercy statue as a landmark, I knew which tree Ben had specifically referenced. The cemetery was large and covered many hundreds of acres—yet another reason why they were no longer used for human remains—but this was also partly why I believed he chose for us to meet there. It was highly improbable that we should be overheard or observed by any visitors, especially at this late hour. Still, it was a creepy place to be alone, especially in the middle of the night.

Once at the big oak tree, I stopped, choosing to sit with my back against its wide base, and waited. I was early by almost fifteen minutes. As I sat alone in the dark, listening to every creak of the tree and rustling of leaves, my imagination created the most outlandish of thoughts in my head. I made a mental note to not leave any earlier than necessary next time.

SEVENTEEN ~ THE ANGEL
OF MERCY STATUE

◆ ◆ ◆

I did not wait long before he arrived.

My heart filled with so much joy over the sight of him it caught me off-guard, and I could not help but smile as he approached me.

He returned my smile, and extended his hand. Without hesitation, I held mine out, allowing him to take it into his own for a moment before letting it go. I was glad that I felt much more comfortable and at ease in his presence this time, and I hoped he could sense it as well.

He sat beside me, positioned so we were almost face to face.

"How did you like Jane Eyre?" he asked.

"It was wonderful!" I exclaimed. It was a pleasant relief to tell someone finally.

He smiled. "I thought you would relate to it. It was always a well-loved story. I'm glad you liked it."

"How do you know about such things?" I asked him. As much as I wanted to discuss the contents of the books with him, I also wanted to understand who he was and what he was doing. It was wildly dangerous, approaching strangers, even if we were all Scourges.

"Yes, let's get started on everything. I've been looking forward to being able to speak to you at length," he said, nodding his head.

I smiled, grateful for the darkness hiding my blush.

"Essentially, I tested high, and was sent to university. I earned a PH.D. and began working in the field selected for me where they thought I may be of the best service. I did this for several years. While I was in school, I used to do janitorial work part-time. You know how the system works; no matter how intelligent or accomplished they believe you to be, they will always hire Scourges for the most menial positions. So I worked as a janitor throughout my years at school. I didn't mind it; it gave me access to the entire campus after hours. I could venture into every department—not just the sciences where I studied. It was there that I could spend time in the Literature department."

He studied my face, making sure I was following. He likely knew that as a librarian page, I probably had to attend university as well, but it was only a two-year program, and it was extremely specialized. They did not give me access to any advanced literature courses; it was almost exclusively focused on the administrative practices within the Primary Library System. Being able to discuss books or authors was never intended to be part of my job duties, and so I was never given the opportunities to learn. Aside from this, my understanding of the program was still limited to what they deemed acceptable literature—and everything taught was readily available through our library system anyhow.

I nodded my head, encouraging him to continue.

"So it was while I was working as a janitor that I made a discovery. The classrooms were generic, the books were all generic—you know what I mean. But I discovered something in the basement of the Literature department that changed everything. It completely changed my life—the life as I knew it to be, the life I had expected to lead, and made me question all that I had ever been told and taught. There was a secret room, you see. A boarded up doorway that had shelves put in front of it. I was cleaning out the mop bucket one night after I finished my duties, and I accidentally spilled the bucket. There were gallons of water all over the cement floor. I quickly grabbed the mop again and began soaking up the spilled water. But some of it had gone under the metal shelves, so I was forced to pull the shelving away from the back wall. I had to remove all the supplies before I could pull the unit away from the wall so I could mop everything up.

"It was then that I realized there was another room behind the wooden planks that had been nailed to the wall. It was a lazy effort to conceal a door frame, simply nailing up some planks of wood and then placing a six-foot metal shelf in front of it, but by the looks of it, no one had been in the room for many years—or had likely even noticed it.

"The building itself was old—you know it was one of the first universities built in Washington, and had been in use since the 19th century. The basement wasn't nearly as big of a space as the rest of the building; I doubted they had ever used it as classrooms or office space. It was too dark, too dreary, too prone to mildew and mold. The damp climate would have been terrible for anyone to spend any proper amount of time in. So I wasn't sure what they could have used the additional space for, but I assumed it must have been more storage.

"You know what they say, don't you? About curiosity killing the cat?" He looked at me, a mischievous smile on his face, and winked.

"Clearly, I had no choice. I had to know what was beyond that door." He laughed, causing me to smile in delight. He was wonderful in every way.

"I found an appropriate tool that I could use to wedge the pieces of wood away from the frame, careful to work quietly even though it was late at night and I knew I was the only person in the building. This was long before they put all the CCTV cameras up throughout the campus, so I didn't have any worries about being overheard or discovered by anyone. No one would have had keys to enter the building other than the Administrator, and it was already late.

"So I got all the planks ripped away, careful not to split any of the pieces. I didn't have any extra nails to put the boards back up. I wasn't expecting to find much—maybe a place where they had dumped old school equipment. I was not expecting what I found. Not in a million years could I have anticipated it, actually."

He grinned at me, raising his eyebrows. He really had the most expressive face of anyone I'd ever seen.

"It was filled with books. Mountains and mountains of books. Thousands. There were shelves lining the room—easily forty or fifty six-foot tall shelves lining the walls—and all of them filled to the brim with books. There were tables and chairs set up throughout the room—it must have been an old library reserved for the Literature Department that was entirely separate from the building that housed the main campus library—I don't know. But there were stacks of books covering almost every table as well. There were books put into crevices between shelves, books towering on top of the shelves almost touching the ceiling, and books stacked on the chairs. I'd never in my life seen so many books outside of a library.

"The entire room was covered in cobwebs, and they had covered all the windows with wooden planks. Of course, there was electricity, and I could have turned on the lights. Some tables had lamps, and there was a librarian station just off to the right of the door. But I only used the light from the janitorial room and a small flashlight I carried as I looked around. I thought any more light might be visible from the small basement windows, and I didn't want the security guards on patrol to notice anything.

"I knew, just from looking at a few of the titles of the books closest to me that they were all contraband books. All of them had been put away—probably all the stacked books on tables and chairs had been the ones pulled from the main library when the new laws came into effect. They were supposed to have been destroyed, as you know.

"What I think happened was...the books were loved. Someone —probably an entire staff full of teachers and librarians, or at least a few—knew that they had banned the books, and they had done their required duty by removing them from the main library on campus. But they were loved, these books. And what they represented! Can you imagine? It was probably heartbreaking for them to have to say goodbye to such books— the history, the memories, the beauty! No matter what a person's political leanings, surely they must have had many beloved favorites among those that were now deemed dangerous, heretical, and anti-government. I'm guessing that there were one or two librarians or professors who were put in charge of disposing of them, but when it came time, they just couldn't bring themselves to do it. They probably understood that they deemed the whole basement library Unfit and would need to be dismantled and destroyed.

"I think there was an angel there—someone who loved literature enough to save the books from destruction—maybe even someone who still visited over the years, making sure they were all still there, still safe, still protected. They probably sat in that room after hours and read in secret."

He laughed, gleefully.

"It's all speculation, of course. I knew nothing about how the books came to be, who put them there, or if anyone still knew they existed. All I knew was that for the first time in my life, I felt free to choose. I felt free to explore a world that I'd never been allowed to before—a world that had existed before I was born, before anyone was considered a second-class citizen, before there was segregation based on genetics, and before any of us were deemed Polluted and Toxic just because our ancestors had once dominated the world through political and military conquest. For the first time in my entire existence, I felt like I had a choice being presented—and right then, I knew, I didn't care about breaking the law, I didn't care about risking my own life, I didn't care about living within the confines of a nation and government that believed me to be less-than my betters and treated me as expendable. If I was going to be used and denied free will, then I would take my chances and make my choices any way I was presented with options—and reading about a world that no longer existed seemed to be exactly what I needed to do."

I stared at him, grinning like a fool, my heart bursting with awe. What a marvel he was. What strength of character, what passion! I wished I had nearly an ounce of his strength and decisiveness—but then I realized I too, had made a choice already, and had risked my safety as well.

"So that was how it began," he continued.

"I needed to develop a plan. I needed to explore ideas of what I could do with my hidden treasures. I couldn't just keep it to myself—it was a gold mine! It was more valuable than anything I could have ever dreamed! Surely there were others out there who wanted to do exactly as I did, and sit down and look through every single title and then discover the contents contained within their pages. But how to do it? What could I do? Where could I take them? Where else would be safe?

"There were plenty of logistics to consider. First, I needed to cover the windows better so I could use the lights. Then, I needed to figure out how I could remove the books. It would take months—if not years—to secret them away one or two at a time. And then I had to figure out how to store them elsewhere—and it had to be a climate-controlled, dry location that no one would ever think to look—but it also had to be close enough I could visit regularly. Luckily, none of them had been damaged by the damp climate and poor building conditions; they seemed to have been preserved as if in a tomb.

"That's what ended up being the game-changer—trying to figure out what I could do. So I started small. I got the windows all blacked out, figured out how to secure the door without needing to use the wood planks but still have it concealed, and I started organizing the books a little at a time. That got me through the first week or so while I mulled things over, trying to figure out my next steps.

"Eventually, I realized I could never pull it off and move thousands of books without having more people. I considered each of the students I interacted with regularly—there were a few that I knew shared my more 'extreme' views, who had a difficult time refraining from letting a few of their more choice comments from sliding. They kept us segregated, as you know, so I was always in classes with other Scourges, but you still never knew who you could truly trust, as I'm sure you can relate to.

"Anyhow, I had one good friend that I'd roomed with my first year and who was also still attending school. He and I had shared many conversations and ideas on how we could really create change within the world—big, bold ideas that would have landed us both in serious trouble had they ever been overheard. So I knew I could count on him.

"In the end, he was the one who came up with the people and the place. He was friends with a few guys who were being trained in a trade program to work in Waste Management. They worked in the sewers, underground, and knew all the tunnel systems. My friend—Aaron—met with a few of the guys and asked them if they knew of any locations that might work, and then again, if they would be interested in helping.

"I think that's really part of where our government has things wrong. They think just because people are well-suited to menial work through the trades that it's because they're not intelligent, or capable of real intellectual growth. They pigeon-hole workers who specialize in the trades as Neanderthals who have no interest in learning or growing. That superiority will eventually be their downfall—and it's likely going to be the key to winning this war between us.

I raised my eyebrows, more than a little surprised at how open he was being, at how dangerous his rhetoric. We could both Disappear just because of this conversation—they'd never let something this openly aggressive go without severe, permanent consequences. I felt a twinge of paranoia—the faintest question arising within me, wondering if I was being set-up. But I pushed it down—it couldn't be. He simply couldn't be false. It would be too tragic if he were.

"So that's where it all began—quite a few years ago now. We formed a little group of rogue revolutionaries—all classified as Scourges, all with the same amount to lose—our freedom. We spent almost two months carrying out the books every night. They wore their work clothes and carried toolboxes—and the plan was to say there were plumbing issues in the building if they were ever caught. But they weren't. There were five of us, including myself, and we all knew the stakes. We all decided it was worth the risk.

"So every night, they rotated in and out, one run each time, usually carrying a half dozen books. I would stay and sort them after my shift, getting them ready to be loaded up. And slowly, over time, we emptied the entire library.

"They knew of old sewer tunnels in the downtown area that had been closed off because of the access they provided to the businesses above. The risk of them being used by criminals to gain entry from underground was too great, and so there were miles of unused tunnels. They worked out a route that began in an isolated area where we could enter and exit without drawing any attention to us—an area secluded enough we could drive vehicles to and no one would happen upon us while we were navigating the tunnels. Uniforms for the Waste Management Services were always used, and they continued to use the toolboxes as book carriers.

"As time went by, we finally began to read and share what we had read. We would check out books just like we did the regular library—careful never to take too many at a time lest we were caught. We got the new rooms organized by genre and set aside all the duplicates.

"And that was when things began to grow. That was when we realized we had an obligation to share all that we were learning and discussing as we read these books. It was also when we realized how dangerous it was to keep all of our books in one singular location. We recognized the historical significance of what we were now responsible for; we understood that the history of our nation as they had taught us had all been based on a lie, that our government had somehow secured their powers, but that their power was contrary to what our Founding Fathers had intended. We learned that our ancestors weren't evil or toxic at all—they were brilliant. In countless ways, we learned about how the world had been before our lifetimes, and we knew that what they had sold us was entirely fabricated. Our Founding Fathers had never intended for our government to be as powerful or intrusive as it was. Everything they were doing was predicated on falsehoods perpetuated by those who stood the most to gain, and once they obtained their power, they had devised ways to ensure they would never lose it again. Everything we had been raised to believe was wrong, and entirely manufactured for nefarious purposes.

"With that in mind, we first found other places where we could establish libraries for all of our duplicates. We made a new rule—no duplicates within the same location, and each location deserved to hold as many of the same titles as possible, especially those based on our Constitution and matters of history and civics. So we created inventory lists—dangerous to have on our person, and thus we committed the lists to memory. We studied the authors. I'm not sure if you noticed this, but many of the books have a page that lists other works that the same authors had published. We committed those lists to memory as well, so we could become further educated about each. We devoured books, eventually creating enough of a palette that we could select our favorites, and then it only grew from there. Those of us who could retain information began tucking away anything that they could—just as Native Americans had done generations back through their long-standing tradition of oral story-telling.

"We recruited librarian page's every chance we could, knowing they were our direct link between what was permissive and what was deemed illegal and had been banned. Who knew more about authors and books than those who worked in the libraries? Of course we couldn't have fully-qualified librarians; we knew they didn't allow Scourges to hold such positions of power. But we could reach out to the library page's—almost all of whom we knew to be both educated in Library Services and also branded Scourge.

"So that's it. We've spent the last several years building an underground empire of contraband books and people, all dedicated to absorbing our collective history. We all know what we risk by being caught. We all know that we will pay with our freedom and possibly our lives.

"We're very careful about revealing too much to one another. We don't allow anyone to learn the specifics about other libraries —only Aaron and myself have a master key, so to speak, and know precisely where each are located. No one else even knows how many there are. No one knows the identities of other members unless it directly involves them, and we try to keep such connections to a bare minimum—we never have more than three or four people physically connected to one another. Everyone knows me and Aaron, but no one really knows much about us beyond our names—which may or may not be real —and that we deliver books through the Services For The Deceased. Even so, we control when and how contact is made— no one really knows where we live, what we do for a living, and they've never seen both of us—they either get him or me.

"You're amazing," I uttered, without thought. I was certain my words were silly—that everything I thought I knew about the world thus far must have appeared almost childish, so naïve and superficial was my existence in comparison to his own. He could not have been more than a few years older than me, but look at all he had accomplished! Look at what he had done!

I was spellbound by him. He had captivated me entirely.

He looked at me strangely for a long moment, his expression unreadable for the first time since I had met him, and then looked away. I thought perhaps I had embarrassed him, but surely he told everyone he shared books with the same story, and it would have been impossible for anyone to respond with any less awe or reverence than I had.

I felt a sudden chill overcome me, and I shuddered. He looked at me, then his timestamp, and told me we ought to call it a night. I nodded, but inside I longed to continue sitting here in the moonlight, listening to him. I was both enamored as well as starved for attention, and there had not been very many occasions where I had ever been showered with as much time or conversation as I had been by him. Given how absolutely wonderful he was, there was very little effort from me to guard my feelings. I knew little of love, and certainly nothing of the romantic variety, but I knew I was incapable of resisting whatever magical force he exuded.

He stood, reaching out toward me to help me to my feet. It felt as though our hands touched for just a fraction of time longer than necessary, but I was almost giddy with devotion by then, so any objectivity was gone.

"So now what?" I asked. Would he want me to go to one of his libraries? Help sort books? Why had he initiated contact, if not to continue building his connections and inviting me in for more?

"So now, you read. You learn. You absorb whatever you can. If you find you have a memory suitable for memorization, well, that will be something else entirely. We desperately need readers who can memorize content—whether it be passages, chapters, or even just poetry. There are many, many thousands of books, and authors, for you to explore. You were given a box of carefully selected books already, plus your book of poetry and then tonight, Anthem. You won't see me dropping off books through the Services For The Deceased—that's part of our protection plan—we seldom interact with one another so we can never be suspected of knowing one another better than we should. But I'm 'around' and have more freedom than most because of the work I do for the Services For The Deceased.

"For now, you're probably good to go for a few more weeks, and I'll have to leave again for another route soon. So maybe, if you would like, we could plan on meeting again just like this when I return?"

He stared down at me, directly into my eyes, and I felt the heat rise again. I knew he didn't mean it personally, but I still nodded my head like a sappy schoolgirl, trying not to smile and give myself away.

"I'll do the same thing when I return. I'll leave you a new book under the stairs, and we can plan on meeting at two again. Did this time work for you? It's not too late?" He looked upward toward the sky, just beginning to have the faintest hint of light, signaling it was probably closer to dawn than we realized.

"It's wonderful. I could probably do 1:30, if that's better for you. I had plenty of time to spare." I answered.

He nodded. "Ok, then. Let's plan on 1:30. It will give us more time before daylight, at least. But soon enough the rain will be here, and we'll have to sort something else out. I know your place is private, but I was concerned that others may hear through your walls. Do you know how many units surround yours? Can you hear your neighbors talking—even a faint murmur through the walls?"

I shook my head. "I don't think I have anyone around me—my unit was converted from the attic, which is why it has a single, outside staircase and only one entrance. And I only have two windows. We may meet there; you'll have to decide after you visit."

He nodded and said we would sort it out later.

"Thank you for meeting with me, Margaret. I'm glad to make your acquaintance." He smiled.

"Thank you for the books, Ben. Thank you for Jane Eyre and the poetry, especially." I responded.

"Head for home. I'm going to walk a ways behind you and make sure you get home safely."

I smiled, gave him a little wave, and walked back through the headstones once more, finding it easier to navigate with the emerging light.

"Oh, and Margaret?"

I turned toward him.

"My name really is Benjamin. I'm not sure why I told you my real name when we first met; I usually tell people my name is Joseph. But just so you know, it really is Ben." He grinned sheepishly at me, and then shushed me off with a sweep of his hand, prodding me to get home.

I smiled, then turned and began walking more quickly toward the cemetery entrance, smiling the entire way home.

It was the strangest sensation, but although everything was almost exactly the same, everything seemed different. Now there was hope.

For the first time in my life, I fell asleep thinking of another, and hoped, with no genuine sense of understanding, that he was somewhere thinking of me, too.

EIGHTEEN ~ A LIFE
WORTH LIVING

◆ ◆ ◆

Life resumed its natural timetable, and the days passed without the slightest break in the ordinary. The head librarian did her best to ignore me most days, and for once I was grateful, so profoundly changed on the inside that I felt it must surely show externally as well. I was careful to keep my eyes downcast and avoided her gaze at every interaction.

What had been most clear to me about Ben was how vibrant he was. They had not beaten him down; he was not submissive. It was a dangerous way to be—dangerous and potentially costly. Those who walked without a broken spirit were quickly targeted. Most within our communities felt it was their 'duty' to ensure that we Scourges were put in our places properly. Even the youngest and lowliest among them had higher stature than us. We were second-class citizens, and we were never supposed to forget it.

It had been that way for as long as I could remember. They would have us believe it had always been as it was now, but I knew it was only within a few generations that the societal powers had shifted so dramatically. I remembered hearing my mother and father discussing it as they talked about my father's parents when I was very young. I recalled a memory of them sitting at our kitchen table, my mother sounding worried, my father reassuring her that his father was not so outspoken that he might face punishment for his political views. I was young, but it was not long after that when everything changed. My father was no longer there, and I was being told that my mother had taken her own life. I was too young to process the full meaning behind what they had been discussing, but I knew enough to keep silent as I listened, and knew that my father was espousing political views that were deemed unacceptable. I believed—now —that he had been objecting to being vilified for the color of his skin rather than the content of his character, and had been protesting against the new laws regarding segregation between races.

I know the shift was not sudden; it began in the 21st century as population numbers changed. There were cultural shifts within the nation. It began innocently enough—under the guise of equality, and was meant to help all races gain equal traction. But as the culture war raged, and the races became more divided into racial factions, the social structure of the country began transforming.

By the time I was around age six, the social stigmas of those considered 'Scourges' had become commonplace. There were unspoken mandates regarding reproduction among The Scourge, all in a concerted effort to obliterate those of toxic bloodlines from the earth. By the time I was seven, my grandparents had died or Disappeared, my mother had been told my father died in a fishing boat accident, and she had committed suicide shortly after. None of this could be investigated or confirmed—these were simply things I took as fact because they were told to me as I was taken away and placed into a group home for others who were just like me. We were orphans— raised by the government, housed and fed by the government, educated by the government, sent to work training programs by the government, and then employed by the government in jobs they had selected for us. Even now, my housing was government housing, and my wages were government funded.

As a Polluted person—as a child of a Polluted lineage, responsible for having caused such extreme damage to the world—my only duty was to spend my life making amends for the atrocities committed by my ancestors, and to do my best to earn my place within our community. It was only because of the tolerance of The People and my government leaders that I was allowed to exist, and it was my duty to remain humble and in service to our nation as a means of paying reparations for all that my kind had done. The alternative, I knew well, was to either Disappear or Die.

Whether I agreed to these terms was not debatable, and my opinion did not matter. I knew, just as every other person with bad blood knew, that compliance and effort were the only options if one wished to live. Choice had never been an option. Free Will simply meant the right to choose compliance and life, or non-compliance and death.

Anything outside of the acceptable range of emotions or actions was not only disallowed, but dangerous.

And so the days passed. I kept my head down, and did my work as usual.

But inside, late at night, as I read through my collection of books, a fire was growing. A hunger for more—a desire for better.

Inside, buried deep underneath the layers of a carefully constructed image of docile submission, I was growing more aware of just how oppressive this existence had become. I was questioning all truths as I had been told. I was speculating about how many Scourges remained within my community and nation—was it in the thousands, or millions?

Since our kind had been advised generations back not to bear children—long before it became an unspoken mandate—our numbers had already been in a steady decline. My ancestors had been told that reproduction was too costly—for the planet and for the other inhabitants—and the only responsible thing we could do was abstain from reproducing. So how well had it worked? Had we diminished to such a reduced count that our own demise was an inevitability? Could we save ourselves from extinction? I didn't know; I wasn't certain anyone knew for sure. Maybe our government kept track of such numbers, but it seemed likely it would be kept secret, lest we know how much power we actually held. If we numbered in the millions, and we united, it would be very dangerous indeed.

I was questioning what sort of life was worth living if one did not have freedom of choice or the right to think or believe as they wanted. I was waking up, and it was well worth the risk.

NINETEEN ~ A SECOND MEETING

◆ ◆ ◆

Finally, during Week 36 of the year, he reached out again. It had been fifteen long, agonizingly slow days before I found another package under the bush. I eagerly took it upstairs, and after following my routine of closing the curtains and bathroom door to ensure no one could see in through the windows, I tore through the brown wrapping paper with zeal.

It was another book of poetry, this time something referred to as an "Anthology of Best Loved Poems of the 19th and 20th Century".

I checked my timestamp, keeping the time in mind as I was expected in the cemetery at 1:30, and then spent a moment looking through the collection. The book by Emily Dickinson had taught me one thing so far, much to my delight, and it was that I had a good ear for poetry, and memorization came easily. I had already committed several to heart, and was looking forward to reading more.

There were several pages marked with bookmarks, and so I turned to them, reading what I could only presume to be Ben's favorites selected for my perusal. I was very excited to read more of the poetry that had once filled our libraries and found it lovely that Ben had provided me with a thick book filled with hundreds of poets.

TWENTY ~ SHE WALKS IN BEAUTY

◆ ◆ ◆

She Walks in Beauty

I.
She walks in beauty, like the night
Of cloudless climes and starry skies;
And all that's best of dark and bright
Meet in her aspect and her eyes:
Thus mellowed to that tender light
Which heaven to gaudy day denies.
II.
One shade the more, one ray the less,
Had half impaired the nameless grace
Which waves in every raven tress,
Or softly lightens o'er her face;
Where thoughts serenely sweet express
How pure, how dear their dwelling place.
III.
And on that cheek, and o'er that brow,
So soft, so calm, yet eloquent,
The smiles that win, the tints that glow,
But tell of days in goodness spent,
A mind at peace with all below,
A heart whose love is innocent!

~George Gordon Byron

TWENTY-ONE ~ ACQUAINTED WITH THE NIGHT

◆ ◆ ◆

Acquainted With The Night

I have been one acquainted with the night.
I have walked out in rain—and back in rain.
I have outwalked the furthest city light.

I have looked down the saddest city lane.
I have passed by the watchman on his beat
And dropped my eyes, unwilling to explain.

I have stood still and stopped the sound of feet
When far away an interrupted cry
Came over houses from another street,

But not to call me back or say good-bye;
And further still at an unearthly height,
One luminary clock against the sky

Proclaimed the time was neither wrong nor right.
I have been one acquainted with the night.

~Robert Frost

TWENTY-TWO ~ A DEEPER UNDERSTANDING

◆ ◆ ◆

As I walked through the cemetery, I was pleased to see that Ben was already there. I was a bit early myself, but I had walked with a light step in anticipation of being able to see him again.

He greeted me with a warm smile, and invited me to sit. I was happy to see he had brought a small blanket to cover the ground; it made me feel as though he intended to stay a while and was thinking of our comfort. I was very much looking forward to being able to spend more time listening to him, talking with him, and mostly just being in his company. It was not very often I shared such moments with others, and I suppose I had not known I was as lonely as I was until it was shown to me what I had been lacking.

"I've met a few more interesting people since we last spoke," he began. "And we have one more location well underway. We're making progress."

I smiled, pleased for him but not fully understanding what 'progress' meant.

"How are you enjoying your books?" he asked.

"They're so wonderful!" I couldn't help but show off, and recited a poem to him. He raised an eyebrow.

"You have an ear for poetry! Isn't that one of the ones I bookmarked just tonight?"

I nodded my head, beaming, glad to have pleased him.

"We're going to have to take advantage of that. We have so much that needs to be put to memory. Our minds are really the only safe place where we know no one can ever break in or take things away from us. We don't have to reveal all that we know, and most of them never even pay attention to us enough to question our intelligence or knowledge."

"Well, I can't speak for anyone else, but I know I'm almost invisible to them. No one ever pays attention to me." I said.

"You do a great job staying under the radar, I've noticed. You're very good at keeping your nose down and not ever making waves. I like that. It means they really have no reason to distrust you, and it shows they never second-guess who you are or regard you as a threat."

I looked at him, unsure if that was actually a compliment or not.

"I've watched you, you know. Not often, but I always take time to observe people before I introduce myself. You're always so good at just going about your business, and I never saw you push the limits with your head librarian. And she's a real peach, isn't she!"

I laughed and he grinned back at me.

"No, I mean it. I would sit in the library, and every time I caught a glimpse of you, she was always badgering you—even though you obviously knew what you were doing and did your job well. And the thing that I was most sure about with you was that you had exceptional patience. See, lots of people—we Scourges still have this streak of brazenness within us, our ego, if you will. We have a hard time being submissive, even if we're young and this is how we grew up, with this whole second-class citizen world. We're a cocky breed, no doubt. And one thing that has always proven difficult is finding trustworthy people who are humble enough, or can act well enough, to fly under the radar. The more we learn—the more our eyes are opened as our knowledge grows —the more rebellious and caustic we become. It's just part of our coding, I think—aside from our innate sense of entitlement to be truly free. We don't appreciate being treated poorly, and sometimes our egos get the best of us and we want to put the other person in their place."

I nodded; I understood exactly what he meant, even if I was cautious enough never to act upon it.

"See, exactly. And if you can relate to that, it's only further testament to your patience, because I never once saw you challenge your head librarian. A lot of Scourges can't help it—they hold their eye contact just a minute too long, they scowl, they have tense body language or they clench their fists. They end up doing something that then draws unwanted attention to themselves and lets 'their betters' know that they still have spirit left inside of them—and they're usually the ones who get reported and then Disappear."

It was true—it was all true. I'd never imagined I could have such conversations, but everything he was saying was exactly as I had both observed and experienced it. It was why I was conditioned to be so cautious around other Scourges—guilt by association was enough to find oneself targeted.

"That's why you're so special. It's what makes you rare. I could see right away that it wasn't because you were passive, and there was no mistaking you for being beaten down. No, not you. I could see you were made of stronger stuff than that. I could see that the wheels were turning."

He looked at me with admiration in his eyes. For the first time since meeting him, I felt color rise to my face uncomfortably. I wasn't used to compliments, and I suppose I didn't really trust anyone, especially if they were being too kind.

I think he sensed this—or maybe he thought I was misconstruing his flattery as false—but he paused, and just studied my face for a moment before speaking again.

"Your personality, your quiet nature, and your thoughtfulness have kept you alive and safe so far. Someday we'll talk more about all of this, but for now, I hope you understand that I only have the best of intentions. Your ability to do your work effectively, to walk among everyone without drawing any unnecessary attention to yourself—that's exactly what I was looking for. You're exactly who I have been hoping to find. We have a lot of work to do, and I can't do it all alone. So please, never think I mean anything negative when I say such things. I have found that I speak freely with you—more so than I do most people—and maybe I shouldn't. But I think it's because I feel I can trust you—and I want you to feel that you can trust me, too."

He reached out and put his hand over mine, clasping it just long enough for me to feel his warmth before withdrawing. I listened to his words, taking comfort in them, and wished, more than anything, that his hand was still covering mine. How starved for human contact I was!

I smiled; an assuring smile, hopefully, a genuine smile to express all that I could not say. Above all, I was simply grateful to have been noticed at all. I was grateful for his time and the trust he had given me. Although I could not be sure, I felt deep within that crossing paths with him had somehow altered the course of my life—given me hope rather than mere existence.

"So here's what I think," he continued.

"I think you and I are going to spend more time together, and we're going to work on a bigger plan than what I've already put together. I think you're going to need to meet Aaron at some point, and the three of us are going to have to consider some long-term goals. How's your writing?"

"I earned top marks in my writing courses, but you know none of it was Creative, nor did I have access to any Literature or Poetry courses. Everything we wrote was Technical English—designed to make us better librarians, nothing more."

He nodded, apparently familiar with the program.

"So I've heard. But still, did you enjoy it? Do you like to write?"

"As much as I could, yes. But I can't say I've explored it enough to know if I'd be any good at it beyond helping with editing, really. I haven't ever written anything of my own, you know? Like, developed my own thoughts, or put anything original down. I've just done assignments."

He nodded.

"Well, that will come. I enjoy writing. Aaron is fine with sharing his ideas when they strike him, but he's more interested in just doing the libraries and recruiting new people to our cause. I think it's time we grow beyond just that."

"What did you have in mind?" I asked. I expected it would hold a certain danger—everything he had done seemed dangerous and risky.

"I'd like to start some kind of newsletter. Flyers. I'd like to drop flyers around the cities. Things that would incite the crowds of Scourges—give them hope. Let them know that there are others out there rebelling against the status quo. I'd like for them to know that not only was there a time when they considered us Equal—but that we were a nation that had laws specifically implemented into our very fabric just to secure it."

"It sounds marvelous—but also very dangerous. How do you intend to distribute flyers without getting caught? Especially with cameras everywhere? And how do you intend to reproduce papers in large quantities without drawing attention to yourself as you purchase supplies? There would be a record of all store purchases—you'd have to have Just Cause for purchasing the paper, the ink, even a printer or computer to do all the copies. You aren't allowed to have any of those things, are you?"

Maybe his job allowed him access to such things. I still knew little about what he did other than working his secondary job as a delivery driver for the Services For The Deceased. Maybe working in the science field, or having a better education and a high-ranking profession allowed him perks.

But he shook his head.

"No, nothing like that. My day job is still just another job for Scourges—they'll never give me access to anything of any true significance there, and it's just lab work anyhow. I don't work with paper at all; I document everything on our computers and mostly work with infectious diseases. Scourges are disposable, you see. So I have the qualifications of my betters, but they don't have to worry about handling the viruses and toxins because we're available to do all that for them."

He rolled his eyes and laughed.

"It really is rather ironic—every day they entrust people whom they consider their inferiors with enough toxins and horrifying viruses that we could technically unleash an epidemic into the world that could potentially kill millions, but they don't ever think we're capable of doing anything without permission, or even thinking freely enough to consider such things."

He smirked, and a look of disdain crossed his face—the first time I ever witnessed him expressing a negative emotion or thought. It seemed contrary to his usual demeanor, but I understood that deep within each of us was a desire to be treated humanely. It seemed that anyone who was ever made to feel "less than" others would feel bitterness and even anger at times.

"Anyhow, wiping out half our population that way wouldn't solve anything; we need a revolution, not mass genocide. Besides, there wouldn't be any way to target the innocent from the guilty with a virus; everyone would be equally at risk. They've never figured out how to isolate any type of contagion so it only targets and destroys specific demographics. Yes, we can do things that affect some more than others—those who are immunocompromised or elderly, for example—but we couldn't really do something that doesn't affect every race. Underneath our skin, we're all made of the same stuff. They probably don't want us to realize that, but if they could have obliterated us as a race by unleashing some sort of pandemic that only affected us, they probably would have done it by now."

That made sense to me, although I had to admit I'd never traveled down such dark corridors in my mind. Somehow, no matter how bad things were, I had always believed we were still regarded as human beings, and no matter how badly we were treated, the vast majority of our fellow man didn't think we should all be dead. I couldn't imagine that the world hated us so much it actually felt they would be better off committing genocide against an entire race just to be rid of us. But I could also admit that my worldview was very small—I hadn't traveled or even gone beyond a twenty-mile radius from my dwelling unit since I had entered adulthood and began working. Like most Scourges, I did not travel unless directed, and my professional position and station in life did not require it.

One thing was becoming clear, the more I listened to the man sitting next to me: I had lived a very sheltered existence until meeting him. I had also been exceptionally complacent in both thought and deed; I went about my business, did as I was expected, caused no trouble, but also did nothing to break free of what I considered to be my only path. It had never occurred to me to challenge our government or the way things were. I would never have even known where to begin, even if I had entertained such thoughts. I found it to be one of the most interesting things about Ben—the fact that he had contemplated so much, and was obviously a man of action as well—especially given the potential for self-harm at any point. His desire to improve the state of our nation and the lives of Scourges everywhere outweighed the value he placed on his own life and freedom, and that spoke volumes to me.

I wondered, as we sat there discussing the future, if it was possible to dare to dream of the world ever returning to the way it once was, or if we could afford to hope for a future in which every person within our nation could consider themselves truly equal or safe from discrimination—either by our government or our fellow citizen.

It all seemed so big—so enormous in both dream and action —that I did not know if a few lowly people could create such a transformation. But as I listened to him, as I stared into his eyes and heard his impassioned speech, I wanted desperately to believe him, and to believe in what he believed was possible.

All I knew, though, was that without such men taking action, without everyone collectively rising, that nothing would change or improve. The only thing we had was hope—and the only hope we had was through ourselves and those brave enough to stand alongside us.

He was looking for soldiers. It was easy to find them among the disenfranchised, disempowered, and the disillusioned. We had nothing left except the will and strength to fight; and we had nothing left to lose by doing so. Our lives and freedom may have been forfeit if we were caught—but mere existence was not the same as having a life worth living.

I knew, in the way that he had stirred such thoughts and passions within me, that he could and would do the same for countless others. He was a natural born leader, a free thinker, and a man of action. He would find his soldiers. He would build his army of revolutionaries. And together, we would either create the changes necessary to make our nation whole again, or we would die trying.

TWENTY-THREE ~ RECONNAISSANCE

◆ ◆ ◆

Being slight of stature and unassuming by nature, Ben seemed to feel that I would be a good person who could do reconnaissance for him. Being a girl likely helped, and even though my 25th birthdate had recently passed, I was still very youthful in appearance. He assured me that this would help me fly under the radar and pass through most parts of the city with no one paying the slightest bit of attention to me. I was inclined to agree with him, but it was still a nerve-wracking idea—me, a person who had never done a brave or heroic thing in my life, being given the responsibility of observing and learning about specific locations for matters of great importance. I was a little person, both literally and figuratively; it was near impossible to imagine myself ever doing what Ben believed I was capable of.

I had great faith in him, his wisdom, and his judgment—even if I did not possess such faith in myself. I also had an almost irrational desire to please him, to do my best for his sake, and to do whatever necessary to win his approval. These were things I did not try to understand, but I did recognize about myself, regardless. I wanted to be pleasing to him, and that was enough.

And so we talked about what he needed of me, of what his goals were, and of those whom he felt he could bring closer into his fold so we could begin training and preparing for what was yet to come. He discussed a variety of ideas, outlined some goals for the short-term, and talked profusely about the people whom he had come into contact with on his travels. His network was already vast—I estimated in the many hundreds, and spanning the distance of at least a thousand miles, given how he spoke of certain places. This was, naturally, a good thing, because it meant he had support far and wide, and if he genuinely equated his movement of Scourges as a revolution against the government and the Common Good, he was going to need both people and resources to accomplish anything significant.

He spoke of small ways we could begin the process, and where I fit into his plans. I was to visit the places where we knew specific work was being done. I needed to secure information regarding both the newspaper publishing plant as well as one of the government factories where the book publishing was conducted —a large facility managed by the Primary Library Services that I knew to be within our city but had never visited. All books published for our libraries originated in the same source. I would have to first discover the location by searching through information held by the head librarian—and hopefully it would not be on her computer, but rather on her desk or on some type of billing paperwork.

Once I had identified and confirmed the locations where both the newspaper and the PLS did their publishing, Ben would attempt to review the facilities on his own, casing the external premises much like I imagined any would-be jewel thief would. He said he would study the security, monitor the work hours, do what he could to study the employees and administration, and try to look for gaps in their security.

The goal, he said, was to gain entry into the building. If it were possible to use the buildings and their resources more than once, then we could work with that, although there would be substantial risk posed to everyone every time they visited.

The alternative was to find a time with minimal risk and low security, break in, and steal the equipment and supplies needed. This was probably the best long-term plan, but if they caught anyone, it would surely result in imprisonment or even death. It also meant that if they noticed supplies and equipment had been taken, it would likely mean a permanent increase in security, making future break-ins and theft impossible.

"Ideally, the best way we could manage is if we can find out if there are Scourges working the locations. Then it would only be a matter of recruiting enough of them to access the facilities routinely, returning whenever we were ready to print more documents. That's why your job will be so important—you'll be able to tell straightaway if you see Scourges working there, or if you can find out any information about the employees or administration through the Primary Library Services. It's a long-shot that there would be access to such details within any of the libraries themselves, but you never know."

It was a bold plan. It was terrifying to consider just how much anyone involved would put their lives at risk. All I had to do was search an office and then—if I could find the addresses—take a brief trip to each location just to verify that they were still being used by the publishers and the addresses were valid. My own minor role seemed safe and simple compared to the dangers I knew others would later face, and yet it still filled me with trepidation. I wanted to be brave—if only for him—but I knew it would require every ounce of fortitude I possessed to even venture into the head librarian's office and snoop through her belongings, let alone travel by myself through the city to unknown locations. It was all entirely outside of my wheelhouse, and I was both terrified and exhilarated to be entrusted with such a task.

How he looked at me, though, how he did not seem to doubt my capabilities, and knowing that he was relying on me, made me believe I could do all that he asked and more.

I was finding, the more time I spent in his company, that believing in his cause—in his desire to see a better world for each of us—was easy. His views may have been idealistic, but he was a realist about the risks, dangers, and outcome should we fail.

Above all, he did not want anyone involved who did not

earnestly support the overall vision of the movement, nor did he want to exploit anyone who was too afraid to take risks. Failure, he said, was much more likely if people seemed scared, hesitant, or nervous. Those were the behaviors that would draw undue attention to the individuals, which would only trace back to the group if they were captured and questioned. Confidence—while simultaneously being humble and unassuming—was the key to success. Acting as though we had a right to be doing what we were doing, as if we were following orders and had a purpose, was the way to travel without drawing attention to oneself. That's where the look of confidence mattered—but it had to be carefully balanced with a submissive nature and meekness so we would continue to be overlooked.

That was why he had chosen me; that was why he was entrusting me. It wasn't solely because I worked in one of the main branches or had access to the head librarian's personal space—although he did state that most head librarians were far less trusting of the Scourges on their staff and seldom granted such leniency to them. I scoffed at that; my head librarian was not tolerant of me, nor did I harbor any delusions that she approved of me. But her indifference—if that qualified as trust—was likely because I had been there since my first day of eligibility for employment. She had sculpted me into the employee she had wanted, and I had kept my head down and done my work without complaint from that day forward. She did not respect nor fear me; she relied on me to do whatever she demanded, and I obliged. After years of service without complaint, with reliable, predictable behavior and results, she ought to have been able to trust me—I had never given her cause not to.

Until now, that was.

Soon, very soon, I would take a rather enormous step away from my usual behavior, and advance toward the most anarchist activity I had ever done.

I knew, however, that I could no longer go back into the quiet, prosaic routine I had existed in before. I could not walk away.

The choices were presented, and of the two, I felt an almost obsessive compulsion to proceed toward the unknown, even though I knew it was full of risks and peril. But only by committing to the danger could I walk parallel with freedom, and personal freedom was something I had tasted very little of. I was standing on the edge of a cliff, but wholeheartedly making the conscientious choice to step off the edge and fly—because only by taking that ultimate step could I finally discover what lay beyond all that I had known. Without taking the risks, I knew what my world would be. The risks were the only hope I had of ever escaping the next fifty years of my life with my soul intact.

And so I chose to leap.

TWENTY-FOUR ~ ECHOES OF CHILDHOOD

◆ ◆ ◆

We talked of things yet to do, of our childhoods, and of our families. He told me how he had come from a family of academics, how his grandfather and father had both been Professors at one of our major universities, and how they had fallen out of favor solely because of the crippling politics which made them the target of contempt. His grandfather had taught mathematics, while his father had been a Professor of English Literature. He said it had been over fifteen years since he had seen either of them—both had gone underground in the early years when men and women began Disappearing. He was only a child, and though his mother would occasionally receive the odd envelope with some funds, they could not communicate in return. He had been raised well enough—away from the city and in relative comfort despite the circumstances.

It was his father and grandfather who had inspired him to focus on the preservation of books and the creation of the underground libraries. Both of them had been ardent readers. His grandfather had lived nearby, and Ben had spent much of his childhood in his company.

Ben told me how his grandfather always spoke of the importance of individualism, of knowing one's own mind, and of using one's time wisely to carve out one's destiny. His grandfather had told him of his own childhood, and how his father had been an artist, beloved by all, and his death had left a significant hole in his life. It clarified the importance of family to him, in being close with his children and grandchildren, and sculpted his desire to instill both his values and a hearty memory of himself into his children. They were his legacy, he would declare, and the best way to be remembered was to be fully immersed in the lives of those one loved.

By contrast, however, Ben's father seemed to have missed the lessons impressed upon him by his father about the importance of family. He had been a man of literary refinement, and his primary interest had always been in his work. Having a family had almost seemed like an afterthought; his time had been spent submerged in his home office, surrounded by his books and writing, barely noticing the small child playing on the lawn. Ben described him as a man who would miss meals, disregard holidays and special occasions, and overlook his personal relationships not out of any form of malice, but merely because his work always took precedence. He worked a full schedule at the university, read voraciously, and in his youth had even written and published important papers and eventually, a novel.

It was his publications that eventually resulted in his need to go into hiding, and had made him a target of the government. Times had shifted significantly enough that the protections of the First Amendment were no longer a guarantee, and any form of self-defense against discrimination had been met with degradation and ridicule. His father was an outspoken critic of the hypocrisy of the People and government, both of whom openly targeted individuals and suppressed the liberties of their fellow citizens. They made examples of those who publicly opposed popular sentiment and implementing new laws which promoted discrimination. Government officials began creating lists of potential terrorists, listing Pro-Constitutional—especially First and Second Amendment Advocates—as primary identifiers for potential terrorism. Ben's father and grandfather had both been placed on that watch list, and were detained and questioned by Law Enforcement. Once the university heard, they were both put on administrative leave pending review. The review was nothing more than the university covering itself, however, and both Ben's father and grandfather were fired, never having returned to work after being placed on administrative leave.

Seeing the writing on the wall, both men determined it was time to flee and live off-grid before they, too, Disappeared as so many of their colleagues had. Their political views resulted in them being heavily monitored by government agencies and classified as the greatest threat to the nation.

It was Ben's father who had taught Ben from an early age the benefits of memorization, and what little time they had shared was usually spent in his father's home office, reading aloud and then repeating what they had read. Ben said his father could—and would—commit long passages of beloved pieces of text to memory, and then recite them both to himself and to anyone who would listen. Ben's recollection of his father was that he was a literary genius, who lived in his head and among the dead writers and poets of old, and preferred their company to that of the living.

As a young child, Ben could feel the tension in the air as things grew more politically volatile. His father would secret himself away with his books once he lost his position within the university, and seemed to sink into a sort of angry, sullen depressive state, where his irritability could no longer be assuaged, and all were instructed just to leave him in peace.

Ben's last memory of his father was that of being awakened in the dead of night, dragged by his father into his study, and then commanded to recite a piece of literature he had been instructed to commit to memory. He recalled his father being near frantic, wild-eyed, and seemed almost afraid. Ben had recited the piece dutifully, and as his father patted his head absent-mindedly, he muttered almost incoherently about how impossible it was to memorize everything, and how could one possibly know how to rank such important pieces to know which to memorize next. His father rambled about how there was no qualitative method to determine what passages or authors had greater value, and there was just too much, too much to do.

Handing Ben a book of poetry, he had ushered him out the door, whispering to him to guard his books with his life, telling him that there was no greater contribution that man could make than to leave a legacy of words behind for generations to come. As Ben walked toward his room, he had looked back at his father, now pacing in front of his shelves, one hand covering his bearded mouth, with tears streaming down his cheeks.

The next morning when he woke, his mother told him his father and grandfather had gone. Had he not received random pieces of mail over the years, Ben would have believed his father to have committed suicide somewhere, so despondent he had seemed at their last encounter.

Ben never saw his father or grandfather again, though he believed they were still alive.

Over the years, he grew up, eventually got selected for university—ironically attending the same one his father and grandfather had both once taught at—and earned advanced degrees in science. His mother had passed away, and as he began his adult life as an employee and a man, life continued on.

Over the years, he would hear stories of people who memorized pieces of literature, sometimes books of the Bible, sometimes chapters of famous works of literature, sometimes entire books. Ben liked to think that no matter where his father was, that he was out there fighting against the current status quo and government in some small way.

Building the underground library system was exactly what Ben believed his father and grandfather would have done on their own had they not fled. Maintaining individualism, free thought, and freedom of expression and speech were cornerstones to a free nation, they believed, and one could not hope to consider oneself truly free if any form of censorship or government control existed over the creators of art.

The suppression of these freedoms had been steadily increasing over the decades, it was undeniable. Ben's father and grandfather may well have seen the direction the nation was taking—parallels to World War II were unavoidable by the time Ben was a boy of ten—and they may have felt it was better to live freely on the fringes of society than to Disappear as so many others before them had.

It was wise for them to have fled, I believed, and Ben agreed. We had both heard the stories of those early years and known it was reputed to be in the hundreds of thousands—if not millions —of citizens who had been taken away for crimes unknown, often without charges or convictions. They had been arrested under the guise of domestic terrorism, and under the broad umbrella of such a label, were seldom given a fair chance for personal defense. Most simply Disappeared, and any questions or inquiries into their absence was met with cold indifference or ignorance, and a wall of bureaucracy.

It was much easier for a government to control a population if it silenced all those who would speak against it, and they routinely did this through both censorship and the permanent suppression of those who had used their voices to express their dissent. After the first wave of arrests, once everyone understood that people were Disappearing, the rest of the citizenry had quickly fallen into step with the new regime. Fear of the unknown, largely supported by stories of horror and dark speculation, heavily influenced the masses. There were even those who reported on others, children against parent, neighbor against neighbor, eager to distance themselves from anyone questionably 'anti-American'. Whether done out of genuine support for the political climate, or to ensure their own security, it was a dangerous time for all Americans, and few felt safe.

Ben was fortunate, in a way—at least more fortunate than I was. I would probably never know the true circumstances of what had befallen my family. There were no records I could access, and no reliable witnesses I could question. My father had simply vanished one day and did not return—with state officials later informing my mother of his death, stating it was a high-risk profession and work-related deaths were a matter of routine. And then later, as state social workers took me away, I had calmly accepted their story of my mother's suicide, again with no means to question the story provided.

At least Ben knew what had initially happened to the men in his family. He knew why they had fled and were no longer a part of his life. He might not have full closure given he did not know what fate had befallen them, but at least he knew why they had gone.

And they had been an active part of the first half of his childhood. He could trace his roots; the family members he had spent his childhood with had left an indelible footprint on his heart and within his mind. He had firm memories of the men they were, how they felt about the social issues of their day, the position they had taken against the drastic transformation of their nation, and the price they were willing to pay in order to secure their freedom. He knew the memory of his mother, could recall her scent, could remember her laugh and the way she had comforted him. He knew they were decent people, obviously intelligent, and possessed a high quality of character. It was not much, but it was more than many of the orphans our generation had.

It had left an undeniable mark on his person; he was strong, confident, and brave. He was a man of conviction; a boy who would grow to become a man willing to risk his life all to help preserve the history of his nation regardless of the risks involved. He had the confidence to know that the men he had been raised by were men of integrity and strong moral character. They had chosen a hard path, but they had ultimately chosen freedom in the only way they could. They could have stayed.

They could have submitted to the requirements imposed upon them by a changing government with far overreaching powers, but instead they had chosen to live the lives of nomads, as outlaws to be hunted for the rest of their days.

I understood Ben a lot better after learning all that he shared, and in some ways, envied him the peace of mind that surely came with knowing who he was and the roots he had come from. But I also questioned if it did not weigh heavily on him, knowing the men in his family had essentially chosen their books and convictions over love for their family. I wondered if he ever felt abandoned, or simply considered inconsequential, to his father and even grandfather. With his mother now deceased, he was just as much an orphan as I, even though he technically still had a father to the best of his knowledge.

Our childhood stories echoed many others I had heard from my peers: We had all lost those whom we loved. Our government had made orphans of us all.

TWENTY-FIVE ~ COURAGE

◆ ◆ ◆

The following week, I summoned the courage to go through the head librarian's office. I did not waver, and I did not delay. There was no way to know how long it might take me to search through her office and locate some type of billing or delivery statement that would have the address of the Primary Library Services factory location, so I wanted to ensure I could go through her office more than once if necessary.

It was much easier than anticipated, however, and I had secured the information needed within moments of being in her office. She had never locked the office door, and though I had never needed to enter the room after hours, I had visited her before she left for the evening on many occasions. There were piles of papers scattered about, books haphazardly placed along her bookshelves and atop the file cabinets, and other signs of untidiness and general disorganization. Without delay, I went first to a box that the Primary Library Services had delivered, and easily located an order form within. The address of the factory had been listed on both the paperwork and the external packaging; I had found it with no hardship.

Just entering her office had required me to draw upon courage I had never before needed. My paranoia made me worry that her office was under surveillance, and the entire time I was in there, I was trying to listen for the sound of sirens over the beating of my heart. But I heard nothing, no one came, and I had done what needed to be done within moments.

Finding the location of the local newspaper office was equally easy, as they printed it on the back page of the newspaper itself.

I went about my business for the rest of the week, walking to and from work and enjoying the onset of Autumn and the cooler weather. Every night I checked the bushes under the stairs, and though I did not expect to find anything for at least another week, I returned to my unit with a general sense of disappointment. I had quickly grown used to Ben's presence in my life, and the long periods between contact left me feeling more lonesome than I ever felt before we had met, and I longed to hear from him.

And so the days passed, with the head librarian paying no mind to my presence, leaving each evening exactly as she always had, and freeing me of any lingering doubts about my having been observed or found guilty over having entered her office when she was not there.

As time went by and I was reassured that I had escaped detection, I felt more comfortable about my deception, and I gained a bit of confidence. My plan was to visit the two buildings on my day off and verify they were in the locations listed. I would have to travel by city bus to get to each of them, and I anticipated the entire afternoon would be spent on the mission. As I never needed to travel outside of my usual walking route, I was apprehensive and nervous about the bus rides and being so far away from home. But I did not want to disappoint Ben. So I did my best to plan my itinerary, and, recalling his bravery for all he did on a regular basis, tried to calm my fears, and conduct myself in a way in which I felt he would have been proud.

TWENTY-SIX ~ VISITING THE FACTORY

◆ ◆ ◆

My next day off, I readied myself in the morning for travel. I packed a sweater in case it was cool, a thick piece of bread with a few slices of summer sausage and cheese, and a bottle of water. I slung my bag over my shoulder cross-wise, took one last look at the route of the bus line and each destination, made sure I had my Identification and Currency Card for travel, and set out for the bus stop.

I had been on the city buses before, but not very many times. There had been no need. I lived within a few blocks of everything I required, and as my life typically consisted of work and a weekly shopping trip at the local market, any further travel was unnecessary.

I entered at the back doors of the bus as required, sitting in the last row. My Identification and payment for travel were documented separately, placing my activities in two separate tracking systems. It was entirely possible I could end up flagged and monitored as a result, if for no other reason than it was uncharacteristic for me to travel such distances. Ben had understood this, and assured me I would lie low for a period afterward, just to ensure no one could pick up on any strange activities. He had also mentioned that we may not have our visits should anything seem out of the ordinary, and I had to admit to feeling disappointed in that possibility more than anything else.

It was almost a full hour by bus to get to the newspaper factory.

I had opted to get off at that bus stop because it would have been less dangerous to explain if anyone ever questioned me, as there were other businesses and shops nearby. The Primary Library Services building was approximately six blocks further north, and I intended to walk the distance after confirming the newspaper factory was active.

At the designated stop, I got off the bus, and clutching my bag tightly, willed myself to be calm and composed. I reminded myself to behave as if I was supposed to be there, as if I knew what I was doing, to walk with intention and purpose. The area was more run-down than I expected, and many of the brick buildings had broken windows and graffiti. There was very little traffic, even though it was a weekend.

I walked along the sidewalk across from the two-story building, trying to mentally document details without being obvious or draw attention to myself. There was a parking lot next to the building with over twenty vehicles filling its rows.

The newspaper factory was much like I expected it would be—an old building with the name of the newspaper in large, bold, faded letters above the main entrance—a reminder of its former glory. I noted glass double-doors in the front entrance, and as I got to the edge of the street, I could see a set of large, metal rolling doors, presumably where the trucks would back in to get loaded. There did not seem to be any CCTV cameras attached to the building or even on the streetlights; I assumed it was because it was a more industrial part of town and crime might have been reduced because of the lack of residential houses and shops.

That was as far as I could see without crossing the road and walking up the sidewalk by the parking lot, so I made my way across the street and casually strolled in the direction of the Primary Library Services building.

Feeling my confidence grow as I walked, I recalled all the details about the building and parking lot, certain that I could give a decent drawing of the place if called upon.

I was glad I had done this trip during daylight hours because the area was growing more industrial by the block. The main road that the bus had stopped on had been lined with brick buildings, and although some of them were obviously abandoned, they still represented a standard city block. The further north I traveled, the more sparse the buildings became, with large, empty lots between them. I crossed several sets of train tracks along the way, and by the time I reached the Primary Library Services building, I was considerably more on edge regarding my surroundings.

The building itself was a concrete monstrosity; it boasted no beautification. The windows were all tinted, the parking lots surrounding three sides were all overrun with weeds and cracked asphalt, and the front side of the building rested on the edge of the sidewalk. The roadway was so old and poorly maintained that it no longer had paint marks, and at least six sets of railroad tracks were directly parallel to the building, a few with parked railway cars covered in graffiti stored on them.

It was not an area that I had any business being in, and there were no shops near enough to justify my being there. Luckily, I did not see any CCTV cameras anywhere—a blessing considering how high crime rates had become, resulting in the nation-wide mandate for CCTV cameras to be installed throughout every major city. But it also appeared that the Primary Library Services building itself was closed down, either for the full weekend or just for today. There should not have been any type of record of my having walked in this area. I did not see any cameras attached to the building itself. It seemed I could walk back the same way I had come without being observed by anyone.

Noting as much as I could once more, I made my way quickly back to the original road where I had exited the bus, and then walked further west toward the local shops. I had looked on the map and noted a particular German shop that sold breads, and had intended to visit to create a legitimate alibi for why I would have gone to such lengths to go to another part of the city if questioned. I intended to say that my walk toward the Primary Library Services had been nothing more than an inexperienced girl—a Scourge girl—getting lost in the city and disoriented after exiting the bus line. It was plausible enough and explained my having walked aimlessly up to the Primary Library Services before realizing I must have taken the wrong road and then turned back.

My confidence returning—along with my sense of security after being back in a more densely populated area—I ventured into the German Bakery, selected two loaves of bread and several pretzels, paid with my Currency Card, and then made my way back toward the bus stop. Once there, my timestamp revealed I had almost a half an hour before the return bus, so I perched along a wide windowpane of an empty building and ate my bread, cheese, and sausage. I felt invigorated—exhilarated, even. It was the bravest thing I'd ever done on my own. I tried to maintain my usual facade of quiet humility and tried to keep my eyes downcast. But I felt very self-conscious as I tore bites from my sandwich, and still uneasy enough about my strange surroundings that I felt compelled to remain vigilant. Above all, I agreed with Ben's assessment, in that we Scourges were always better off appearing to be slow-witted, afraid, and meek. I believed that most of us gave this act away through our eyes— intelligence being such a difficult thing to conceal long-term to anyone observant enough to notice. It worked to our advantage that no one typically gave us too much credit. And we had been beaten into submission enough that the humility and meekness came much more naturally to most than pride would have them admit. But it was always better to be timid and submissive than to evoke the negative attention, harassment, and potential violence from our betters.

The bus eventually arrived, and taking my extra bag full of German breads, I made my way back home without incident. I had left a decent account of my travels by visiting the bakery, and although it might have seemed like a long trip just for specialty bread, my time was still my own enough to have the freedom to shop where I preferred. And since it was done on a day off, I felt comfortable that even if questioned, my alibi was more than adequate to justify the entire trip.

Once I returned home, I stored the breads and two of the three pretzels in my freezer, closed my curtains and bathroom door, and then settled down to relax with my book of poetry.

I was exceedingly pleased with myself and felt remarkably brave. I wished I could have shared my exploits with Ben right then, but I knew it would be at least another week, or possibly even longer, before I would see him again.

So I did the next best thing, and set about memorizing some of the poetry contained within the book he had given me.

TWENTY-SEVEN ~ IN TOO DEEP

◆ ◆ ◆

I met with Ben in the cemetery a full sixteen days after my day trip to the newspaper factory and the Primary Library Services building. This made it over three weeks since the last time I had seen him.

He looked tired, and his right arm was bandaged.

"We hit some trouble while we were scouting one of our locations. We thought it had been cleared and would be a safe place to put another library. All of our intel indicated it was a deserted location in a town that had little government presence. They didn't even have a local library, let alone CCTV cameras everywhere. We were told by one of our local supporters of an area that had been used as a storm shelter a few decades back. So we checked it out.

"I went there with the local guy and the two others who were within an hour's drive who would have been in charge of the place once it was operational. Our local guide was wrong about it being abandoned. He didn't know any better, I'm sure, but we ended up being confronted by the landowner. Things got messy.

"We couldn't exactly tell him what we were doing on his property, and he was clearly bigoted and hated Scourges. He might not have been the sharpest tool in the shed, but he knew something was up when four Scourges from out of town were found casing his property late at night. But then he spotted our local guy—and we knew right then that he was going to report us.

"As soon as he reached for his phone, things turned south. One of our guys attacked him, trying to get his phone away from him, and as soon as he did, all hell broke loose. He had two German Shepherds—one of which lunged at me and bit me on the arm. The other attacked one of the men. The guy started screaming for help, so the two other guys jumped him, trying to get him to shut up. One of them used a rock on him, and it knocked him out."

He looked at me, his eyes reflecting the sadness and shame he seemed to be feeling.

"I'm not sure how much of this you want to hear..."

His voice trailed off. His spirit seemed heavy, and he was nothing like his usual self. Rubbing his temple, he sighed heavily.

I put my hand over his, giving it a squeeze. I wasn't squeamish. I wasn't innocent. I knew what we were doing was dangerous. I accepted this. I wasn't sure how far I was prepared to go myself, but I had no illusions that we could ever hope to make progress without some violence. They had been mercilessly, intentionally, and vindictively targeting us for decades now, and getting away with it because we had no recourse. Although I did not advocate for violence, I knew it was an inevitability, and felt no guilt over giving back that which they gave so freely.

"We were in a mess. What could we do? If we left the man there, he would regain consciousness and report us to the authorities. If he had any sort of description, we'd all be caught eventually and then hanged. If we killed him with any obvious signs of trauma, we'd be hunted as murderers, and they'd never stop with the surveillance and trackers until they had traced it back to at least one of us—and if they managed that, how long before they eventually found the rest of us or we cracked under interrogation and gave everyone else up or confessed all we knew?"

He shook his head, looking down at the ground.

"We killed the dogs. Well, I didn't, but two of the guys did by bashing them with rocks once they had knocked the farmer unconscious. So we were already in it; it was already violent, and we were already dead if they caught us.

"The one thing we had going for us is that we were close to the river. It wasn't very fool-proof, but it was the best we could do. We carried the man down to the river with his dogs and watched them as they got pulled into the rapids. We couldn't risk the man regaining consciousness and saving himself, so we held him under. We all did it, too—so our guilt and responsibility were equal—none more or less than the next. After a few moments, we sent his body out to the rapids, too.

"Our hope is that when his body is discovered, or that of his dogs, they eventually put the story together that we thought seemed most reasonable: He was a farmer out on his land one night, maybe one of his dogs went into the river by accident, or both, and the farmer tried to save him. Technically, they were all knocked unconscious or killed by wounds to the head, and that could easily have happened if they fell into the river; they'd have gotten knocked around. Or even if the farmer had fallen in and gotten knocked unconscious—his dogs would have jumped in and tried to save him. Luckily, because the property ran along parts of the river that were full of whitewater rapids, either of those scenarios is plausible. And it's a clean story—no unnatural violence, no signs of attack, and no evidence of other people ever having been involved."

He looked at me, his eyes almost pleading for forgiveness.

"We're at war," I said.

"I'm sorry that you had to go to such lengths, and I'm sorry that you now feel you have something you're going to have to carry with you. But guilt will not help anything. This is a war. It may not have bombs, or fighter jets, or trench warfare on the front lines, but this is still a war, and every war has casualties."

He raised his eyebrows, surprised at my firm tone and the weight of my words.

"We're fighting for our right to exist and to be treated as equal human beings in a country that our own ancestors founded. We're treated like garbage—less than garbage—by everyone because of the way we look and the actions of our ancestors— neither of which are within our control, and yet we are blamed and vilified. We've had our rights denied to us—rights that not only were Constitutionally guaranteed at one point, but that even our Founding Fathers had declared to be unalienable— given to us by God, not man. And yet our government, along with most of our fellow citizens, is perfectly happy to violate our rights every chance they get. They've been slaughtering us for decades—for generations. I'm sorry, but I just don't feel any guilt over the death of one man—a man who was going to report you and would gladly have watched you all get hauled away to face torture and death."

I squeezed his hand again.

"It's unfortunate, but necessary. We're at war. This is war. And it's a war without middle ground—you're either on one side or the other. There's no room for passive, non-political people anymore—everyone who doesn't choose to fight against what has been happening to us has allowed it to happen—and they've made their decision where they stand. And if they're not for us, they're against us—and that makes them the enemy just as surely as our government is."

I smiled at him, hopefully giving him a bit of reassurance.

"It's one thing to feel upset about your own role in things, in feeling bad because two dogs were involved—even in the loss of life because it should be sacred no matter who he was or what he believed. And I can even feel bad for his family if he had one. But what I can't feel bad about is that you handled it the only way you could so that you could extract yourself from that situation without ending up captured and dead. You did what had to be done—and as a leader, as a soldier, that's what you needed to do."

He smiled faintly, and nodded his head.

"You're right. Thank you."

We held eye contact for a long moment before I looked away, suddenly feeling very self-conscious.

I realized I was in far too deep to back out.

He had just confessed to murder, and I hadn't even blinked.

I had no frame of reference to know if this was what it meant to fall in love, but I was invested now. His future was tied to mine, and neither of us would have one worth anything if we did not have the same basic freedoms everyone else was given.

TWENTY-EIGHT ~ RECIPROCITY

◆ ◆ ◆

I met with Ben several more times over the next few weeks. He had decided to stay close to home while his arm healed. He wanted to be able to verify his travels, and had advised the other men he had been with to do the same. The man who lived near the farmer had sent word to Ben that the story had been reported locally, but they had listed it as an unfortunate accident. They had determined that the man must have slipped into the water, and it was believed he had either tried to save one of his dogs or both his dogs had attempted to save him. Both scenarios had been cited as possibilities, and most hailed the farmer as having died a heroic death. There was not a prolonged investigation.

Even still, Ben had decided to tread with caution for the time being, and they had halted all further activities regarding the development of new libraries until they were confident things had stabilized once more. Everyone was on heightened alert, instructed to remain vigilant, and advised to report anything suspicious at any of the locations.

Ben's uniform for his day job required him to wear a lab coat, so concealing his bandaged arm did not prove to be difficult. His hours working for the Services For The Deceased were typically sporadic and only part-time, and as they listed him as a Scourge, he remained mostly invisible to the community at large.

He had gained many contacts over the years, and some worked within healthcare. They provided him with medical care after his injury and monitored him to ensure he did not develop an infection or rabies. As the weeks passed, his arm healed until it was finally nothing more than a series of small scars, all of which were easily concealed with a long-sleeve shirt.

It was during these weeks that we discussed many things, including our vision for what we would most like to see transform within our nation. We talked of books, authors, and the social issues that were prevalent during their lives that made their way into their stories. I shared with him the newly acquired poems I had committed to memory, and listened to him while he softly recited the sonnets of Shakespeare and countless other poems—an endlessly beautiful collection of works he had spent his entire life committing to memory.

There came a time, as I walked one evening to meet him, that I came to accept that although I could recall my life before he had become a steady presence in it, it was not something I ever wanted to experience again. I had grown accustomed to his voice, his mannerisms, his familiar scent, and the way he winked and smiled. We sat near one another, rarely touching, but even then, I had never known such closeness or intimacy in my life.

I could not know how he felt, but I had to believe my feelings were reciprocated, given the time he spent with me.

I knew there was a difference between love and attachment, and between friendship and romance. But these were not subjects I had first-hand experience with. All I knew was that when he spoke, expressing the love conveyed by the poets of old, I understood, and found beauty and truth within their timeless messages.

TWENTY-NINE ~ A STEP FORWARD

◆ ◆ ◆

We had been meeting in the cemetery thus far, but Ben said he thought perhaps it was time that I met Aaron. He was no longer living in the same city as the two of us, so it would require a day trip on one of my days off. He and Aaron had divided the state in half so each could work in designated regions. Although they were the original two creators of the underground library system, they had built libraries as far out as a thousand miles, resulting in zones covering Idaho, Montana, Oregon, and parts of California. There were dozens of men and women in charge of maintaining the libraries within their respective areas, all operating independently and typically without direct knowledge of any other locations or persons aside from Ben and Aaron. It was enough just to know that there were so many others out there doing the same thing and facing the same risks.

Ben and Aaron had been friends with shared common interests and values since their college days, but it was only after building the first library together that they had cemented their friendship with respect and loyalty. Ben referred to Aaron as his 'brother', and stated that he did not feel he could be any better connected to him other than having served in combat with him. Combat, he said, was not out of the realm of possibility, anyhow, and he was grateful to know he could rely on Aaron should things escalate to open warfare.

He wanted for us to meet so we could discuss possibilities for what we could do to take things to the next level. It was one thing to build libraries and to get people into the mindset that they were not only entitled to regard themselves as equal to everyone else in their country—it was quite another to get them into a position where they were willing to go to war to fight for those rights. Their primary plan had simply been to wake people up enough to see that they only had to be victims of society and their government if they chose to—they wanted them to realize that they had the power to create change, provided they did it all together and were willing to take chances and accept the consequences for their involvement if caught. The libraries were working in that regard, but it was a lot safer to weigh the risks of borrowing books and reading in secret than it was to contemplate dying on a battlefield in a Civil War against your own countrymen.

If the overall goal was to recreate the equality that once existed within our nation—to put an end to the bigotry and discrimination now plaguing almost half of the citizens in our country—then millions of people would need to be prepared to rise against it collectively. Violence, though unwelcome, had to become a recognized possibility—and it had to be more than just words. People had to be willing to fight, and willing to die, for their country and fellow countrymen.

The only way that could happen is if there was a significant movement propelling them—and just getting them to read outlawed books was not enough. Yes, they were risking their freedom by visiting the libraries and reading the books. But it was not the same as asking them to fight—to risk their lives, the lives of their families, to go to the front lines and fight against their fellow man—when they were seldom soldiers or trained in the art of war.

We worried it was too much to ask. We worried it was a movement that could never gain enough traction because people were simply too afraid to step beyond their comfort zones, to take a step that was, literally, going to put their lives on the line. We worried that their fears were too well-grounded to make any type of rebellion a realistic endeavor, that the government agencies and Law Enforcement were too militarized to challenge, and that the extreme restrictions on firearms had already rendered most of the citizens powerless to fight back.

It was complacency and the steady erosion of their rights that had resulted in us being exactly where we currently were. Apathy of the people had made it easy for the government to overreach, encroach on liberties, and take things away from the citizens one small measure at a time. Slowly, incrementally, but with dedicated purpose, the government had progressively gained power and control while citizens lost freedoms they had always taken for granted.

Many people had watched it happen but were too helpless to do anything beyond protest against it. The People were not organized enough, didn't have enough financial backing, and lacked the leadership to take a firm stand against what was unfolding before their eyes.

How could we expect them to rise against the tyranny that now plagued the nation when their own ancestors had allowed such powers to seize hold? How could we expect them to understand the importance of unifying and fighting back before things only got much worse—which history itself had proven was an inevitability?

These were discussions we needed to have—likely the same discussions our parents and grandparents had also had—that were extremely dangerous.

There was no choice, however.

It was necessary.

As Thomas Paine had said centuries before, "It is the duty of the patriot to protect his country from its government."

We not only had to be prepared for violence, we had to convince half of our countrymen that it was better to rise alongside us before their own children and grandchildren were rendered so powerless they could never shake the yoke of authoritarianism.

THIRTY ~ MEETING AARON

◆ ◆ ◆

We went to meet with Aaron on a crisp day at the end of October. It was now the 44th Week of the year, and the days were getting shorter. It was a pleasant drive, though we had to set out early. I was not used to traveling by vehicle, nor did I have much experience outside of the city. Like most urbanites, I had spent the majority of my life within the same five-mile radius. Given the restrictions on our freedom and the potential need to justify our travels, it was typically safer to remain within one's prescribed boundaries. There had been no legitimate reason for me to travel outside of the city, and so I didn't.

Ben had far better reasons, however, and working with the Services For The Deceased had given him ample opportunities to venture out than most would have. He was able to travel freely within the state, and by using the same van that was used by all Book Collectors for the Services For the Deceased, he had never been pulled over by Law Enforcement although it was often a concern for many Scourges. Everyone recognized the vehicle and dismissed it; such vehicles traveled everywhere at all hours, and were not distinct from one zone to the next. It was an ideal way for him to travel under the radar.

As we made our way to our destination, he told me about Aaron, and more about their plans.

"Ideally, what we could accomplish could be done with just a few of us playing in the majors. The fewer people we have on the top doing the bulk of the work, the safer it will be for everyone. As it is, once we start getting things printed, we'll need to branch out and get more people involved in distribution—and with that, they'll be taking on greater risks and responsibilities as well."

"How many people do you think you would need for that?" I asked. A thousand miles, hundreds of different library systems, and thousands of people—millions, even, was a lot of ground to cover.

"Well, I think a lot of it will get passed along once we get the originals out there; people will start sharing the papers—at the very least, they'll start whispering to each other about it. But we need to recognize that anyone caught with it will be basically considered traitors and our message would be an act of treason. So we need to choose our messages wisely, keep their word count to a minimum, and try and distribute it more like a flyer than a newspaper. Even still, we'll have hundreds of distributors, and each one will have to take a few thousand copies I would imagine."

"So we're going to have to figure out how they can conceal and carry around about 4 to six reams of paper. That's about, what? A foot by a foot for 2500 pages. We get boxes of paper at the library, and each has five reams of 500 pages each. So assuming we can use the Primary Library Services or the newspaper factory to print everything, we still have to figure out how to get thousands of pages printed and then packed and relocated somewhere else while they prepare for distribution."

It was an awesome undertaking with countless variables that could go wrong. Where would we get the paper from? How many people would it take to get it printed, stacked into the boxes, and then have the boxes loaded into multiple vehicles? Who would drive the vehicles? Where would they go? The process of creating an underground newspaper was much more complex than simply finding a few competent writers capable of selling war to a reluctant audience.

"So the one thing we have going for us is that we can utilize the Services For The Deceased vehicles in quite a few zones. We've built up a pretty good system within that department, and have intentionally been placing people to work there precisely to gain access to the vehicles and books. It's still going to be a nightmare trying to figure out how to get the flyers loaded all from one centralized location though, especially after-hours and in such a prominent building. We have a lot to sort out."

"Ok, so what about this? You have the library system broken into regions, right? So what if you get the printing and distribution set up regionally as well? Wouldn't that almost be better anyhow —to create several hubs just in case one gets busted? I mean, it's higher risk to have multiple prints happening—but really, if one of them were to be found out, you would know and could vacate the others or stop using them until you felt things had cooled down."

He nodded, smiling softly as he drove.

"All you need is for each location to have a master copy of the flyer. They could each do their own recon and sort out the details for how to manage it. My guess, though, is that each of the Primary Library Services buildings stick to the same exact schedule, which means they would all be vacant and available at the same time. They are government buildings, after all; they should keep the same hours as any other agency. So technically, if you printed from there rather than the newspaper factory, you could do all of the printings simultaneously in different regions —which probably reduces the risk as well."

"But something else to consider," I continued. "If you did plan on creating multiple printing and distribution hubs, not every region or city is going to have newspaper factories. They'll all have a Primary Library Service building because they're the main production and storage facility for each region and the libraries within their zones. But there aren't nearly as many newspaper factories; I only know of two—the one near us and the other in Spokane. So if the plan is to delegate and create multiple hubs, the Primary Library Services might be the only option."

"True," he responded.

"The good part about concentrating on the Primary Library Services as our building is that it wouldn't be suspicious at all to see the vehicles from the Services For The Deceased—no matter what the hour. No one passing through the parking lots —including Law Enforcement—would even think twice if they saw these vehicles on site."

"The PLS is also set up to print on book size paper; they print textbooks on regular 11x8 size pages. We likely wouldn't have any problem with the settings of the machines either, unlike the newspaper factories. I don't even know if we could adjust them to print smaller pages or if they would be stocked. If we used those locations, we might end up with newspaper-sized flyers, and we'd either have to distribute those or figure out how to repeat the flyers multiple times per page and then cut them into smaller flyers. It wouldn't be nearly as uniform and would require a lot more work."

"Yeah, I think we just figured out that it's going to need to be done through the PLS," he answered.

He grinned and looked over at me. "I'm so glad you're here."

I couldn't help but return his smile, glad I could contribute meaningfully, but also just to be sitting there as well, enjoying his company.

Things would get more complicated and likely more dangerous. But for this one moment, everything was perfect.

THIRTY-ONE ~ A PLEASANT VISIT

◆ ◆ ◆

Aaron was a stocky, dark-haired man with thick eyebrows and a beard. His hair was long enough to curl over his ears and the collar of his shirt, and he had a habit of pushing it out of his face as he talked.

After Ben introduced us, Aaron shook my hand warmly and said, "It's nice to finally meet you!"

With a quiet delight, I blushed and smiled, glowing internally because it meant Ben had mentioned me.

Aaron lived by himself in a country setting, almost as if he were a homesteader. His electricity was solar-generated, and his water came from a well and collected rainwater. It was a marvel to tour; I had never seen a Scourge person with the level of independence he had acquired. It was, apparently, because they had trained him in forestry and ecology.

He had greater freedom to travel than most, had his own vehicle parked alongside the Department of Ecology truck he used for work, and was left on his own with no direct supervision for weeks at a time. The disadvantage, I supposed, was the isolation. But for his lifestyle—working extensively in an underground setting and reading books at his leisure—he had a better situation than most Scourges could ever dream of anymore.

His freedom made him an invaluable asset.

We finally settled down for a cup of tea inside his small cabin —a simple building of a mere 800 square feet with a kitchen on one side, a designated living room area, and a small bedroom and bathroom in the back. It was the loveliest place I had ever visited, and I was enamored with how cozy it became with the fire crackling and the plaid curtains closed. There were no books present, and he stated he kept a container buried on the property to conceal them and protect them from damage. It seemed a delightful way of life, and I was enjoying our visit immensely.

For a while, I sat and listened as the two men discussed various issues and mutual connections, absorbing their knowledge and devotion to their enterprise. Then Ben summarized the things we had discussed on the way out, letting Aaron know that the PLS buildings would be the best way to go. He said he still hadn't gone to stake the building out and establish a pattern—mostly because of the incident with the farmer and his arm still healing —but at this point they might as well have a handful of the other leaders do the recon for their particular location so we could ensure they were all on the same schedule.

Aaron agreed, and said he would get in touch with all the leaders on his side of the state, and send word to those in the surrounding states to do the same. They guesstimated that if there were at least two regions creating pamphlets per state, they could divide into two regions and manage the distribution without too much difficulty or strain. Most of the leaders were in professions that allowed for more privacy and flexibility—as was often necessary. The two of them were clearly excited to advance to the next level.

"So we still need a few writers, don't we?" Aaron asked.

"Yeah. We have enough leaders who can delegate distribution within their own zones, and I'm fairly certain we'll be able to handle the printing itself—not to mention figuring out how to break in every time and all the logistics associated with that. But yeah, we need to figure out what we want our pamphlets to say, how long we want them to be, and who has enough writing experience to do a good job. We really need someone who's gone to school for English, or who can do a fairly persuasive writing style, and edit it, too. We won't have a lot of extra time to plan it out or do a lot of revisions, so they need to get it right without too much work. We need it to be one of the leaders—or a few of them. We probably need someone who's been in long enough to understand what we're doing, or at least have enough of a vision for our goals that they can write about it enough to convince people to join."

They both faded into their own thoughts, mulling over potential candidates.

"We'll have to figure it out. We can start asking our people discreetly if they have any interest in doing it or if they would be good at it. Surely we've got some writers in our group, even if they haven't had a lot of practice or experience. We can't all just be readers."

Aaron nodded his head and shrugged his shoulders. "I know what we need to say, but I'm not the one to say it. And I don't want to be. I've got enough going on managing the region and expanding. I'll do what I can to get the PLS part going because that's the next step, but I already have someone else in mind for who would do a better job running it than I would, so I will not be directly involved in any of it. But I can ask them if they know of any writers, too."

"Yeah, it won't do us much good to have the PLS buildings all set up if we have nothing written to get printed and distributed." Ben paused, still preoccupied. "Well! At least we have a plan! I'll see what I can do on my end, and maybe I can get some notes written out so we can know what we want them to say once we get someone."

"Sounds good," Aaron replied.

It was interesting to watch how the two men interacted; they were very comfortable with one another and seemed to have an easy friendship. They bounced ideas off one another, and the conversation drifted from the libraries to other topics with the fluidity of long-time friends who were around one another often.

By the time we set out again, Aaron hugged me and apologized for having monopolized so much of the conversation. I assured him I hadn't minded. I couldn't help but express my delight over the visit, telling him I hoped we could visit again soon. With a gracious smile, he kissed my cheek and gave me a wink. He gave Ben a hearty hug, and the two men parted ways casually, as if knowing they would see one another again soon.

It had been a pleasant day, and I was very happy to have been invited along.

We drove along the bumpy dirt road as the sun set behind us. Ben took my hand in his and then brought it to his lips, lightly kissing my fingertips. He kept my hand in his, resting them comfortably between us as we made our way home.

It had been a good day.

THIRTY-TWO ~ THE
EVOLUTION OF SELF

◆ ◆ ◆

The days passed with purpose and joy. I worked my shifts, read as much as possible, and saw Ben as often as time allowed. His arm healed, and he resumed his travels, but he made a concerted effort to return weekly—I believed, though it was unspoken, so we could spend time together, as it always seemed to coincide with either the night before my day off or on my day off.

The weather had transitioned into blustery days, sharp winds, and biting rain. Although I had never been to his dwelling unit, the weather changes had made it necessary for him to visit mine. And so we passed the time, often sitting hours alongside one another on the sofa, quietly reading our respective books and sharing things of particular interest with one another.

It seemed an idyllic courtship, and we were well-suited companions.

The more I read, the more my mind was opened to fresh ideas and possibilities, all of which seemed to delight Ben. He frequently shared all that he knew about the history of our nation, as well as various other notable world events. Uprisings and Civil Wars seemed to hold a particular interest, and he loved to share his knowledge of our Founding Fathers and the tyranny they had escaped. He was a proud citizen, even in a nation that had turned its back on him. Poor leadership and bigotry were dominant forces that had led to the deterioration of our country, he said, but it did not alter that the foundation upon which our nation had been framed, or that it was the best example of a free society.

He impressed upon me the words written within our Declaration of Independence—words that we were no longer allowed to recite without being branded terrorists and a danger to our fellow countrymen: "That whenever any Form of Government becomes destructive of these ends, it is the Right of the People to alter or to abolish it, and to institute new Government, laying its foundation on such principles and organizing its powers in such form, as to them shall seem most likely to effect their Safety and Happiness."

We did not have all the answers yet, and we knew we lacked the resources to fully take on our own government; we were nothing but flies for them to swat at as we were. We posed no danger or genuine threat—yet.

But we were changing. We were gaining power. We were gaining influence. Each time we spoke, Ben shared how new libraries and people were being added regularly. The message was spreading, even without the pamphlets underway yet.

I felt, deep within me, that I was changing. I was finding new purpose in living, and was driven by an innate desire to learn all that I could, and to explore every new idea presented to me. It was a glorious feeling, being able to think critically, to contemplate how I felt about everything, and to discuss such philosophies with Ben. He was very encouraging of my self-education, and seemed to appreciate that I devoured books with a fervor. As much as I loved classic literature and poetry—which I continued to commit to memory—I had found a particular interest in history and books related to civics and government. It seemed I had a mind for it, and I absorbed all that I could.

It was around the end of December—the time Christians would have marked as the Birth of Christ—that I decided I wanted to try my hand at writing. I had never taken any type of creative writing course, and I wasn't sure how much actual 'talent' would be required.

But over the months, I had felt a growing desire to see Ben's movement progress—indeed, I considered it now my cause as well. I wanted to see my nation transform back into the ideals which I had read about through our Founding Fathers and Framers. I wanted to see equality, both in practice and reflected in the law. I wanted the people to demand fair protection and representation from their government—no matter their heritage or genetics. I longed to see an end to the routine violence against those who were considered minorities, and I wanted both Law Enforcement and our government to do their duty to protect victims of crimes borne of hate rather than turn the other way and ignore them.

I wanted to choose my own mate, and to have children if I desired to. It wasn't too much to ask—I just wanted to have the freedoms that at one point my nation had fought against their own fellow man to ensure were provided to everyone in our nation.

And so I set about gathering writing materials—pen and paper—and secreted them away from the library so I could see how well I could put my thoughts down. For a long while, I wrote nothing. Instead, I sorted through my ideas, trying to organize my message in my head, and determining what was most important to share.

Then, one night after work, when it seemed the entire city must have been sleeping, I closed my curtains, removed my stash of writing materials from their own secret place hidden within another wall, and began writing.

PART ~ TWO ~ 2043

MARA O'REILLY

THIRTY-THREE ~ THE FIRST MESSAGES

◆ ◆ ◆

It was a new year. January 1st marked the beginning of the Year of Our Lord, 2043.

I continued with work, continued spending time with Ben as much as possible, and continued writing. Ben and Aaron were still increasing the number of libraries, growing their army of dissidents by the hundreds, and advancing their geographical boundaries mile by mile. They still hadn't found anyone either capable or willing to take on the role of writing the pamphlets, and the plans to access the Primary Library Services buildings and create messages set for distribution were still on hold.

I had not been idle with my time, however, and I believed myself to be leading a purpose-filled life. My personal growth and knowledge was ever-evolving, and I absorbed as much new information as possible. I was doing a considerable amount of writing, and was working on developing both a brevity of words and competency of persuasion to make my writing substantive. I wrote my messages as a sculptor might work with clay, constantly revising, cutting, reworking, and transforming my blank canvas into precisely what I needed from it. My initial thoughts were typically sorted and organized within my head—conserving my usage of paper, as I was forced to steal it from my work—and also because the less I put to paper the less evidence could potentially be used against me. The books in my walls were enough to result in severe consequences, but writing messages against my government with the intent to stir up a revolution would have led to the brutal end of my freedom and likely my life.

I was exceedingly cautious in all that I did.

It was during the second week of the new year, 2043, that I finally showed Ben the messages I had been writing. As a general rule, I tried to keep each message to a maximum of four pages total—front and back. Ben had said long ago that two pages would be easily stapled and folded in half, but anything more than that would require significantly more work. Ideally, we would only have one page per publication, which could then be printed on both front and back and folded. Given that we had never attempted to mass produce anything yet, it seemed risky to do anything more than single page pamphlets until we had a firm handle on the process. As it was, if we folded the pages manually, it would require countless hours of manpower, a secondary location after using the Primary Library Services building to print, and then we would still have to box them and transfer them to various locations for distribution. Single pages, unfolded, would be the best way to transport them—at least from the PLS building itself. Once we had managed that much, we could sort out the details.

With that in mind, as I organized the messages I had written, I put them in order of lowest word count to highest. Unfortunately, because I did not have a personal computer— and it would have been heavily monitored even if I had—I did not have the means of presenting Ben with a type-written copy. My hand-writing was small and neat, and I had made pristine copies with no errors, but they were still hand-written. At some point, we would have to figure out how to get them typed before printing. Anyone's hand-writing could be analyzed and used against them. If Ben proceeded with any of the messages I had written, that was fine, but it would have been suicide to allow copies to be made carrying my hand-writing. We would have to find a way to type out the messages if they were to be used. It was, unfortunately, another complication.

This also reminded me of another forensic disadvantage we faced. Anyone who handled the papers was likely to leave fingerprints behind. If government officials were to secure a copy of a pamphlet, it could—and undoubtedly would—get analyzed for fingerprints or any traces of DNA. We would have to distribute the flyers with no residue or incriminating evidence, and everyone who touched the pages afterward would be at risk as well. The best way for us to prevent this from occurring was to anticipate taking extreme protection measures during production, and then to encourage everyone to destroy their copies after reading them.

Should our government find such messages, they would know of our existence as a movement, and this alone would create a massive manhunt and investigation. Our one advantage we had for now was that we were—as far as we knew—flying under government radar, and no one knew of the existence of an underground movement which was steadily growing in size and geographic area.

With all that in mind, I readied myself for a visit from Ben. I was expecting him late in the evening; he rarely arrived until after it was considered too late for social calls. Even though I had not had a single visitor in all the months that I had known him, it was still a level of care he insisted upon. By arriving late—and it was always dark anyhow since it was winter—he ensured we would not be interrupted, and there would be no reason for someone to be on the stairs. Even though we were quiet, even whispering if we read aloud to one another, and even though technically it was not illegal or wrong for us to have visitors in our dwelling units, it was still wise to be cautious. I imagined his efforts to take great care in securing his privacy was how he had survived without incident thus far, and I trusted his methods.

THIRTY-FOUR ~ SWEET HAPPINESS

◆ ◆ ◆

Ben read through my pages, occasionally writing something along the border. I had never done anything that required collaboration with another person, and though I had been hesitant to show him my work originally, I was excited to see how pleased he had been when I shared everything with him.

It took him the better part of two hours to read through the handful of messages I had written. I sat alongside him, patiently attempting to read a book, unable to prevent myself from sneaking the occasional look in his direction. By the time he finished, I nervously awaited his comments.

He set the stack of pages and his pencil on the coffee table, and turned toward me. His smile reassured me that all was well, but the pride in his eyes warmed me to my core.

"You're remarkable," he said. "This is exactly what I was hoping we could say."

I smiled, relieved.

"So it's not too terrible? You can work with most of it? I saw you made some notes."

He nodded.

"Not much more I could add to it—the writing is excellent, and there isn't really any need for editing. But I found a few areas where we could add a sentence or two just to elaborate or draw the point home a little better. Really, most of it could be printed and distributed as-is. But if we have a bit of time to fluff each piece and tweak it, we may as well. What's really great, though, is that we're not really going to need to do much more than this. There's enough material here we can distribute one message a month or every few weeks and we're still set for the first year. You did a great job. There's a lot to work with."

I beamed, so happy to have pleased him.

"I wish you would have told me! We could have worked on these together! I didn't know you had any interest in writing. It never even occurred to me to try doing it myself or to ask you. But you really nailed it. You knew exactly what needed to be said."

Holding my hand, he lifted it to his lips and kissed my fingers— something he did from time to time, and I adored.

"Do you mind if I take them? I think they're ready to be typed up."

I shook my head. There was nothing more I needed to do with them.

"I found an old typewriter a while back—including a few extra ink cartridges. It's not a long-term solution unless we can replace the ink, but I bet we have enough to type all these out, and if we space them out, we should have enough material to get us through our first year."

"Aren't typewriters noisy?" I asked, concerned.

"Where could you type with no one hearing it?"

He nodded his head.

"Yeah, we'll have to do it at Aaron's place or have Aaron do it. He can use the generator, and he's really the only one who has an isolated enough location to ensure complete privacy. It'll be a lot for him to do—a bigger risk for sure. He'll have to hide everything, too."

With a faraway look in his eyes, he considered everything.

"I'll have to take it out to him tomorrow. I know I was planning on taking you with me, but it will be too dangerous now. I don't want you to be with me if I have all these pages, plus a typewriter with me in the rig. If I were to get pulled over, they would probably search it just because I had someone else with me who wasn't an employee of the Services For The Deceased. I don't want to put you that much at risk."

I was disappointed, but I understood. I had been eager to spend more time with him, that was all.

He stood and held out his hand to help pull me up alongside him so I could walk him to the door. He picked his jacket up from the edge of the couch and put it on.

"Thank you for doing this. I can't tell you how amazing it is to see everything written out like that. I don't think I really gave you enough credit for seeing my vision to the extent that you did. You said everything I wanted to be said."

He smiled again, and picked up the stack of papers, carefully folding them in half before stuffing them into the inside pocket of his jacket.

Tenderly, he put his hand on my cheek, then leaned down and kissed me. His lips were soft, his kiss gentle and slow.

Years later—too many to count—I would look back on that moment as being one of the most precious in my entire humble existence, and I would come to recognize it as the moment that I understood what it meant to love and be loved.

He left me then, my heart bursting with such sweet happiness I could neither have described nor concealed, as the words of Sir Philip Sidney echoed through my being:

THIRTY-FIVE ~ MY TRUE LOVE HATH MY HEART

◆ ◆ ◆

My True Love Hath My Heart

My true love hath my heart, and I have his,
By just exchange one for the other given:
I hold his dear, and mine he cannot miss;
There never was a bargain better driven.
His heart in me keeps me and him in one;
My heart in him his thoughts and senses guides:
He loves my heart, for once it was his own;
I cherish his because in me it bides.
His heart his wound received from my sight;
My heart was wounded with his wounded heart;
For as from me on him his hurt did light,
So still, methought, in me his hurt did smart:
Both equal hurt, in this change sought our bliss,
My true love hath my heart, and I have his.

~Sir Philip Sidney

THIRTY-SIX ~ THE RELATIVITY OF TIME

◆ ◆ ◆

I waited, as patiently as I could, for Ben to leave word—another book—to let me know he had returned safely from Aaron's house. I didn't expect to see him for several days at the very least, and likely not again until the night after my last workday for the week, or even on my day off. I knew he had a full schedule, and I had grown accustomed to being available to him at his convenience, waiting patiently whenever he reached out, and simply having faith that he would when he could.

And so the days passed without anything noteworthy, a steady routine of work, reading, and sleep. It was an uneventful life I led, and Ben's absences only made this more noticeable. He was my only lifeline, really, and although I enjoyed his company, his absences served as a reminder that dependency was a dangerous weapon. Caring for another was often ammunition by those who desired control over others. He was both the man who had saved me from my own slow march to death as well as the sole reason I could end up having my life ended prematurely through a government Death Sentence. Prior to his entering my life, I had never given cause for the government or any of my betters to even notice me, let alone target me. Ben was Danger. But he was also my Salvation, and as the choice was mine to make, I chose to risk everything rather than have nothing.

He did not arrive on my doorstep until almost midnight on the evening of my day off. I had waited anxiously all the evening before and then my whole day off, growing more and more concerned with each passing hour. When he finally arrived, he said he had walked the back roads and alleys between his dwelling unit and my own rather than risk driving.

He came inside, taking off his coat and hat and then bent over, unlacing his boots. The hour was late, and though my floorboards were not usually creaky, it was always better to be cautious. I turned and began walking into the living room, but he took me by the hand and pulled me against him, wrapping his arms around me and pulling me close. We had never hugged before, and I could not recall the last time I had touched someone. I had likely been a young child. Tentatively, I allowed my hands to hold him as he pulled my head toward his chest. He was warm, even through his layers of clothing, and I could feel the steady thump of his heart against my ear. "I am so glad to be here," he said. "You have no idea how long of a week it has been."

I did not know of all that he had toiled with, but time had moved just as slowly for me. It had left me with too much to think about, the haunting worries of his being pulled over and the typewriter and documents found, and my fears of his being apprehended. All of those worries subsided with him here. I had spent my sleepless nights overthinking, worrying about his well-being. I would ruminate over the wisdom of developing feelings for him when it was so dangerous.

I had a pragmatic realization that if something were to happen to him I would never know—that I would only ever be able to conclude something had happened because he would have simply Disappeared and stopped coming to visit. I worried about all the risks that I was taking, knowing I could have my heart broken, and that it could leave me grief-stricken and alone once more. I had weighed it all out time and again.

I wished for time to stand still right then. I was safe, he was safe, and all was right in the world.

THIRTY-SEVEN ~ FREEDOM
TO CHOOSE

◆ ◆ ◆

"I took the typewriter and your pages out to Aaron last week. I'll admit, I was more nervous carrying around your pages and that old typewriter than I ever have been carrying all the contraband books. Your writing was pretty powerful stuff—and I knew if they caught me, I'd have been in serious trouble. I know I face those risks with the books, but I never really felt like it was as big of a deal."

He looked at me as we sat on the couch and took my hand in his.

"I was weighing out the risks differently than I used to…"

He smiled and continued.

"Anyhow, Aaron was really excited to read them. Neither of us ever really considered what we would say if we were to sit down and write everything out; I don't think we consider ourselves leaders or spokesmen, although I guess that's what we are."

I nodded—of course they were leaders. They'd already accomplished so much, unified so many people, and built an entire underground movement. Even if no one could ever know their names, surely there were whispers about the men behind the curtain who were making it all happen, or at the very least, who had initially started the whole movement.

"Well, anyway, I got everything out to Aaron's, and it was pretty late already. I stuck around as he read the pages, and we ended up talking til almost dawn about everything you had written out. He read through the bit of notes I had included, and we worked out the changes. I don't think we removed a single line you had written, just so you know. We elaborated a few of the ideas, expounded upon some of the key points, but you really did a great job outlining everything."

I smiled. As much as I appreciated his praise—it felt like the sun beaming directly down on me, enveloping me in a bouquet of warmth—I was mostly just so glad to be sitting alongside him, touching him, watching his beautiful face as he shared everything with me. I wanted to have him near me always; his presence ignited my soul, and when he smiled, my whole world was happier.

"So I got a few hours of sleep before heading back. He assured me he could get them all typed up without any issue, and that he had a place where he could hide everything that was separate and away from the cabin. He says 'Hello', by the way, and wanted me to tell you he was really excited about your work."

He yawned.

'That was about it. I got home later that morning and got called out to do another job for the Deceased. Spent a long, boring week doing my lab work, and had a few calls for the Services For The Deceased—but none of them resulted in any finds. Not a single one. I swear, sometimes that job isn't worth the time, but I know it's necessary. I might never have crossed paths with you had I not been able to use that job as a cover," he said, winking.

"Do you want anything? A cup of tea? Are you hungry?" I asked.

He shook his head and pulled me close to him, turning me around so my back was leaning up against his chest.

"No, I think this is all I want right now, thanks. I was really looking forward to being here tonight."

I took his hand into my own, letting it fall around my middle.

All of this was alien to me—and likely to him. The intimacy, the familiarity, the physical contact, the expression of emotion, and yet we both seemed to embrace and accept it as a matter of course.

"Do you think we will ever reach a point of true freedom?" I asked him. "Not just freedom to choose school, or work, or where to live, but freedom to choose personal things."

"What? You mean, like having a family?"

"Yes, I suppose so. At least the ability to choose."

The room fell silent once again. After a long moment, he spoke.

"I don't know. I really don't. It's not even that we couldn't or shouldn't already have those choices—technically, they should never have been taken away from us. They were Human Rights, and they specifically designed our Constitution to guarantee those basic rights. The issue is that we're no longer regarded as human; we are less than in their eyes, and that's how they justify what they are doing to us now."

"They'll never consider us equal without an Uprising." I said flatly.

"No…" he responded softly.

I sighed.

"If we do nothing, we will never have the life we would choose for ourselves. We'll never be allowed to have anything normal. We'll never have the life that our parents and grandparents had —the ability to choose one another, to get married, to choose whether or not to have our own family."

He bent his head toward mine and kissed my forehead softly.

"We have the freedom to choose who to love. We just don't have the freedom to do what we would like to with that love. That alone seems like enough of a reason to fight."

"Even if it means risking our lives and dying?" I asked. It was heartbreaking to consider.

"Is there any greater cause worth dying for?"

I sat up and turned to him, kissing his mouth softly. Then, without a moment of hesitation or feeling of doubt, I stood. Taking his hand, I led him to my bedroom.

Time was working against us, and fate was conspiring to serve more misery than joy. I did not want to waste another precious moment.

THIRTY-EIGHT ~ THE
FIRST PAMPHLETS

◆ ◆ ◆

At the end of February 2043, we set our plan in motion to print the first pamphlet. Aaron had painstakingly typed out every page I had hand-written, including the edits by Ben and himself weeks earlier.

They had sent out reliable people to do reconnaissance for a dozen Primary Library Services buildings over a geographic area of almost 1500 miles. Leaders of each zone had selected a handful of faithful soldiers who were willing to do the most risky of all actions and do what was required to get the pamphlets printed. These brave citizens were placing their lives and freedom on the line simply by being on the property of the PLS buildings after hours without permission—breaking and entering after that was taking the risks to a whole new level. But beyond that, they were also going to be on the premises with contraband materials—and if they were caught with either the original pamphlet or the thousands of copies they were hoping to make, their lives would surely have been forfeited.

If they were caught, the government would become aware of the existence of a group of dissidents who were plotting against our nation. It would result in our being hunted down, and it would never have ended until we were all caught.

To say that there was a lot at stake was an under-statement.

But Ben had full faith in those he and Aaron had chosen as the leaders of all the different zones, and they, in turn, were being asked to choose only the best men and women whom they believed in for this monumental task. Most of those who were asked were strangers to Ben and Aaron, likely never even having heard of them. The chain of command was firmly in place with a 'need to know' policy, and it was already being affected. It was too big of a job for only a few people, and although many had been using the library system for years, the secrecy and risk had still made most of them isolated and unknown to one another.

Gathering a dozen people together in each of the zones, expecting them to meet one another and place their lives into the hands of strangers, trusting that they had been vetted and were all 'safe' was a profound act of faith, and it deserved recognition.

What was being attempted—the publication of treasonous pamphlets—was monumental, both for us as a collective whole as well as for us as individuals. If they could pull this off, if everyone was successful, and no one was hurt while our people were there, it was likely going to be easier to do each time after. The first time would be the most scary, and likely the most time-consuming and disorganized. But if they all managed to do their role, if they remembered every single piece of paper and left no trace they had ever been there, and if they could enter and exit without damage to the buildings as we had planned, then there was no reason to doubt their success.

Still, it was incredibly nerve-wracking to contemplate, and the night that everything was put into motion was a long one.

THIRTY-NINE ~ LEADERSHIP

◆ ◆ ◆

The night of the first publication passed slowly. I waited in my dwelling unit with Ben by my side, silently willing him to remain patient enough to not leave or attempt to investigate what was currently happening at our local PLS building. I knew he wanted to be there, to be directly involved in the entire process. I also understood that he felt an inherent obligation to take part in anything dangerous; he felt liable for all who were daring to risk everything for what he still considered to be his cause. His sense of responsibility affected his ability to accept that people were electing to place themselves in Harm's Way because they had their own set of convictions and dreams of a free society.

I was not so sensitive to this issue—but I could also readily acknowledge that it was because I had nothing left to lose, save Ben. We needed soldiers. We needed people who were willing to pick up the banners and lead us into war. This was too big of an undertaking for just a handful of people—we needed as many as possible, and each of them needed to be willing to die for our cause if necessary.

We needed for them to put their lives on the line if called upon, for them to enter any task or mission we needed of them with purpose and clarity—we did not need those who were indecisive or afraid of death or capture because they had Loved Ones depending on them and clouding their judgment. Fear of death was an honest fear, but it also depended on why one was afraid to die. A fear of dying because one could not comprehend or verify an Afterlife was decidedly different from fearing death because one didn't want to leave Loved One's behind. One was a rational fear, the other emotion-driven. We could not risk people being compromised if captured because they had ammunition that could be used against them; we needed soldiers who were willing to sacrifice everything because they had nothing to lose other than their lives.

Somewhere deep within, Ben knew this. But it did not change his sense of responsibility. It made him more human, and certainly a better man. Yet I also knew this would not serve him well as a leader—as the leader—of this revolution. This uprising was necessary—it meant the lives and freedom of millions of citizens. Everyone, at some point, would be called upon to take a stand, and even if they were reluctant to get involved, there was no guarantee that they would be left alone. There was nothing to prevent our government from rounding every one of us up and murdering us in cold blood. There were those who had called for precisely that to happen—and it wasn't considered Hate Speech, it wasn't met with shock and awe—it had been socially acceptable, and that alone should have struck fear into the heart of every single person deemed The Scourge of the Earth by their 'betters'. The time would come when everyone would be required to take a stand—for many, possibly hundreds of thousands—it would become a battle which could be their last.

So there was only one question I felt I needed to answer for myself, and I believed every other person needed to consider for themselves, and that was whether or not it was worth it. Was it worth potentially losing one's life over—to take a stand even knowing it may be their Last Stand? Was it worth it to know that we could ask them to sacrifice themselves for a war in which, even if it were won, that they might never be given the privilege of seeing the positive results of? Was it worth them risking their lives so that their children or grandchildren could have a better future than the one they were currently on the trajectory to have?

Assuming we could take this stand—assuming we could all rise collectively together and weren't slaughtered by our own government—was it worth the potential loss of life not only for ourselves, but those of our fellow citizens? Were we willing to stand by their side, risk everything, and help them stand as well, even leaning on one another for strength and courage?

What was worth sacrificing, if not our very lives, for the sake of a future in which everyone could live as a free people, coexisting in a world peacefully, without discrimination or violence? Was Free Will not worth paying the ultimate price? What was worth dying for, if not freedom—especially freedom of speech? For hundreds of years, the soldiers of our nation had thought it was. They had been willing to fight and die for our nation and our fellow citizens with very little reward in return. They did it because it was what made our nation so exceptional; they did it because freedom was worth it.

That was what we needed to remember. That was what Ben needed to understand—we were all soldiers now.

Soldiers had leaders, and we needed those leaders to remain alive. Every life mattered, and any who would eventually fall would be a tragedy, but they would fall as soldiers fell during times of war.

A good leader needed to delegate risks and responsibilities. He needed to understand the value of his own life and its significance. His role was not to be on the battlefield and directly in Harm's Way—entire kingdoms had been lost because their kings had chosen to fight alongside their men during times of war. This was counterproductive and far too costly, especially for honor.

We needed Ben alive. He and Aaron, even if only a handful of people knew them, were the leaders of this entire movement, and as such, they were both invaluable. The entire future depended on it.

These were the thoughts I tried to share with Ben as I watched him nervously pace the length of the room that evening. Secretly, a part of me half-expected a group of government officials to burst through my door and kill us both. The odds of gathering that many people across so many miles with no one being a turncoat, attempting to confess all they knew beforehand out of fear, or things happening flawlessly in so many different locations was a miracle.

Nonetheless, I prayed for one, and I prayed for Ben to carry on until our vision for a better future was realized, and our nation began a Great Reformation, as was necessary.

Of all that he had done thus far—the years of networking and the building of an underground community—none of it was as significant as the steps he was taking now. This—this plan to distribute his message and begin recruiting those willing to fight—this was what would change everything. This was action. We were about to embark on a journey we could no longer control. We were about to start a war, and in war, no one could control everything.

I prayed he could embrace these realities and come to terms with the enormity of his role as well as his limitations.

FORTY ~ MEETING OFFICER REN

◆ ◆ ◆

Everything changed after that night.

Aaron and Ben had both set up a chain of communication so they could receive reports regarding the activities of the night before. Ben left me before dawn, promising to update me as soon as he could.

I was walking home from work shortly after midnight when I heard a vehicle driving slowly behind me. I typically walked along the alleyways just to avoid interacting with anyone. Nothing good ever happened in the city after dark. The danger levels were much higher, and it was not uncommon for women to get abducted, raped, and murdered. They did not hold us in high regard, and there were seldom investigations made by Law Enforcement on our behalf. In a world high in crime and low in compassion, the value of human life for people diminished, especially for those considered The Scourge of the Earth. At any rate, Law Enforcement numbers had dwindled to the bare minimum, and most crimes, including rape and murder, were often disregarded. In some areas of the city—those with the highest rates of crime, violence, and attacks against Law Enforcement—murders occurred so frequently that bodies would often rot where they fell.

The only security or protection one had against such a fate was to avoid congested areas, avoid all confrontation and sketchy, unstable people, and never appear to have anything of value. I had also learned the importance of only going into public areas during daylight hours—and never shopped in the evening. Walking to and from work was a necessity I could not avoid, but even then, I typically clung to the shadows, walked with a light step, and never used a flashlight to guide my way. After years of being ignored and overlooked by most of society, I was used to being invisible.

The vehicle creeping along the alleyway behind me was disconcerting, but even more so when I glanced over my shoulder and realized it was a Police vehicle. Initially, I merely moved to the side so he could pass. I wasn't worried about being stopped or questioned—luckily I did not have any contraband on me and had not taken any paper from the library in several weeks. I had permission to be out because of my work orders, and I was on a direct path between work and home. Despite this, it was still unsettling to know Law Enforcement had noticed me.

They weren't, as a general rule, a demographic I needed to fear. But they were the long-arm of the government, and when people began disappearing over political conflicts, Law Enforcement had arrested many of them. I knew they were in a difficult position. Much of the citizenry of our nation hated them, and our government had used them for their own nefarious misdeeds for decades already, forcing them to choose between their livelihood and their oaths to our Constitution. It was not an easy path, being a member of Law Enforcement. Even law-abiding citizens had grown distrustful over the years; they knew that by obeying an authoritarian government that they were responsible for causing just as much harm as good. Their job descriptions had grown far beyond 'to protect and to serve' the citizenry, and for many, it was an inexcusable line to have crossed. Much of the nation believed Law Enforcement to be little more than rogue oath-breakers, America's gestapo.

The vehicle pulled up alongside, put on its brakes, and then cut the engine. I stopped walking. A moment later, a police officer got out of the driver's side. The man stood still for a moment, adjusting his hat, and then walked around the front of the vehicle. The alleyway was dark, and there were no streetlights.

He took a flashlight from his waistband and directed it toward me.

"ID?" he asked.

I fumbled through the contents of my handbag, searching until I found my work pass and picture ID. Handing both to him, it surprised me to see my hands trembled slightly.

He read my name, flashed his light into my face to ensure the photograph matched, and then handed both documents back to me.

"I have a message for you from Ben," he said.

Immediately, I relaxed and breathed a deep sigh of relief. I was surprised, though. This man was not one of The Scourge. How did he know Ben? My paranoia set in, and I said nothing.

"He said to tell you everything went well with the PLS, and distribution was underway. He wants you to be more cautious than ever before. He's concerned that once the docs circulate that they'll be looking at some Scourges more closely than others, and library staff are likely to be at the top of the list."

He looked me in the eye as he spoke, his voice low but steady. I nodded, too afraid to speak, still skeptical of who this man actually was, and uncertain it was not a set-up. What if they already had Ben? What if they'd already made him talk, and they were now trying to incriminate me?

"He says he's not sure if it's safe to do anything outside of normal routines, so he wants you to lie low and not to expect a visit for a week or two. He sent me just so you have another point of contact; he wants me to make sure you're getting home every night. I won't approach you again, but just know that I'm out here if you need me."

I nodded my head again. Did Ben really think the risks were that high?

"My name is Ren. If anything happens, I will be in touch as

soon as I can. If you're approached by anyone or questioned by anyone, contact me at the 2nd Precinct. Just call and ask for Officer Ren. Can you remember all that?"

I nodded my head again, still not sure I could trust the man before me.

"I'm sure everything will be fine. I'll hear about any reports if they get filed regarding the docs. And I've known Ben for a long time. He's cautious because he's smart. Don't worry about anything; just go about your usual activities and keep your head down."

He smiled.

"Everything is about to change," he said.

With that, he touched the brim of his uniform cap and started walking around the front of the vehicle again.

"Remember, head straight home. Do your shopping on your day off, but otherwise stay home. And don't miss any work!"

I nodded again. "Th-th-thank you," I said, and started walking toward my house again. I heard the door of his vehicle shut softly behind me, and then he drove past me, turning right at the end of the block.

I made my way home quickly, but it was not until I was safely inside with the door locked that my legs finally stopped shaking. I turned on the living room lamp, and then, entirely out of paranoia, I peeked through the curtain of the window in the kitchen. Sure enough, sitting at the edge of the corner and facing my unit was the police car. He flashed his lights, flipped a U-turn, and was gone.

FORTY-ONE ~ PERSUASION

◆ ◆ ◆

Every night for the next two weeks, I noticed Officer Ren during my walk home from work. I could only assume he intended to be seen, as more often than not, he would park within sight of my kitchen window and flash his lights before leaving.

I still had not heard a single word from Ben, and as the days passed, I grew more and more concerned. I understood he was being cautious, but it was difficult to go so many days with no communication. Not only was I worried about him, I missed him. After spending over six months in his company, the last several on a much more intimate and regular schedule, it was lonely to not have him there to speak with regularly.

There were so many questions I wanted to ask him—how did he know Officer Ren? How had he come to know him well enough to entrust the very secrets that could cause his being given the Death Penalty if discovered? And why had he asked him, of all people, to monitor me rather than someone else—someone of my own standing that I would have been more inclined to trust?

Officer Ren, while dutifully monitoring me as he had promised, did not approach me again. I was thirsting for information about Ben, the night of the PSL, and the results of the distribution. I wondered if Officer Ren knew I was the one who had written the pamphlets, or that I was intimately involved with Ben. How much did Ben actually trust him? If he knew about the pamphlets and the distribution, he must have surely known about the entire library system, and likely Aaron as well.

I felt I had too many questions left unanswered, and as the days passed without word, I grew increasingly restless.

Spring was now upon us, and the days were getting longer again. It was raining almost every day, but as it was mid-March, that was to be expected. I wondered how Ben was doing, what he filled his days with, and whether he thought of me as often as I thought of him.

I didn't have any solutions for what Officer Ren had explained to me to be the reasoning behind why Ben remained absent. The plan was to release new pamphlets every month. I understood the reasons for being cautious, but if he insisted on the two of us not being able to see one another because of the heat directly following the release of the pamphlets, then we would never be able to spend time with one another again. As long as our people were breaking into the PLS buildings, we were at risk of exposure. And as long as there were pamphlets being distributed, there would always be danger, should any of them be discovered by the wrong people. If the criteria for visiting were going to be based on whether there were increased risks involved, then they would never be low enough for visits again as long as we were producing pamphlets and conducting PLS activities.

During these long nights, I initially occupied my time reading and memorizing poetry and passages from other books. But as the days and nights added up, I finally decided I needed a more constructive outlet for my restlessness and frustration. And so, despite the risks, I began to write once more.

I wrote about the importance of freedom, and how without the freedom to choose one's life path and profession, one could not truly consider himself his own person. I wrote about freedom of reproductive rights for both men and women, and how freedom to choose whether or not one desired to bear children or have a family needed to be the choice of the two individuals involved rather than the state—that parenting was a personal choice, regardless of the genetics, social or financial status of the parents. I wrote about the importance of freedom of education, and why granting individuals the choice of schools and education pathways would only help society, because people working passionately toward learning and careers in a field of their own choosing would work harder and invest more into the process.

My time was spent absorbing the words of our Founding Fathers and Framers, in reading as much as I could access on their accomplishments, and what their intentions and vision had been for our new world. Through their eyes, I saw my nation not as it was, but as it was supposed to have been—and what it may once have been. They awakened within me a sense of injustice for how things had become during my lifetime, and a growing resentment for all that my fellow citizens and government had done to those they had decided were less than their equals.

I read about similar countries throughout the history of the world where such imbalances of power had taken place—how thousands and even millions of people had been subjected to genocide by those who had deemed them Unworthy to live—just as our own government had. I read of the horrors of socialism, Marxism, and communism, and how powerful leaders could manipulate entire military populations into doing their ugly bidding—choosing to obey immoral and unethical orders given by corrupt, evil men rather than doing what they surely must have known to be the right thing.

I learned what it meant to be a Christian nation, and how without God, we had spiraled into a self-loathing, hedonistic, self-serving country where little hope remained.

I studied every resource I had that captured the essence of what had been happening across my nation since before my birth, and learned just how easily history had repeated itself regarding global atrocities.

And then I wrote. I poured my heart into my blank pages, creating message after message—issuing warnings about how we were slowly being eradicated, how genocide was already happening, even if we thought things seemed normal. I likened us to frogs in the water pot, oblivious to the fact that the water was slowly coming to a boil, and by the time we realized what was happening, it would be too late.

I shared all I could about what the vision had been for our nation as outlined by our Founding Fathers and the Framers and then wrote about how far removed we had become from the free world they had designed and then fought to uphold. I wrote about how many of our fellow citizens had been complicit in granting too many powers to our government, then allowing their powers to advance their own agendas to target those whom they considered their enemies, openly calling for discrimination and restrictions which then resulted in inequality, injustice, and open bigotry. I called for Scourges to stand behind and support Law Enforcement as they once did, to come to their aid if they ever saw them physically assaulted or ambushed, and then called upon Law Enforcement to remember that their original purpose was to protect and defend their fellow citizen—not do the evil bidding of a corrupt government.

Every night, with the window curtain drawn and only the low lighting of the living room lamp to keep me company, I wrote of what I knew to an audience that I would never meet in the hopes that my words would resonate within them and serve as an inspiration for their own desires for freedom. I wrote to them as if I were a voice worth listening to—a person with the strength and knowledge to lead them from the darkness and into the light —a person who they could, and should, trust. I expected nothing from my work—I knew I would never attach my name to my words, that there would be no claim to fame because of what I was doing. I knew it would always be too dangerous to ever be known for the messages I was creating, and that remaining anonymous was paramount to our continued progress and success.

Even so, I wrote with passion and fervor. I shared every important detail I could to compare and contrast the current events unfolding within our lifetime and the horrors and atrocities that had been committed against other human beings throughout history. I wanted them to see what was happening —to understand that everything we were experiencing had been done before by other people in other nations, and that it had always ended with violence and genocide, regardless of how slowly it progressed to that point.

I wanted them to learn from the past—a historical legacy of genocide that our government had intentionally removed our ability to read about and learn from through censorship and information control.

My messages were a warning, and they needed to serve as a warning, to every person who believed in the good of humanity, in human rights, and in true equality. Our government had done their best to ensure they left us sitting blind in the dark so we could never question the status quo. I intended to change that.

And so I wrote. I did my best to write with authority, conviction, and persuasion. I did my best to present my arguments with solid research and facts; I used relevant, applicable contributions directly from our Founding Fathers and the Framers and I did my best to compel readers to fight for the preservation and restoration of their freedom and rights.

I knew there was much to say—far more to put down on paper than would ever be printed or distributed. But it was therapeutic to write everything out. It made me feel as though I were doing something productive and useful for my fellow countrymen.

I wasn't trying to control their thinking—I was merely hoping to encourage them to access the same information I had, to read the words and intentions of our Founding Fathers and the Framers, and to come to their own conclusions about whether their government could be trusted or was working in their best interests. I wanted them to question why they should trust a government who had worked so diligently to control their access to the written word, to points of view that were contrary to the messaging being delivered and controlled only by them.

Our nation could only have an uprising—a true revolution—if there were enough people out there who were willing to fight for it. This went far beyond the decision that each person might someday be required to make regarding possible Civil War. It went beyond whether they were willing to risk their lives on a field of battle.

What I was asking people to do was to recognize that if they continued on the same path they were on, that there was only one outcome—and that was genocide. I wanted them to understand that fighting was not a debate—that they either needed to accept their fate, accept complete submission and defeat, and accept that one day their entire families and themselves would be hunted down and exterminated by their own government—or they could rise together now before it was too late.

I wanted them to understand that there wasn't a choice being presented at all—it had never been about risking their life in battle or maintaining peace through compliance, because even compliance meant their eventual death—and a violent death at that.

I needed for them to recognize the truth, which was that if their parents and grandparents had fought harder against these issues in their time, it wouldn't have fallen on us to correct. I wanted them to see that it had begun long ago, this genocide, and it had started insidiously, slowly, and quietly through the constant—if subtle—eradication of rights one small measure at a time. It was exactly the same thing that had occurred during World War II against the Jews, only this time it had happened on American soil and during a time when human rights were supposed to have been internationally recognized.

I longed for people to see the truth, to search for it on their own, and to arrive at the only sane conclusion I could imagine—the reality that if they did not take a stand now, they would never have another chance.

I did not want my words to come across as overly dramatic, which was why I encouraged them to seek more information through our underground library systems and read the words and history for themselves. I didn't want to fear-monger or to make bold declarations designed to strike fear into their hearts. I wanted them to examine their own options and come to the same conclusion—to see the merit in choosing to fight back now while we still had the strength and numbers.

I needed for them to understand what was now perfectly clear in my mind: We either fought back or we accept that our apathy would eventually kill us.

If we did not take a stand—one Last Stand for our nation—then we were doomed. We could only begin working toward a new future and rebuild all that we had lost after we resolved the tyranny, segregation, and discrimination we were all dealing with currently. The violence we faced—the deaths of hundreds of thousands of good people throughout our nation every year —had to stop before we could rebuild. The attacks on our Law Enforcement, the ambushes and hunting them down for sport with no true repercussions—it was all just another example of how far our nation had fallen into the clutches of an indifferent, hostile society and a government that did not care about the Sanctity of Human Life or the Value of Human Rights.

If we were to survive this—if we were to stop being victims and start being our own advocates, we had to be prepared to take a stand once and for all. If we were too afraid to rise collectively against our government, then we had already lost everything.

I refused to surrender without a fight. I believed my fellow citizens were worth fighting for—that freedom was worth fighting for. I believed in true equality—that we had all been born equal and that we all deserved to seek the best that life within our country could offer. We deserved to pursue Life, Liberty, and Happiness—we did not deserve to live our lives devoid of basic freedoms and human rights, treated with discrimination and segregated like farm animals being led to the slaughter. That wasn't what our Founding Fathers had intended for us, and as our Founding Fathers had instilled in us, we had the right to rebel when our government acted against our best interests.

I shared with them the very words that granted us this right:

'whenever any form of government becomes destructive of these ends, it is the right of the people to alter or to abolish it, and to institute a new government, laying its foundation on such principles, and organizing its powers in such form, as to them shall seem most likely to effect their safety and happiness.'

The Declaration of Independence made it unequivocally clear: "when a long train of abuses and usurpations, pursuing invariably the same Object evinces a design to reduce them under absolute Despotism, it is their right, it is their duty, to throw off such Government".

I was not writing my messages to advocate for insurrection or a simple rebellion. I was providing my fellow countrymen with the unquestionable truth that our Founding Fathers had not only fought their own war for, but had instituted within our very framework its message so that future generations would never forget it should their own government become too powerful and tyrannical.

This was the truth of my message—and it was because of this truth that I knew my life would be forfeit if the government ever found my words and could attribute them to me. But it was a truth that could not be hidden from our citizenry, no matter how much our leaders had tried. We The People were more powerful than the thousand men and women 'elected' to lead our nation. We had always been more powerful—we had simply never risen together to show our strength.

The time had come when we needed to.

Ben, Aaron, and I had created the means for people to self-educate and form their own conclusions. Action would follow. There were already thousands of citizens out there who had been vilified and painted as evil for no other reason than because they were of a certain lineage. We were being demonized for the sins of our fathers, and denied basic human rights.

Our message was spreading, and we were gaining both numbers and power.

All I could do was continue to write and compile my words into digestible concepts to help warn people of what our future would be if we didn't rise together now while we still could.

I only hoped it was enough.

FORTY-TWO ~ PREPARATIONS

◆ ◆ ◆

Ben arrived in the Fourteenth Week of the year, stressed and exhausted. He said he had been working both his full-time job at the lab, shifts at the Services For The Deceased, and spending a significant amount of time coordinating things within his underground network.

The first batch of pamphlets had been printed with no issues and was delivered to the distributors without incident. The distributors had traveled far and wide dispensing their portions of the pamphlets, and as the days passed, Ben received word that they had been dispersed as far out as 2000 miles away. Word was spreading.

"The whole underground system has ignited!" he said, beaming.

"It's a little terrifying how successful everything has been, actually. I wasn't sure if it would work, or even if it would make a difference other than putting everyone in danger. But, man, was I wrong about how hungry people were for the truth and a little bit of hope."

"You know we couldn't have done any of this without you," he said, pulling me close and kissing my forehead.

"Your words changed everything. It's really been difficult to keep track of everything, but we've had reports coming in from as far away as Indianapolis. That's over two thousand miles! We expected it to spread a fair bit through the more rural areas, but to know that we're getting recruits from larger cities and we're covering that kind of distance is tremendous."

"But how will you ensure that you're not getting set-up? How will you possibly be able to vet new people, especially if there are so many of them and they're all coming in from different zones?" My concern was valid; I didn't want any greater risk for either of us than necessary, and it didn't seem possible to remove all potential risks.

"Well, I can't, really. But we've known all along that there would be a certain degree of risk involved even when we were just moving books. One book, Margaret. One book, and we could lose our lives. So if those are the standards—then one book may as well be a thousand, or a thousand libraries—it makes no difference. And if one contraband item can result in death, then one pamphlet would definitely result in a death sentence—and if one pamphlet is enough, then we may as well have a million out there. The risks are equal—and the more people we have, the more power we have in the long run."

He picked up my hand and kissed my fingers; an endearing, reassuring habit of his that I had grown all-too-accustomed to.

"Don't worry. My risks aren't any greater than they ever were. Yes, there's now a much greater chance that some member of Law Enforcement or another government agency will catch wind of it. And if we're really given some bad luck, they'll even get their hands on a pamphlet as evidence. But no one except a few people could ever trace those words back to Washington State, let alone to us. It's just traveled too far now to know the original source—and as much manpower as our government has, because we've printed it from so many locations, even if they knew they had been printed through the PLS system, they wouldn't have any reason to think the main source was in Washington versus one of the other states."

I smiled, as best as I could, and tried to find comfort in his reassurances. I knew, logically, that all he said was true, and it was a fair assessment of the risks we had undertaken. I knew he had been living on a razor's edge for years now—and that he had decided it was worth it from the moment he did something with the books in the campus library.

I wondered if my fears were legitimate, or purely emotional. I questioned if I was being reasonable, or if I ground my fears on the possibility of losing him—of something happening to him which would ultimately leave me on my own once again. Surely death for both of us would be better than my having to live the life of quiet solitude I had known before him. Anything but that. Going back to that life would have been a prison sentence; the silence, the loneliness, the endless days of nothingness—it would be impossible to endure. But to know that I could end up there once again—it was too much to even consider. I would grieve for his loss, mourning in silence and solitude for a love that no one ever knew about, for a man that no one knew had been the most magical, lovely person in my life. Yes, death would be better.

"So now what?" I asked, steering the conversation away from the dark thoughts that clouded my head. There was always time for morbid dwelling; for now, he was here, and that was enough.

"Well, I suppose we decide what one we want to send out next, and we get prepared for our next trip to the PLS. We keep recruiting new people. We keep expanding. We take stock of our assets—if we have people who had ever served in the Armed Forces, if people have caches of weapons, if people have experience in matters of warfare."

"That makes sense. But that's going to compound the risks once again—and people who might have weapons or supplies, or even skills, might not want to let anyone else know. Everyone will have something to lose and no reason to trust strangers with such information."

"True enough, but we won't have much of a war if we don't even have any weapons. We need to tell people to prepare. I know supplies and funds are limited and restricted for most of us, but we need to tell everyone to stock up on some basics at least— try to stockpile food reserves. They should all have enough food storage to feed the people they share a home with for a while. At least what? Store a minimum of three months? Do you think that's realistic? Could most people start storing extra cans of food, rice, oatmeal, and stuff like that? It's cheap and plentiful. And maybe dehydrated corn or fruits? It seems they always have lots of that in the stores since fresh produce isn't always available. If people buy just a bit extra each time they shop, they could start building their storage without drawing too much attention to themselves."

I agreed. Food storage was always important, and there was no question whether or not it was necessary; it wasn't uncommon for food supplies to suffer regularly, and the shelves were frequently lacking in various items. It was one issue that had been protested against throughout my childhood, and it had gotten no better over the years, even though they had outlawed such protests. Still, it would not be easy for people to buy up extra stores of food. Too high of a rise in demand would draw attention from the government without a doubt.

"It would be a good recommendation, but you would also have to advise caution in purchases. No large bulk purchases all at once of any product, and no excessive shopping trips outside of what they normally would do. They would need to do it casually—a few extra things each time, and nothing in bulk."

He nodded his head and smiled at me. "See, this is what's so good about this—we have each other to bounce ideas off of, and you bring so much clarity to it. I might be a good one for big ideas, but when it comes to the fine-tuning, you're much better at it than I am."

With that, he winked and pulled me into his arms.

I forgot entirely that I was planning on asking him about Officer Ren.

FORTY-THREE ~ A STRATEGIC PLAN

◆ ◆ ◆

The following day off, Ben and I drove out to Aaron's. Before we left my dwelling unit, I showed Ben my newly written messages and watched as he fastidiously packed them away in a secret false bottom of a workbench in the back of the van before we set off. He told me he would prefer not to travel with me and contraband during the same trip, but as I had only shown them to him, he said it was better to remove them from my unit sooner than later.

Aaron smiled happily upon our arrival, and greeted me graciously with a firm hug. Although I was initially taken aback by his friendliness—I was not used to being touched, even now, and could not recall the last time anyone had hugged me aside from Ben—I was glad to see him. He was in such high spirits; it was contagious.

He had been hearing good things from his contacts, and the messages in the pamphlets were resonating with many people.

"It's almost as if people don't like being treated poorly, and they're tired of being subservient to those whom they feel they are equal to—or at least should be, according to our Constitution," he said, with more than a hint of sarcasm.

Ben removed the papers from the secret drawer, and then the three of us walked from the van into the house. Aaron put on the water pot for tea, and we sat comfortably in his small living room, chatting about things of no importance.

Ben sat near me, his arm casually resting along my shoulders.

It struck me as a very masculine thing to do, an almost unconscious display of possession, as if he wanted to ensure Aaron knew I was spoken for. It amused me, as I was certain Aaron would never have expressed an interest in me romantically, and I also believed the two of them to be friends close enough that they had likely discussed me already, and Ben would surely have stated how things had been progressing. But such was the way of humans, I assumed, to mark one's territory and to thwart off any potential suitors by asserting one's place. I could not deny I was pleased that Ben would be so direct about our togetherness, on whatever terms it was. I liked the idea of being known as his, and he mine.

"So after hearing from some of the newly established zones further east, we are now growing in the suburbs of Indianapolis, and we also have a small library taking root just outside of Milwaukee. Nothing in the cities, though—far too dangerous," Aaron stated.

"Well, at least the one advantage to having libraries around the big cities is that they aren't likely to get discovered or busted by Law Enforcement, given their numbers now," Ben responded.

"That's true, although it doesn't make it any better for anyone trying to live in those areas. The crime rates alone make it terrible, but their murder rates have sky-rocketed to unprecedented levels these last few decades. But that's what happens when you defund Law Enforcement and allow criminals to run the streets. My cousin is in Chicago, and he says it's so dangerous now that they've been on nightly curfews for almost a year, with no signs of it being lifted by the Mayor anytime soon. He's trying to get out of there, but he can't get the relocation or travel passes approved. They have him working in one of the jails as a night janitor. He says the only good thing about his job is that at least he knows where the predators are, and he doesn't have to walk the streets after dark."

"We're pretty lucky, all things considered—at least we're not in one of the major cities, and Washington doesn't have nearly as high of a population as most states." Ben replied.

Their conversation reminded me of Officer Ren, but I didn't want to bring him up in case Aaron didn't know who he was, or perhaps that Ben wanted to keep his contacts discreet. I didn't have to worry about it though because Aaron mentioned him.

"I wonder if Ren ever gets orders to work in Seattle. I hear they're stretched so thin along the I-5 corridor now that all Peacekeepers are being worked anywhere from Vancouver to Seattle. They could be assigned to Olympia one day, but then have to work in Seattle the next. The last time I talked to him, he said they weren't even responding to burglaries or home invasions anymore unless there was a rape, assault, or murder. They just don't have the manpower."

Ben nodded.

"Yeah, we talked about that, too. He said his wife wanted to stay on the Force, but because of the new structuring and risk levels, they decided it was better if she resigned. He said they offered her a re-enlistment bonus—something they hadn't done before, but because of the national shortage, they were willing to fund. He said they thought about it—apparently it was a pretty sizeable chunk of change—but he said it was just blood money. He said Washington State was on the top five list for the lowest numbers of Law Enforcement per capita now. California and New York were the top two, and I think Illinois and Texas were the other ones. He said they cut the Academy training by two-thirds the time, just to get more officers on the streets, but they still can't fill the positions."

"Doesn't surprise me, the way they get treated. I mean, would you want to risk your life for all this?"

The two men looked at each other and laughed, causing me to laugh myself. They were clearly willing to risk their lives—and were even doing it for the same citizenry, only they weren't getting paid.

After we had some tea and tasty treats, the conversation shifted back to the expansion of the libraries and the deliverance of pamphlets.

"So next, I think we need to see if we can print a double batch. I got the numbers, and they each spent roughly forty-five minutes to an hour at each location. They sent the first few guys in to get it printed, and the remaining guys stayed in the parking lot areas monitoring traffic and keeping watch. Then, when they had it all printed, they changed places, and the distributors—all the van drivers and their co-pilots, went in, boxed everything, and got it all loaded. It was a good system because it split the risk in half—each team was inside the buildings for about half the time, and the other guys could have escaped on foot if anyone came into the parking areas. As we had discussed, each team had a designated guy who would run inside to ring the warning bell if trouble showed up. But it was all pretty flawless. There wasn't a single report of a security guard, patrol unit, or Law Enforcement sighted while they were there."

"Yeah, I think they pick some pretty isolated locations for the PLS buildings—most are in run-down industrial areas from what I could see," Ben replied.

"Has anyone actually been able to confirm or deny if the PLS employs a security service?" I asked. "I know our building doesn't have a security guard, and I've never seen patrol cars around or in our parking lots during my shift—and you know I work until midnight. Maybe none of the buildings have security, even if they're not necessarily the same."

"No," Ben responded. "The most we've been able to verify is that each of the PLS buildings operates on a Monday through Friday schedule, and everyone's out of the buildings and gone by six every night."

"I'm guessing it's a funding issue, aside from arrogance," Aaron replied. "I mean, what do they have to fear? That someone is going to break into a building that has nothing of value beyond paper, ink, and printing machines? Our guys said they only had a few computers that run everything, so it's not like there's a lot that would be stolen or would even be worth stealing. No one could take any of the printing machines without some serious manpower and a big truck. So why would the government pay to have the buildings guarded or even patrolled? What, because so many people want to read? Pfft."

We sat in silence for a moment, and I wondered if they were thinking about stealing an entire printing press machine like I was.

It could be done, I thought. Why not? If the plan was to keep breaking in, it seemed an inevitability that eventually someone would get caught. Increasing printing to twice a month only doubled that risk. Plus, it endangered a dozen people at each location—and the more they expanded, the more PLS buildings would get involved, and the more people would be at risk.

"Why couldn't we just steal a machine and computer then?" I asked.

The two men stared at me incredulously, giving a quick burst of laughter.

"Damn, Ben, she is a fireball." Aaron laughed.

"No, seriously!" I said, laughing. You said all it would take is a truck and some manpower, right? Well, you have plenty of both. And you said yourself, you're wanting to take things up a notch —to get on the board. Well, what better way to start trouble than to have a massive, coordinated attack on all the PLS buildings across the country? Or at least for about 2200 miles of it?"

I looked at each of them, and seeing that I was making sense to them, I continued.

"So think about it: You already have teams picked out. Use the database for the Services For The Deceased and get a listing of every PLS building in a 2000 mile radius—however far you can organize people. Find out what guys from each zone are willing to do some dangerous work and then plan a massive attack. You'll need some fire accelerants, and you'll need a bunch of guys to move the equipment. Plan it out, break in, load the equipment—one printing press per building and a computer to match plus a ton of paper and ink—get it all loaded up in the vans and move it out, and then have a group of guys stick around to set the buildings on fire. If you burn the buildings enough, they might not even be able to inventory what's left. And if they can't inventory it or prove computers, supplies, or even a printing press were missing, they wouldn't be hunting for it. All they would have to go on would be that there was a major attack against the PLS. It would still be terrorism, but they would believe it's just a political statement against the censorship or government-controlled Library Services System—they wouldn't even be looking for the stolen materials."

"It's a good plan...But it would still mean we were risking ourselves. If we keep on breaking in, we could probably stay under the radar for quite a while. Torching a hundred buildings in a simultaneous attack would definitely prove to them that there were some rogue people out there—and the hunt would be on. We'd never be able to relax again. We would all be at risk." Aaron mused.

"But it would be the shot heard round the world..." Ben remarked.

We sat in silence, considering all the possibilities.

By the end of our visit, we had not only agreed on a plan, we had solidified our union. If we were to take the plunge, we three were going to do it together. By raising the stakes—by even discussing Acts of Terrorism, let alone strategically plotting it so we could bring our ideas to fruition—we had all committed crimes that could result in our demise. We would surely receive the death penalty if one of us betrayed another. We were not just planning how to start a Civil War; we were learning what it meant to place our faith and trust into other people after a lifetime of forced independence and separation from Loved Ones.

FORTY-FOUR ~ REINFORCEMENTS

◆ ◆ ◆

The two men I had grown to care about more than anything else in the world did their best to protect me from everything they considered too dangerous, violent, or ugly. They protected my identity and existence at every turn—they alone took credit and blame for all that was to come in the following months. No one knew I was the person responsible for writing the messages that reached coast to coast, no one knew there was a third person behind the highest echelon of leadership. There were some half a million followers and growing, and an unknown number of leaders within their ranks, both male and female. Most could not say who or where the top tier of leaders lived, or how many of them there were. Information was on a need-to-know basis, and most accepted that it was much safer all around if they knew only what was necessary in order to perform their duties.

I knew that Ben and Aaron spoke with a handful of leaders and had developed genuine friendships and relationships with them. Some they had known for years, while others were newly appointed, but had a verified track-record and reputation for shared political views and love for their country. The people within the movement contributed in meaningful ways every single day and placed themselves at significant risk. For the vast majority of citizens, just spreading the word about the movement and trying to find like-minded people was the best and most effective way they could help, and most did it with passion and a steadfast loyalty. We were blessed to have so many of our fellow citizens willing to take a stand against their government, risking their lives and everything they held sacred in order to do so.

The plan to take the printing presses and other supplies from the PLS buildings was underway. Groups were organized, leaders were selected, reconnaissance missions were conducted to ensure there weren't any security patrols occurring, and the materials necessary for the destruction of the buildings were obtained. My initial thought had been to start fires, but as both Ben and Aaron pointed out, mere fires would not destroy the metal printing presses sufficiently enough to disallow investigators to take a full account of what remained—and so they could verify that not only were the buildings damaged, but items had been stolen. This would result in a considerably different response from our government. One would be perceived as coordinated Acts of Terrorism, while confirmed theft of items would provide them with the first—we believed —evidence of proof that there was an underground movement gaining momentum.

For the sake of our continued anonymity, we needed to destroy the buildings entirely—at least sufficiently enough to disallow an accurate assessment of the contents within. For this, we needed bomb-making materials, and people with the training and knowledge to know how to make such things possible. Locating people with this sort of resume was risky, but it was also like finding a needle in a haystack. No one in the last twenty years would have ever been given access to such information, nor could they have learned it through formal education. The government was very careful about the production of both the information as well as the materials required. Because of these limitations, it would be necessary to look for much older candidates—men and women who had been around decades before the government had gained the bulk of their power and before The Scourge had lost most of theirs. People possessing the knowledge required were likely already known to the government, however, and it was highly probable that most of them had been rounded up decades earlier, never to be seen again.

Even if we could locate people with the required experience, there was very little chance we could find enough to have well-qualified persons in every region, let alone zone. This meant we would have to train each zone separately, and from there they would be expected to both build the bombs successfully as well as plant them. And they'd have to do this without any formal education except a brief training session.

Everything was delayed while the leaders assessed the people within their zones to search for viable candidates. Several weeks passed, and still only a small handful had been found—and none of them had an extensive knowledge or first-hand experience worth any significance.

It was late one night—a night in early May—and Ben was staying over when we finally received the break we needed.

There was a knock on the door, a quiet rapping that was completely unexpected and made my heart stop when I heard it. It was near 2:30 in the morning, and Ben and I had been quietly talking on the couch.

After hearing the knock, he put his finger to his mouth, reminding me to be quiet—as if I needed any direction for that.

He walked quietly to the door in his stocking feet, bending down to look through the peephole. Within a second, he seemed to relax, and then unlocked and opened the door.

Officer Ren entered, and Ben quickly shut and locked the door behind him.

The two men shook hands, and Officer Ren looked beyond Ben toward me, and gave me a quick tip of his hat just as he had on the only other occasion I had met him.

They both walked into the living room. Ben sat beside me once more on the couch, and Officer Ren took a seat on the only other piece of furniture in the room—an old, worn-out, overstuffed chair.

"I have someone for you. It took a bit of time," he said. "I've been talking to him for a while, and I trust him. But it's one thing to know he agrees with how things are happening, and quite another to ask him to train Scourges to help build bombs."

I felt Ben tense next to me.

"So he's a LEO?" he asked.

"Yeah, he's on the bomb squad. The head of it, actually. And I've known him for most of my career. We were at the Academy together, then he left to go do more training and they put me on the streets. But he's been here at the 2nd Precinct since his training ended, and we've worked together ever since."

"How well do you know him? Are you sure he can be trusted?"

Officer Ren gave a little laugh.

"Yeah, I think I can trust him. It's June's brother. You know Charlie—you've met him a few times, I think. You know he wouldn't do anything that might end up with me getting hurt. He'd never forgive himself if June's heart was broken."

He looked at me for a brief moment, and said, "June is my wife."

Then he looked back at Ben. "Besides, I've talked to him about everything—not about you or anything, but just about how things have been going these last 20 years, and I know he's a good guy. He sees what's going on. There's never been a need to involve him any further, so I never have. But after we last spoke, when you told me you were having problems finding anyone with the right experience, I knew it was time to get Charlie involved."

"And he's ok with all of this?" Ben asked, incredulously. I still hadn't ever really learned the connection between Officer Ren and Ben, and didn't know how they knew each other as well as they did. But by Ben's tone, it surprised him to hear another member of Law Enforcement would actually be willing to help.

"You can't do this all alone, Ben," Officer Ren said. "At some point, we're going to have to start trusting people and letting them in. It's dangerous out there for all of us."

Ben nodded his head.

"You and Charlie might not have the same passion, but he has plenty of reasons for wanting to see things change. His job is extremely dangerous. There was a time when anyone working S.W.A.T. or on the Bomb Squad would have gotten extra compensation based on their risk levels, but they haven't had it for years now under the current regime. They used to get Life Insurance that would compensate for their deaths, including a separate policy that would pay off their mortgages if they were killed in the Line of Duty. They have taken away all of that from them. And because the risk levels are so high with such little compensation, they can't fill more than two-thirds of the job listings they have for S.W.A.T. or the Bomb Squad—so he's constantly working without overtime. He might not care so much about the inequalities between the Lessors and the Betters, and he might not be fighting for The Scourge directly, but he knows that true change can only come if there's a major political shift of power—and the only way he sees that happening is with a major reformation movement. That's what I've been talking to him about all these years—I just haven't mentioned that such a movement already existed until now."

I watched Ben's face change as he listened to Officer Ren, and I could see he was acclimating to the idea. Of course, it would never hurt to have members of Law Enforcement in our ranks; they were a great asset for many reasons. They had access to technology and information we didn't; they weren't allowed to be Scourges, so they had more social standing, and they also carried weapons and had experience with them. For those reasons alone, we should have considered ourselves lucky to have any of them within our ranks—but to have one who was willing to help us learn how to make bombs when his job was to diffuse them, well, that was something very remarkable indeed.

Officer Ren did not stay long after that. He shook Ben's hand, gave me the faintest flicker of a smile and nod of the head, and then made his way to the door once again.

"I apologize for dropping in unannounced, ma'am," he said to me.

I smiled, reassuring him it was not a problem, and he was welcome anytime he needed anything.

With that, having made arrangements with Ben for the two men to meet, he slipped quietly out the door.

"He's a good guy," Ben said after he'd gone.

"I still don't know how you know him, or how it came to be that he knows all about your work," I said.

"Oh! Well that's easy! He was my neighbor when I was growing up; he and my father were good friends. After my father left, Ren tried his best to help out. He sort of took me under his wing, filled in the role of father whenever he could, and basically took care of us. My mother was a total wreck after my father left, and there never seemed to be enough of anything. Then, after my mom got sick, he was the one who took care of things. He and his wife June were the ones who got my mother into Hospice Care, and then got the house all taken care of once she had passed. They gave me a room afterward, helped me get into a program for school and training, and you know, just looked out for me. He's always been there."

It explained a lot—why they both trusted one another despite the forced social constraints that would have them at war, and why they could speak so openly without fear.

"And how about Charlie? Do you know him well enough to trust him for this?" I asked.

I wasn't all that concerned, surprisingly enough. I believed

Officer Ren cared about Ben, and if he did, then he wouldn't endanger him by talking about him to someone potentially dangerous, nor would he bring him into that part of his life. If Officer Ren trusted him, then it made sense that Ben should as well. Besides, Officer Ren had technically already broken enough laws and incriminated himself that if one of us went down for Acts of Terrorism or Treason, then we would all go down. Not to mention that Officer Ren would face ample abuse just for consorting with us.

"I suppose we need to, don't we? We don't really have any better options."

"Maybe it's not about options," I said. "Maybe it's about things falling into place."

FORTY-FIVE ~ MASTERING NEW SKILLS

◆ ◆ ◆

It was now May of the year 2043. Officer Ren had made good on his promise to introduce Officer Charlie Cohen to Ben and Aaron. Although I did not prefer that either Ben or Aaron work directly with the explosives, both insisted on receiving the training themselves. I did not want either of them transporting any of the dangerous materials, either, but once again, both took it upon themselves to do the most risky aspects of their plan rather than delegate it.

Officer Cohen had one condition before he connected with Ben and Aaron, and all parties had to agree to it. He didn't want to meet anyone other than Ben and Aaron, and he didn't want any direct communication with either of them after they had completed their training with him. The possibility existed that their paths might cross organically at some point, considering Ben and Officer Ren knew one another. This was vital for creating a reasonable connection should agents of the government ever notice or question anything. But times were no longer such that Officer Ren would socialize with the likes of Ben anymore, so it was best if there were never any associations made about any of it.

They met several times a week at Aaron's cabin for four weeks total. Officer Cohen, according to Ben, was a meticulous instructor, and his knowledge regarding various types of explosives and bomb-making was extensive. He was a strict mentor, always demanding perfection from his two students. Whenever I could see Ben during those weeks—which was not for very long, and the visits were few and far between—he always seemed exhausted. Mentally, however, I could tell it exhilarated him to be learning everything he could, and it was apparent he valued the opportunity.

There was no margin for error, he said. One mistake in calculations, one improperly installed device, and it could all be over. Because of this level of risk involved, all three men were extremely cautious and respectful of what they were doing.

I questioned how well they could teach it. The people they taught would ultimately create the many dozens of explosive devices that would be used on the PLS buildings.

"We're having the leaders sort it out," he responded. "They're vetting everyone now. Ideally, of course, we'll have a selection to choose from, and we'll be able to choose those with the most applicable experience in this sort of thing—at least some with a bit of education in a related field. It's not enough to just have brave people willing to risk their lives being around such danger. We need people who can learn this information in a crash course and then take a leadership role for the entire process. They'll need to create the bombs, transport, plant, and then activate—even if they have people doing the transporting and planting, we still need them to build what will be required and then ensure they work properly—at the right time, too."

"It seems like it's the most dangerous thing to date," I answered.

"Oh, definitely. The ingredients by themselves are fine, overall, and aren't dangerous. But after we put everything together, it's immediately a volatile risk."

"So have you gotten any feedback about the increase in risk?" I asked.

"Well, we're being very cautious about who we share this information with. We definitely don't want anyone to go to the authorities because they think we're taking things too far. So for now, we're really only working with the zone leaders, and we're not telling them what our big picture plan is so much as just asking them to find out if they have anyone capable of working with bombs within their ranks."

"And? Are they finding qualified people? Will you have enough to do what needs to be done?"

He shook his head.

"No, I think you're right—most of the people who had this sort of skill set have already been rounded up years ago. They didn't want to leave anyone around who had tangible experience who could have led an uprising or created violence against them. In that regard, they handled it just the same as they did with eliminating most firearm ownership. They were good at getting rid of anyone who they thought might fight back. "

"So, what options do you have? Do you think the zone leaders will find enough suitable people? How many do you think you need per zone?" I asked.

"I really don't know. I mean, I can be optimistic, and I think each zone is going to pull through—meaning, I think every zone is going to have enough volunteers signing up that we'll be able to get people trained. I don't think the problem will be that we won't be able to find enough people—we have many people who have been ready for battle for a long time and they're going to be happy to do anything that takes this to the next level. But I think we're going to struggle to find people who are actually well-suited for this type of work."

I grimaced, and said, "Well, it's not going to do anyone any favors if they get blown up before they even construct any bombs. In fact, if even one were to go off accidentally before we intend for them to, it could bring the attention of the government down on all of us. The last thing we need is to fall under their radar before we even get started."

Ben agreed, and we talked more about the locations we were hoping each of the zones could find where they could work on gathering their supplies and constructing their bombs. Just as there would be a certain level of risk in the production process, we would be asking people to risk their lives gathering the ingredients as well. We would have to do reconnaissance missions to find facilities that stored the materials needed, and then we would have to have those facilities broken into so we could steal as much as we could.

Every step we took was fraught with danger now, and there was much greater risk being placed on the lives of those who followed the movement.

I chided myself, though, for having an emotional response to this type of thinking. This was war. We were being victimized daily by those who believed we were less than they were. This was not just my battle, or Ben or Aaron's, and we were not the only ones who made decisions. There came a point in one's life when one needed to determine what they were willing to fight and die for, and what level of risk to self they were willing to accept. This may have begun as a movement to help bring about a new era of enlightenment to the oppressed, but it had evolved since then, and everyone who chose to actively take part was doing so because they wanted to fight for their own freedom and future. They knew the risks and had deemed them worthwhile. Far be it from me to deny them the opportunity to take direct action when action was necessary.

I reminded myself once again that by my own words I had called upon people to rise and join with those who were willing to fight back. I had written an impassioned message specifically hoping to inspire people to take a stand; I had warned them that if they did not do it now, they may miss any future opportunities.

It was not my place, nor Ben or Aaron's, to decide if working with explosives was too dangerous for anyone—no matter how ill-equipped or under-qualified they might have been. We needed to have faith that only those who felt capable and competent would volunteer for the more technical aspects of the mission, and trust that between the individuals and their zone leaders that the best people would be selected for each of the jobs that would need to be done.

This movement had taken on a life of its own, and just as any business owner could tell you, once a corporation or industry reached a certain size, there were simply too many people and moving parts for one owner or leader to handle. This was why the zoning leaders were so vital, and their judgment and knowledge of those in their care would be so instrumental in our continued success.

Ben and Aaron had started something tremendous that was entirely capable of changing the entire future of our nation. Their intentions likely never envisioned something of this magnitude, but here we were.

All that could be done at this point was proper training and enough faith in our fellow citizens to believe in the best of everyone.

FORTY-SIX ~ THE BIG PICTURE

◆ ◆ ◆

Aaron's right-hand-man was the zone leader who was in charge of the eastern-half of the Washington State border. His zone traveled along the Columbia River and was relatively unremarkable terrain had it not been for one major feature: the only Super-Maximum-Security Prison in Washington State. There were only twelve functioning prisons throughout Washington, but as violence continued to skyrocket, the Supermax had been designed solely to house the overflowing Supermax cells that had previously been part of each existing prison.

As preparations were made for the bombings of the PLS buildings, Ben and Aaron had been broadening their list of targets. Aaron's zone leader, James Dwayne, was a guard at the Supermax. He had been a prison guard for over fifteen years and had worked exclusively at the Supermax for the last decade.

Formerly known as Washington State Penitentiary, the facility had been repurposed and upgraded into a Supermax in the mid-2030s. Once the renovations had been completed, all the remaining prisons in Washington had transferred their Supermax prisoners, thus freeing up more space for additional inmates. The prisons, however, aside from the Supermax, were over-crowded and above-capacity. The population of criminals requiring prison time had been steadily on the rise for decades.

James Dwayne was sitting with Aaron when we arrived, having traveled from the Walla Walla area just to meet with us. We exchanged greetings and settled into Aaron's living room comfortably.

"So James has a few things to say that I thought might be worth hearing. I'm not going to say I'm on board with this entirely, but I'm not opposed to any of it, either. It may just be part of the bigger picture that we might need to address later. At any rate, I figured it was a good idea to talk things over now while we're focusing on the PLS, so we can start strategizing about what we're going to do afterward."

Aaron finished speaking and then nodded to James, indicating he now had the floor.

"Well, first, I'm really glad to be here. Thanks for taking the time," he began.

I smiled at him. He seemed nervous, as though he thought he was being presented to the King.

"Well, I suppose I should preface my thoughts by saying I've done this job for a long time, and I've spent plenty of time around some truly sick, evil men. I don't want to offend you, ma'am, so if I cross any lines, please let me know."

All three men looked at me, but I think only James Dwayne was of the mindset that I might have any 'delicate sensibilities' which could be offended. I gave him another smile and reassured him that whatever he had to say—however he wanted to say it— would be fine. He seemed to find this comforting and continued on.

"Well, the way I see it, we're never gonna make any type of significant change in the way things are unless we completely wipe out most parts of our government. We have to take away most of their power and leave enough of our politicians weak and exposed that they either quit or go into hiding somewhere. We're gonna have to use a lot of violence to get this country back on track."

I nodded. A man after my own heart.

Feeling more comfortable with the stage, James Dwayne

continued.

"We know our government has been using the prison system for years to control the population. I'm sure y'all have heard the rumors that all the people who have disappeared over the years are being kept in some prison somewhere. Well, I've been trying to see if there's any truth to it, and I don't believe there is. I think they're just taking out anyone who they think is a danger. I think they've been capturing them and then having them executed as political prisoners. I think they're branding them all as domestic terrorists so they can lock 'em up and then kill them without any problems regarding the violation of their Constitutional rights."

He looked around the room at each of us. I glanced at Aaron and then Ben. Neither of them seemed surprised. I had guessed as much, but I'd never put much thought into it because, to date, we'd never had any way to even investigate any of the disappearances, and so no one ever had. We only had theories to go on—that, and that no one ever returned once they were taken. Death or imprisonment seemed the only viable answers.

"So anyhow, I've gained a lot of traction with the other guardsmen. And not just the Supermax—we're a pretty tightknit community, and we meet up throughout the state pretty regularly because we're all unionized and have meetings. Aaron has me as his zone leader, but you might not know that I'm also the representative for our union. So I'm used to being in the spotlight and speaking for the guardsmen. I'm not sure if you know this, but we have about a half million guardsmen throughout the state."

I felt Ben shift beside me and could feel his excitement surge; he was thinking about the possibility of those numbers.

"What are you thinking?" he asked.

"I'm thinking that most of the men who work in the prison system are fed up with our government," James responded.

"I'm thinking they're pretty fed up with getting killed by

violent offenders who will never be rehabilitated and who have no business ever being released again. I don't know if you know this, but we're now looking at the same rates of ambush and violence against prison guards as we're seeing with Law Enforcement. They're exploiting our weak criminal justice system to get away with murdering us by the hundreds every year. And because our 'leaders' in D.C. keep lessening the sentences and allowing for early release, we're caught in a vicious cycle of catch and release that's only killing us and endangering everyone on the outside."

James adjusted his position in the chair. He was a beast of a man, standing at least 6'4 and weighing probably at least 250 in solid muscle. Sweat glistened on his forehead, and his mouth tightened into a snarl as he spoke.

"I know what you're planning on doing for the PLS buildings, and I think that's a good move in the right direction. But we're never gonna make any true progress with taking this nation back until we do two things: We have to get rid of our government, and we're gonna have to kill a lot of evil monsters in order for our streets to be safe again."

There it was.

Aaron watched Ben carefully, as if he were uncertain about how far Ben was willing to go, and he wanted to see if James Dwayne had shocked him.

For a long moment, no one said anything. I imagined we were all weighing out the philosophical debate posed before us. What, exactly, constituted genocide? Was there such a thing as mass murder in the hopes that it could create a better world for the good of the community? Wasn't that exactly the reason so many other countries and regimes had used in order to justify their own heinous murder sprees and attempts to annihilate entire races and cultures? Shouldn't there be a distinction between the innocent and those who have inflicted violence and harm against their fellow man? What was the true value of human life—especially if that human life was little more than human excrement, and responsible for having caused unspeakable horrors to innocent victims? And if one could justify such mass murder, where was the line to be drawn? What crimes merited a death sentence versus a lesser punishment, such as incarceration or even exile?

Our country had no system in place to deal with violent offenders save incarceration. We'd never explored alternatives such as exile, and slowly, state by state, capital punishment had been eradicated. As such, we had been filling prisons with inmates who had committed the most egregious acts of violence against their fellow man, but there was no harsher consequence other than containment and some loss of freedom. James Dwayne was not wrong about his assessment; we had almost four million violent offenders incarcerated throughout our nation, and more than half of those were convicted of violent crimes that would have resulted in a death sentence at any other point in history. Aside from the obvious financial burden this placed on our country, it was a weak consequence given many of the crimes.

"So what are you proposing?" I asked.

"I think we should blow up the prisons after we destroy the PLS buildings," he responded, without blinking an eye.

Ben cleared his throat and shifted again, sitting more upright.

"And you think you could get the manpower and access we would need in order to pull something like that off?" he asked. His tone was neutral.

"I do," James replied.

"But you know we don't have access to people nation-wide yet. We've made great strides, and we're now as far east as Indiana… But we don't have the resources to access prisons or recruit people any further than that. It's one of the biggest reasons we've refrained from any fantasies about actually overthrowing our government; we don't have the means to access anyone in D.C."

"Yet," I said.

Ben nodded, and repeated, "Yet."

"Well, there's nothing that says we have to take down every prison across the nation all in one simultaneous, coordinated attack," Aaron interjected.

Ben looked at him.

"True," he said. "But what are the odds that we'll be able to get another shot once we've done it? Even if we could coordinate it so we could hit all the prisons in the state, don't you think that all the other states would just increase their security, making it even more impossible to coordinate another wave of attacks?"

James Dwayne nodded his head and shrugged his shoulders.

"Well, one thing I can say with confidence is that I think we've got enough guardsmen here in Washington that we could probably spread the word and coordinate attacks through a hell of a lot more prisons than just the ones in our state. And aside from that—how do you think the other states are going to increase security, if not through the hiring of more guardsmen?"

Ben raised his eyebrows, surprised at the ideas James presented.

"What do you think would happen if all the prisons were hit at the same time? What would happen to the guardsmen? Do you think they'd just sit around until they could find other jobs, or do you know of a way that they could end up out of state? I'm not familiar with how anything within the prison system works."

James Dwayne smiled broadly.

"Well, that's where the union comes into it. We're national. Now, in the past, that just made it easier for us to transfer if we wanted to, allowing us to move jobs and locations without losing rank or years. But in this particular circumstance, if the other states were to increase their security, our union would relocate all of us as needed. We have a lot more power now that all the prisons have been privatized."

"Well, I think it's brilliant," I said.

"We can't rebuild a country until we gut it from the ground up. We can't fight for the people if the people are still at the mercy of a toxic, tyrannical government and dying at the hands of violent criminals everywhere. If we're truly intent on trying to repair our nation, we can't focus on one aspect while completely overlooking the damaged byproduct of their actions."

Aaron seemed relieved. I wondered if he thought either Ben or I would consider it too extreme.

"I mean, think about it," I continued, mostly for Ben's benefit. "Say we can gain some long-term traction with the government. Say we uphold the parts of our Constitution and laws that the current regime has obliterated. We still have two major issues—even if we can put an end to this whole Scourge nonsense. We still have a major issue with violent predators wreaking havoc on our citizenry, and we still have a national Law Enforcement system that's been decimated and is drastically understaffed. There's no way we're ever going to restore law and order if we can't recruit new Peacekeepers, and no one is going to apply for jobs if we can't guarantee their safety. Like it or not, getting rid of this government and its evil politicians is only one problem. If we don't tackle Sentence Reform, we won't ever really create substantial change."

Aaron and James both smiled at me. Ben seemed more reserved, but I knew him well enough to know that for as light-hearted as he usually was, he was also introspective and prone to long periods of thoughtful contemplation. His actions, though they often seemed light-spirited, were usually only a result of carefully measured decisions made beforehand. He was not impulsive; he weighed everything out, and like most strategists, imagined every possible outcome long before ever making a move. I knew we would not get a confirmed opinion or plan of action out of him immediately, or even today. He would take this with him and process it in due time.

"Well, that's only one aspect of it, I suppose," Aaron said. "We would still need to figure out how we could launch attacks at all the prisons and hit the entire populations while also keeping all the guards safe. We'd have to figure out how to get the materials necessary to make more bombs, and we'd have to gather tremendous amounts—which as we already know from the PLS plan isn't always easy to come by."

"We'd have to have recruits from every zone where there's a prison," Ben said. "Not just guardsmen. We'd have to have recruits for both securing the materials and the build, and then they'd have to have access to the prisons themselves."

"I know I can get enough guardsmen involved we could either do it all ourselves—with training, of course—or we could figure out how to get some extra men in the gates." James said.

"Can you think of any way you can get the entire prison population into a specific area? We can't possibly get enough materials to make explosives that could destroy all their cells. Is there a way to get them all into a certain area—preferably indoors?" Ben asked.

James nodded his head.

"Well, for the Supermax, that's easy because they're not separated by security levels. There's a separate population isolated in the solitaire confinement ward, we could do it though, so when it was time, we'd have to have guards move them into the general population. But yeah, with enough guardsmen, we could do it for each location."

"And you think you know enough men who could be trusted to do all this—or you think you could recruit them? And do it all without having any of them report in to higher-ups or betray you?"

James lifted his hands as if to say, "Who knows", but then he said, "Look, I can't guarantee a certain number of men until I can coordinate it and work with a few of my most loyal guys. But what I can promise is that we have enough control over the union that even if we can't secure the men in each prison, we can control the men enough to put men into each of the prisons as needed."

Aaron looked expectantly at Ben, searching for some degree of positive affirmation that Ben was at least considering it as an option.

Ben raised an eyebrow, looked around the room at each of us, and said, "Well, it all sounds good to me. I think we have a lot of work to do before we get to that point, but I think it's the direction we need to go in."

He looked at James. "Your work is just beginning. You're going to have to figure out how to get blue-prints or decent drawings of each prison. You'll have to coordinate your men and have a complete roster of men you know you can trust throughout the state. You'll have to share our pamphlets with some of your most reliable guardsmen so they can pass them along to their contacts in other states, and you'll have to keep your feelers out for any talk that might come your way—good or bad. You'll need to remind everyone to keep quiet. We can't even put any of this into motion for at least a few more months. There's far too much that needs to be done before we're able to take action. And all it's going to take to ruin all of it is loud gossip."

James and Aaron both nodded their heads in excitement, smiling despite their best efforts to play it cool.

I realized then that although Ben never really claimed the title, and was always quick to credit Aaron as his equal, both James and Aaron himself regarded Ben as the final word.

Ben might consider this to be a democracy, but he was wise enough to know that his opinion carried the most weight, and no one would make a move without his blessing.

"One last thing," I said. "We need to get more pamphlets out. More people need to be recruited—and mostly, we just need for people to know that there's a growing sentiment across the nation that not only disapproves of our current government, but that we're actively pursuing other options. This might not seem like a big deal, but there's going to be a lot of really unhappy people out there once we start blowing things up. It's very easy when we're all surrounded by those who share our views to forget that we're in a nation that is filled with citizens who have allowed it to become what it is today. And even if we know we can garner support from all the people who have been victimized by them, all those inmates still have friends and family out here that might not take too kindly to their deaths— no matter how altruistic we think we're being. It could lead to even more chaos. So we need to be sure that we have the public support we believe we have. And we can't discount that there are a lot of Scourges out there who are completely content to remain part of the status quo—they're complacent and comfortable with how things are, and they won't think twice about turning us in. So we need to be very cautious from now on. We can't assume anyone agrees with us, and we can't risk mass genocide unless we can be sure the public opinion will not turn against us. Because it's one thing to have our government hunting us—it's going to be a lot worse if we can't trust anyone. If we fail, we're all going to be hunted down and slaughtered."

We were playing a dangerous game, with high stakes.

Thinking out loud, I said, "It's really too bad we don't have a system in place where we could account for every single friend and family member of those who had lost a loved one through a random act of violence—especially violence by repeat offenders. You know, not only so we could keep a database of all of the victims, but so we could truly understand just how many of the bereaved were left behind to grieve. What a powerful voice they would have, if they could all rise in unison and show to the world that a lax criminal justice system only resulted in more casualties. Imagine the impact they would have —an entire ripple effect brought about by the death of each victim. The magnitude of loss each death had created, an empty space in time that could never be filled again—and all because our government betrayed every victim and their grief-stricken friends and family by enabling violent predators to commit one evil act after another with no permanent consequences…"

The room was silent. What power we would have as a collective whole if we could only unify and stand together!

It seemed we had all come to terms with our next course of action. It was all so big. We were just a handful of people, conspiring to do something that truly defied all imagination. Never did I ever believe I would become an integral part of a movement that so casually discussed both the overthrowing of my government as well as the construction of bombs and even the mass genocide of an entire population of peoples—no matter how heinous they were.

But I knew, deep inside, would that I could, I would add the deaths of every evil politician in our nation to the list, along with all those who were openly bigoted against everyone whom they deemed inferior. Would that I could, I would tear my nation apart, rid it of the toxic poison that had infected it, and then implement the changes I wished to see in this world. And if it required exile and the deaths of millions of my fellow citizens, I was completely comfortable doing whatever was necessary.

On this note, I completely agreed with James Dwayne. Unless we gutted our nation of all who would destroy it, we could never create the reform we needed.

I was willing to do anything to restore my nation to the one my Founding Fathers had envisioned. We owed our citizens that much—especially all those who had paid with their lives, and those who had been left behind to grieve over them.

FORTY-SEVEN ~ THE PLAN

◆ ◆ ◆

As much as I took everything into consideration, I could not reconcile a way in which we could steal printing presses from each of the PLS buildings without being discovered by our government. Our best plan remained the most destructive: to blow up the main rooms within each building where the printing presses were stored and hope the wreckage created would be enough to prevent investigators from discovering the theft.

We were unquestionably going to be better off viewed as domestic terrorists with a grievance solely about censorship than as thieves. This wasn't just because the investigation would take a different turn if they knew we had stolen property. It was because there would only be one purpose for what we had stolen —and that was to print something. Our government officials would spend a great deal of time publicly proclaiming that we were anti-government and dangerous domestic terrorists, although they would likely never delve into what sort of reasons we might have had which would motivate us to bomb the PLS buildings.

But if they knew we were printing pamphlets that promoted legitimate reasons why we should all work together to overthrow our government, we would be hunted to the ends of the earth. We would never be safe again.

There were approximately twenty PLS buildings we intended to rob and destroy, spread out over two-thousand miles. Zone leaders had converged in Washington State in small groups over the last month to spend time with Ben and Aaron. It was a brief window of time, but each zone leader and their elected bomb technicians were all given a crash course in the intricate process of bomb-building.

The plan remained the same: a team would remove the printing presses, then a second team would enter the buildings, set up the bombs, vacate the buildings, and then they would detonate them once they were safely out of Harm's Way. A secondary location had been arranged for everyone to meet and for the printing presses to be moved to.

Neither Ben nor Aaron would take part directly in the PLS bombings, and for this, I was grateful. Their lives were too valuable to risk.

By the end of June 2043, approximately two-hundred volunteers had been trained for the PLS bombing. So far as we knew, no government officials knew of the existence of any type of dissidence or an underground movement of revolutionaries who were about to escalate from disgruntled rhetoric to declaring open war against their tyrannical government.

Everything was riding on our ability to secure the printing presses and supplies necessary to continue the production of our pamphlets. They were our primary method of communication, and the only authentic form of connection we could guarantee was sharing the exact message we wanted our fellow citizens to hear. We lost too much in translation when we relied on people alone sharing our message. It was ambitious to consider stealing such large pieces of machinery—not to mention countless boxes of printing ink and paper—but we were at a point that it was necessary if we wished to further our work. By the time we were ready to destroy countless prisons and commit mass genocide, we needed to be certain that we had the support of the public.

FORTY-EIGHT ~
SIGNIFICANT DETAILS

◆ ◆ ◆

We chose the date for the PLS bombings. The buildings were all closed on the weekends—both Saturday and Sunday—and would be empty. Ever since the plan was set into motion, Ben and Aaron had advised the zone leaders to post surveillance on the buildings to ensure consistency. Their intent was to have as close to a guarantee as possible that there would be no casualties involved. To do this, surveillance would monitor the buildings every weekend, confirming that no random employees or security personnel would be present. After a multitude of weeks, with each location under constant surveillance, the reports had confidently confirmed that there should not be any persons on the property between Friday evening and Monday morning.

Once the date had been settled, things went quickly. They had spent the months of May and June gathering supplies, learning proper procedures, and doing trial runs of the impending event. The groups of ten men and women would travel in nondescript vans to the PLS buildings. Each location would have two vehicles on site. One would carry supplies—stockpiles of paper and printing ink—and the second would carry the printing press. A third van would be on standby, carrying an 11th driver and a 12th man as a back-up driver should anything go wrong.

Our plan was simple, and according to the zone leaders, basic enough it should be able to be carried out without too much conflict or variables. The first team would arrive, break in, and begin the laborious move of getting the printing press from its resting place and into the van. The machines would need to be dragged across the floor because of their weight, and for this reason, the first job Team A would do would be to attach a cable around the printing press so the van could pull it toward the wide doorway with the overhead rolling door.

Team B would enter and begin loading the boxes of paper and printing cartridges into their van. I did not expect these items to be extremely heavy, but moving them would require constant trips back and forth from the storage room to the van. The idea of using a rolling cart had been considered, but the passageway from the storage room to the rolling doors weaved through the machinery, and as it would still require time and effort to load and unload, we determined it might be faster just to have individuals make multiple trips. This also reduced the issue of the carts being large enough to cause congestion within the passageway, or the possibility that they blocked and impeded traffic flow altogether.

Once both teams had completed their tasks, members from Team A and B would close the doors of Vans A and B—now loaded with supplies and the printing press—and then they would all load up in the third van. Van C would leave within moments of the first two vans, and all three vans would drive out of the city through various routes.

Meanwhile, a fourth and final van would transport the bombs and the appointed bomb technicians. They were expected to arrive once the first two vans had been loaded and as Van C was preparing to leave, carrying everyone.

After receiving confirmation that all participants were off-site and accounted for, the bomb technicians would enter the building, plant their devices, and then leave. The bomb technicians, being driven away by a fourth driver, would then detonate the bombs remotely.

All four vans used at each PLS building would be black and have stolen license plates affixed to them. We would use cargo vans, designed to carry heavy loads or up to fifteen passengers. None would have windows on the sides. The teams would sit on the floor both on the drive there as well as leaving, as none of the vans held seats.

There would be ten men and women responsible for moving the supplies, four vans with two drivers in each, and two bomb technicians. Each PLS bombing would have twenty people. We had planned attacks for twenty PLS buildings, giving us a grand total of 400 individuals taking part.

Aside from the intricate planning and oversight required to be done beforehand, it illustrated that at least 400 of our fellow citizens valued their country and rights enough to risk their lives to implement change.

Our government would gain important information from these attacks. They would learn that they were well-coordinated —enough to span several thousand miles and occur almost simultaneously. This would cause extreme measures by the government to protect their own and launch a series of relentless investigations.

Investigations could verify that printing presses and supplies had been taken during the attacks. This would serve as confirmation that each attack was done with more manpower and coordination than they originally believed—and this would make the situation even more dire.

They would realize that a coordinated attack on twenty buildings could technically be carried out with as few as twenty people—one in each location. But robbing the buildings, maneuvering heavy equipment, and hauling supplies—all of that meant additional labor—and that was a revolution, not a handful of rogue domestic terrorists with a grievance. Our numbers would give away the extent of our power and the strength of our movement.

I sincerely hoped and prayed we could pull everything off without the loss of a single life. It would be extremely disheartening for everyone if things ended up going sideways, and we found ourselves under attack before we even secured all that we needed to move on to the next phase. It could also demoralize everyone—force them to look hard at the possibility of the loss of their own lives, and that could prove detrimental to our plans.

All I could do, though, was wait and see.

FORTY-NINE ~ INDEPENDENCE DAY, 2043

◆ ◆ ◆

Independence Day, 2043

Independence Day, 2043. It was here. The day that We The People finally begin taking our stand—The Last Stand we could hope to take before it was too late. We had been fighting the clock for decades, waiting and watching as our government imposed restrictions, laws that promoted inequality, discrimination, and segregation. For years, we had watched as our leaders imposed one law after the next to suppress our freedoms—especially our First and Second Amendments.

We had tried to fight back within our respective states against the growing tyranny, but when half of the nation's citizens were not only willing to go along with unconstitutional laws but openly supported them, it was difficult.

Civil War had seemed imminent for many years—decades, even—as a growing populous within our nation had rejected the extreme measures being introduced and forced upon our society. But they had failed; previous generations had failed us. We had thought them to be capable of resisting the radical changes as they were implemented, but people had been too afraid to rise or take direct action. And by then, it was too late. They had rounded up those who were likely to become dangerous—those volatile, with well-known anti-government rhetoric. And once they began to vanish, people became more afraid and less inclined to speak out, lest they disappear as well.

Civil War had been stomped out because those who were willing to rise had been monitored for months—even years—by our government agencies. By the time our leaders began taking drastic measures to control the masses, they had eradicated any potential dissidents. This left those who wanted to rise, but feared doing so without motivational speeches by impassioned leaders. Oppression and domination had come easily after that.

But all of that was about to change. Tonight, hundreds of our fellow citizens were going to alter the course of history. The citizens of our nation were going to show our government in no uncertain terms that we would fight back against tyranny and unlawful abuse of power. Tonight, we would take a stand.

FIFTY ~ 4 JULY, 4 A.M.

◆ ◆ ◆

4 July 2043. Saturday. Independence Day.

We would attack during the early hours of the morning versus the night of the 4th while fireworks went off. There was a reason for this: we wanted to affect Independence Day by drawing attention to the bombings during the entire day itself rather than on the 5th. We wanted everyone at home on this federal holiday to see the news and headlines and know what had occurred. We wanted for the world to know that America was no longer free, and Independence Day in 2043 was a lie—but We The People were doing something about it, and we were taking our nation back.

And so the plan was for the attacks to happen at 4 a.m. on 4 July. The night sky would light up with explosions, but the early summer sunrise would show the plumes of smoke throughout every city that once held a Primary Library Services Distribution Center. Anyone who went outside of their residence could see the billowing black smoke. The call for freedom would be on full display.

The original plan meant that neither Ben nor I could see the explosion or take part. Aaron would remain at home as well. We knew the risks would go up immediately after the explosions, and anyone observed traveling afterward could be targeted by Law Enforcement. Ben and I had no legitimate reason to travel together; it was a tenuous enough connection for us to even explain how we knew one another.

Despite this, Ben showed up at my door just after midnight

on Friday night. Saturdays were usually my day off, so I had expected to see him. But to my surprise, he told me we were going to go to the PLS building so we could observe our plan in motion at 4 a.m. As worried as I was initially, I was also delighted. So much planning and preparation had gone into what we were about to do. It seemed a shame that we couldn't take part or even watch from afar. I was glad he had changed his mind and we would be allowed to bear witness to our work. Even if we weren't directly taking part, it was the culmination of our ideas and effort to create change that was inspiring, and I had wanted to see the end product of our planning.

It was too far away for us to walk, and the bus system did not run past 7 p.m. We would need to drive there, and that meant driving the van from the Services For The Deceased.

"The return trip is going to be where things become more high risk," he said. "As soon as the explosion happens, every CCTV camera will focus on that area. The one advantage everyone has is that there aren't any within about a mile in any direction because it's an industrial area. Our recon teams also did extra prep this week and severed the wires on a handful of the ones closest to the buildings. It needed to be done to ensure that all the vans could make their getaways without getting tagged by the cameras. We had to make sure they all had a means of egress—either back roads or freeway entrances. Some locations had more cameras than others—we couldn't dismantle each individually, so a few of the locations ended up taking out entire grids. They made it look like it was unintentional, though—a faulty wire, a fallen tree, whatever they needed to do to destroy the master box enough that it would require a few days to get them operational again."

"So, how do they intend to get rid of the vans when they're all done? Won't they all have traces of DNA and other things that might identify them?" I asked.

All the vans were the same because they were all being taken from the Services For The Deceased. Ben had said acquiring them had been the easy part—the movement was full of people who were employed by the SFTD. He had intentionally promoted the message years back that it was one of the best means of gathering contraband materials and books. There were some SFTDs in which every single employee was part of the movement. And because each location used the same 15-passenger, basic black van, gaining access to them had been easy enough. Using them had been smart; they were unlikely to be missed or reported missing since most of the drivers kept the vans in their possession full-time since they could be called upon at any given time.

"Well, we can't get rid of the vans without drawing a lot of attention to everyone. I'm hoping that they're so generic that even if an investigation shows the vans on CCTV that they're unremarkable enough to not create any genuine leads. All the markings on the vans have been carefully concealed, and they were all instructed to put stolen plates on them. There shouldn't be anything to tie them to the Deceased Services other than matching the same type of van they use regularly."

"That's all well and good, but it's still just too optimistic to be enough. And if it doesn't seem like it's enough of a precaution to me, I can't imagine it's enough for your standards." I replied.

He laughed.

"True enough. Well—realistically, each location has four vans, and we have twenty buildings in the works. So that's 80 vans that will be in use tonight. All of them will have DNA residue to some extent. Fingerprints, sweat, saliva, maybe even blood. It would take the destruction of every van in order to eradicate any possibility of being linked to any humans—and that's a problem because we need the vans for the Deceased Services—because if they report them missing or stolen, we're really going to be in trouble."

"So what precautions have you taken?" I asked.

"Well, for starters, we only took vans that the drivers had legitimate rights to be in. So all the vans were already supposed to be in their possession. The guys we selected to be their co-pilots were also already employees of the DS. Like I said, we had to get a lot of moving pieces in place before we could get this right."

"So that's fine for explaining how the guys have the vans, and it's probably a good enough alibi if any of them get pulled over tonight. But how do you explain the extra twelve guys?" I pushed him.

He raised an eyebrow and smirked at me.

"I'm sure you're probably going to be disappointed, but I really only have blind optimism for the rest of it. If they get pulled over on the way there or as they leave the area, they're probably all going to be arrested and end up getting the death penalty. If they piece together that the vans used were all from the SFTD, they're probably going to investigate every employee they've had in the last five years, and since we're almost all Scourge, we're probably all going to be thoroughly investigated and likely monitored. The best we can hope for is a clean getaway, an incompetent team of investigators, and for them to never figure out we took the printing presses or where we got the vans from."

There wasn't anything I could say after that. I hadn't ever questioned his strategy or ability to organize a plan. He'd created countless libraries over the years and had hundreds of thousands of people following his lead. If there was ever a man capable of strategy, it was him. It hadn't even occurred to me he wouldn't have every angle analyzed and prepared for. I couldn't see any quick fixes to account for why there would be DNA of non-employees in the vans, so I was inclined to agree with him: the best hope we had was that no investigation turned its eye toward the Services For The Deceased.

Hopefully, if God was smiling down on us, none of these potential risks would become realities.

FIFTY-ONE ~ BOOM

◆ ◆ ◆

We drove through the city in silence, our path marked by the glow of the streetlights between patches of darkness, occasionally passing cars or pedestrians. The crime and violence rates were usually a deterrent for the more cautious, but there were still many who maintained blind optimism in their fellow man. I was seldom out at such hours other than walking the alleyways on my return trip home after work, and though our traveling blended in with all the other vehicles on the roads, the anticipation and knowledge of what we were embarking on heightened my excitement and paranoia.

We were going to have to park several blocks away from the PLS building, and like everyone else, our exit would be the most dangerous aspect of the plan.

I had vague memories of the route Ben drove from my own venture on the bus. It seemed ages ago that I had spent my day off trying to locate the building, and it reminded me of how things had changed over the months.

Ben must have driven through the area and done his own reconnaissance with this night in mind, because he drove directly into a darkened parking area on a hill about a half a mile from the PLS building. He parked between several cars, killed the lights, and then cut the engine. From our position, we had a wide, panoramic view of the city through the windshield. Were it any other point in history, and were we there for any other reason, it might have been beautiful. But there was nothing magical about any of our cities anymore; they were filthy, dangerous, poverty-stricken cesspools filled with crime and violence. Urban areas were places filled with misery and death; there was little regard for the value of human life and seldom was consideration or care given to the suffering of its many inhabitants. The twinkling lights did little to disguise these facts —a harsh reality learned the hard way by most of its citizens.

He reached across the space between our seats and took my hand into his, bringing it to his lips as was his habit, gently kissing my fingers before letting our hands fall onto his leg to rest.

We passed the time in whispered conversation, keeping a close eye on any passing vehicles. We were still in the industrial part of town; streetlights and CCTV cameras were few and far between. Traffic was sparse given the late—or early—hour, and as it was both Saturday and a holiday, the streets were mostly empty.

"I know we need to do this, and I know we've done all that we can to mitigate any risks. But I'd be lying if I didn't tell you I'm worried—and I've spent a lot of time going over everything in my head trying to figure out how we can create the changes we need without us ending up in open warfare on our own streets. I just don't know how else we can do it," he said softly.

"I know you've done your best to protect everyone—even taking on more risks yourself just to carry the burden for others," I replied, looking at him.

"I just don't want anyone to die," he said.

I squeezed his hand. His heart was good. It was in the right place. But this was war. We were at war already, and had been for decades—he, like most people, just had problems accepting it. He was still trying to take the high road when the truth of the matter was that our side was the only one trying to maintain non-violence or honor. It was endearing to know how gentle and thoughtful he was, but the battlefield was no place for self-doubt or a soft heart.

"Try to remember that everyone involved has assessed the risks and has decided for themselves that they're worth it. Of all the things you cannot shoulder or take responsibility for, it's their decision to take part. You're not the only one longing for change. What you should concentrate on is how willing everyone is to step forward and take action. They're all volunteering, despite the risk of harm or loss of life. They're doing it for their own reasons."

I put my hand on his cheek, then along the nape of his neck, feeling his soft hair between my fingers. I would never tire of touching him or looking at him.

"Also," I told him, "These people may have been drawn to you because of what you were initially offering—a rogue, underground library system that thumbed its nose at the government and refused to submit to their classism and discrimination—but they're staying because they've been preparing for battle for years now. They're warriors at heart. They're ready to fight. They want to fight. This is their nation—they've been too afraid to stand up individually, but you've given them the means to stand together collectively. You may have started this, but it's taken on a life of its own since then, and you can't control how big things will get."

He smiled at me, a sad, small smile—one that carried the weight of the world within it.

"I understand what you're saying, and I've tried to tell myself it a thousand times. But I already feel guilty just for putting them at risk. They're still acting on my orders—and they're still looking to me for leadership. It's a lot to carry."

I smiled back at him. We had all suffered so much already. Most of us had lost someone during the height of the Disappearances. Many of us were orphans, having lost both of our parents. They had ripped apart our families. Children were separated and put into different homes, seldom able to reconnect with lost siblings as adults. We knew and understood grief from a young age. We learned it was too painful to grow attached to anyone, and too risky to place our trust in the hands of strangers.

His feelings were not surprising—they were the reaction I would have expected from someone who had been required to grow up too soon; the burden of being a child who had lost his father and grandfather, and watched his mother suffer in the wake of their absence. He carried responsibility and grief like the heavy cloak of death, burdened by its weight but unwilling to cast it off or share the load.

"We must remain positive," I said. "We've organized everything as meticulously as possible. You've made every provision you were capable of controlling and have gone over every potential outcome. All we can do now is pray that it all goes as planned, and that everyone makes it through without any bloodshed or loss of life."

He looked at the timestamp on his arm; it was now after 4 a.m. and our teams should have been working their way through the buildings. We expected it would take about fifteen to twenty minutes to get everything loaded once they were inside, and it would be approximately 4:30 a.m. before we could expect to see the explosion.

Ben leaned over and kissed me, allowing his head to rest against my own for a moment before sitting back upright. Together, we watched the PLS building off in the distance, waiting in silence for the moment that would change everything.

FIFTY-TWO ~ THE SHOT
HEARD ROUND THE WORLD

◆ ◆ ◆

In the Year of Our Lord, 2043, on the 4th of July, twenty synchronized bombs went off throughout the western United States.

Just as the shot heard round the world changed the course of events, so too did the destructive blasts which decimated twenty government buildings. Each building, it would come to be known, was left in such ruin that nothing remained except rubble.

They would secure the areas surrounding each building with temporary chain-link fences and layers of barbed wire across the tops. They would install CCTV cameras to ensure all traffic surrounding the blast zone was monitored and logged. An endless parade of government officials, investigators, bomb technicians, and bureaucrats would traipse through the rubble, searching for anything of substance capable of granting clues as to the party responsible. They would find very little. News crews would report on the blast and subsequent progress of each investigation with carefully scripted reports designed to alleviate public fears whilst also promoting the evils of domestic terrorism. Government leaders would routinely condemn the attacks and promise that all persons responsible would one day soon face 'justice'.

And throughout it all, no one—not Law Enforcement, the national guardsmen appointed to guard the blast zones, not the bomb technicians, bureaucrats, news reporters, or politicians—

ever came out and directly stated that the buildings had been selected because they were the embodiment of censorship and government suppression of the First Amendment. Not one news report dared broach the possibility that the attacks might have been done for a valid cause or to make a legitimate political point.

No one dared. It was a conversation that was quietly discussed between those who knew and trusted one another. The silence and unwillingness to engage in discussion among casual acquaintances only validated that the truth was too contentious and dangerous to hold opinions about or to risk being overheard.

It was a time of fear for all citizens, not just those considered The Scourge of the Earth. For the first time, every citizen knew what it meant to live in fear of their government and its obscene authoritarianism. Unlike decades before when only those labeled as The Scourge were targeted, no one felt safe. Everyone was suspect, and no one was trusted. A new level of polite society emerged as people masked their true selves and painted on plastic, smiling faces to show they were happy and content with the state of the nation. Common complaints ended as neighbor feared being reported by neighbor, and disgruntled family members worried about being betrayed by their more compliant relatives. Everyone feared that the day might come when government officials knocked on the door and investigations ensued. People from all walks of life and all along the political spectrum feared they might someday simply disappear, and in the quiet of the night, they tried to recall any commentary that might have been considered offensive or anti-government. They worried that casual conversations would be recounted, and their comments misunderstood or perceived as threatening, which could then result in their being turned in as potential suspects.

It was a dangerous time for all Americans as tensions ran high and fears swallowed people whole. They deemed loners high-risk, and hysterical neighbors feared the single, unattached persons living in their complex might be harboring explosives on-site. Law Enforcement was stretched thin with anonymous tips as thousands of citizens sought to expose those whom they were 'certain' must be up to no good while simultaneously showing that they themselves were dutiful, obedient, and helpful citizens of These United States.

It revealed the true nature of humanity during those early days and weeks. Hysteria, fear-mongering, and bigotry against others were on endless display.

The only peace that came readily to those who had taken part in the events of that fateful day was that the true magnitude of the explosives had been unknown, and the size of the blasts had all but guaranteed their success and anonymity. There was simply nothing left that could link anyone to the bombings. The investigators were at a loss, and eventually were required to admit that they could not even create an accurate profile for who might have been involved or how many individuals there were.

For all intents and purposes, the most widespread, coordinated Act of Domestic Terrorism on US soil had been committed by ghosts. And with no one claiming responsibility, issuing demands, or declaring their intentions behind it, the American People were left to speculate.

No government official ever provided a plausible explanation or theory for who or why the attacks occurred, and eventually, the news coverage slowed until it was seldom mentioned. Like so many other heinous attacks of terror and violence that had occurred throughout the West, there were simply more questions than answers, and the government, for all its infinite resources and funding poured into endless investigations, provided no answers.

In due time, the attacks against the Primary Library Services buildings faded from memories, and since there weren't any casualties, there was little reason to dwell.

As time passed, even those who were directly involved moved on and pushed their involvement to the corners of their minds. Life carried on. Ben and Aaron began working on their next plan: the destruction of the prison system and the end of all violent offenders. Preparations were made, supplies were gathered, blue-prints were acquired, and volunteers were selected and trained.

My path took me in different directions during the months following the PLS bombings. I continued to write and share my messages with a few key contacts, who then passed them along to each of the zones that now held their own printing presses. We focused on the printing and distribution of our messages, and as a byproduct of this, continued to build our numbers.

At times, I feared a knock on the door—the type of knock that would mean the end of all I knew and loved.

But the knock never came. It seemed, at least for now, that we were safe.

FIFTY-THREE ~ ONE GLORIOUS YEAR

◆ ◆ ◆

August 2043 marked the one-year anniversary of the date Ben first entered my life. It had been the most significant period of time I had ever experienced, and it was not only because of the romantic relationship that had grown between us.

I thanked God every day that Ben left that box of contraband books for me in the hopes that I would take the bait and take them home with me. I counted that night—and every moment after—as the date my life truly began. Through him and his movement, my own life had been given purpose and meaning. I had learned and grown in all ways that mattered. His books had expanded my mind and intellect, and opened up a world entirely unknown before. Without him, I would never have learned what it meant to love and be loved. I would never have experienced the joys of a loving, romantic relationship, or what it meant to be treasured by the person who held my heart. He had transformed me from a shy, introverted, sleeping girl into an impassioned, brave, and dedicated woman with a strong sense of personal and national identity. Through him and his faith in me, I had discovered a talent for writing, and had been allowed to embrace and magnify the untapped potential within myself.

I owed him everything, and I began each day entirely content and full of gratitude for all that my life had become.

FIFTY-FOUR ~ AUTONOMY

◆ ◆ ◆

By the end of September 2043, Ben and Aaron had met with James Dwayne a handful of times to gather intel and get everything organized. James Dwayne had stepped up into the role of leadership within the movement, capitalizing off of his position within the union of prison guards.

It was a miracle to me that no government agencies or officials had caught wind of our underground movement. We were rapidly approaching one million confirmed members, and had allies in every state coast to coast. They distributed my pamphlets far and wide, quietly sharing them.

It was during this time when Ben told me of a few zone leaders who had approached him with a request to plan out more bombings against the PLS buildings in other states. Knowing that the movement had grown beyond his control, and recognizing that we were on the precipice of creating fundamental change through open rebellion, Ben selected a group of his most loyal zone leaders and appointed them to the highest position of authority he could create.

Because the movement was technically a loose-fit collection of people, and because there had been such need for secrecy, no formal hierarchy had ever been established. There were points of contact in various positions, and there were zone leaders who had been selected by either Ben or Aaron over the years, but as the movement had grown, it had taken on a form of its own. In principle, everything was similar throughout the nation. The fundamentals remained the same: create an underground movement of illegal libraries filled with contraband books, and build an army of citizens who would work toward changing the country. But from zone to zone, state to state, how those activities were achieved had been as diverse and varied as its members.

The advantage to this was the level of responsibility that either Ben or Aaron had an obligation to bear; the greater the cause, the more moving parts, the less control the men had. For matters of security and accountability, this mattered a great deal. Ben, with an inherent sense of ownership and duty, would have gladly borne the burdens and guilt that arose through any events that might have led to a member getting caught or dying—even if he didn't know them personally, hadn't sanctioned their actions, and could not have controlled the events leading up to their demise even if he had known. As the creator of the movement, he took each blow to their efforts personally. Should things ever turn into open warfare, this tendency would eventually eat him alive.

Discussing this, Ben and Aaron agreed that each state must become its own chapter, and become accountable for their own members and actions. They may have been the founding members of a movement that originated in Washington State, but it was now greater than anything a few people could hope to own or control. With both reluctance and trepidation, both men agreed the best way to move forward was to relinquish all control and for each state to appoint their own form of leadership and itinerary.

As long as the goals remained the same, and as long as unity could be counted on if there was a national need to collaborate and work together, then it was for the best if they delegated by encouraging each state to work within their own perimeters. Not only would self-governance be better because of distance, it allowed respective leaders to address the specific needs and desires of their own zones and states.

Ultimately, the movement was not supposed to have ever

become a well-known or well-organized group of individuals. The only thing such an accomplishment could have ever guaranteed was recognition by government agencies and placing targets on the backs of all involved. It was risky enough for zone leaders to be known to those under their command; if members readily identified their names and faces, it made it all the easier for them to be picked up by investigators and interrogated.

For these reasons, it was time for each of the states to embrace their own autonomy and start strategizing their own plans. Ben and Aaron had provided instruction with enough zone leaders they could continue reaching out to other leaders and share their knowledge of bomb-building—which was really the most complicated feat of accomplishment within the movement thus far. If the individual states were determined to destroy important buildings such as the Primary Library Services, then it was vital that each state have the fundamentals of bomb making that we had learned.

And so, as time permitted, each of the states broke away from one another and began working as independent entities. As these changes took root, less information trickled in, and the level of involvement of both Ben and Aaron slowly dissipated.

One of the final national agendas Ben passed along through his chain of command was regarding the Primary Library Services. Sharing his recommendation for each state to continue forward by following in the footsteps of the original bombings, Ben encouraged all states to obtain printing presses and supplies and then destroy the PLS buildings. Although it was unlikely that communication and the sharing of messages would all continue to stem from the same source—my writing them and sharing them—he wanted to ensure that the messages could continue. This meant new writers would need to be found, and once the printing presses were acquired, new distributions could begin.

The movement, Ben said, must continue to grow and develop,

gaining both in size as well as strength. Where one soldier might fall, another must be ready and prepared to take up where they left off. We were not powerful individually, but as a collective whole, we were unstoppable.

Time changed everything as the states became more independently organized. Meanwhile, Ben and Aaron were finding more freedom to plan out their most important attack —that of the prisons. Only after these synchronized explosions took place would they share the intel and experience they had gained. The risk of discovery was too great to allow it to be commonly known, and each man was heavily invested in ensuring this plan was brought to fruition. Once they had succeeded, the rest of the nation could begin working toward their own plans. It was, as far as ambitions went, the most dangerous, organized, and complex undertaking to date, and because it required dozens of committed soldiers willing to contribute, it carried a significant risk of betrayal. If it worked, though, it would be well worth it.

FIFTY-FIVE ~ FIGHT OR FLIGHT

◆ ◆ ◆

"I may have to go underground," Ben told me.

"What do you mean? For how long?" I asked. Surely he couldn't mean permanently. He would never be able to resume any sense of normalcy if he disappeared for too long or disrupted his job and responsibilities.

"Permanently. I don't want to—it reminds me of my dad and his choices. I don't want to give up on society; I want to be here to make it better. But I'm not sure I can lead as effectively if I'm constantly hindered by my job, and that doesn't even address the issues regarding the constant paranoia of being monitored. I always feel paranoid now; I feel like they're watching me and I'm about to get picked up. I can't shake it. I used to travel and do all my usual things, knowing the risks but still able to do it without this sense of fear. Now I have this constant sense of foreboding that I just can't shake. Every time I drive somewhere I feel like I'm being followed."

I sighed. I understood more than he realized. I had felt a similar pressure, although I doubted it was to the same extent. But I felt a growing fear as well. It was a feeling of living on borrowed time, as if I knew the simple goodness of my humble existence couldn't stay the same for too long. I had to wonder if it was because we were a people who were used to losing the things that we loved. We were no longer familiar with a healthy level of satisfaction or bliss—we were constantly waiting for the other shoe to drop, and for all we loved to be taken away from us.

"But have you seen anything out of the ordinary? Anything at all to give credibility to your feelings?" I asked him.

He shook his head, his eyes almost pleading with me to recognize that his fears were valid.

"But where will you go? What will you do? How will you support yourself?" I tried to ignore the hint of hysteria and fear within my voice—my fear of losing him drawing out a shocking level of panic I was not used to feeling and which surprised me.

"I don't know. I haven't sorted anything out yet. I don't have any answers."

His eyes were sad, full of regret and worry.

"I don't even know if it can really be done," he said. "I mean, who knows if people who tried to do it years ago are even still alive— they could have all been tracked down, rounded up, and thrown into prisons or killed. We only have rumors to go on that they're even still out there."

"Rumors from long ago—and usually nothing more than stories told from person to person—never any first-hand accounts," I reminded him.

"I know you'd like to believe that your father and grandfather are out there still, that they're just getting by on the fringes of society, that they're safe and just doing what they've chosen to do... But when was the last time you had any concrete proof of their existence? How many years? You were still a child, weren't you?"

Slowly, he nodded his head, sighing.

"Yeah, it was back when I was still living with my mother, right before she started getting sick. He had mailed a letter to Ren with some cash. He said he was living off the land, hopping trains as necessary. It was the last letter I saw of his, anyway. He said he was proud of me for taking care of my mom."

"So how many years ago was that?" I asked him.

"I dunno. Probably close to ten, I imagine."

"Look," I said. "I'm not trying to shoot holes in your plan and I definitely don't want you to imagine the worst about your father. There's a good chance that he's still out there with your grandfather doing exactly what you think they're doing, and they're surviving just fine. But they're also much older now—and that lifestyle is only going to get harder with age. I just don't understand why you would want to run into a situation where it could be so much harder on you in the long run."

"Because this isn't living, Margaret! No matter how much we've gotten away with, no matter how lucky we are to have found each other and been able to at least enjoy some part of this time, this isn't what life is supposed to be. It never will be. We don't have the freedom to choose anything—we can't even choose each other! We're never going to be together, truly together, like our parents were. I mean, for God's sake, you haven't even been able to visit my place because it's so heavily monitored. I can't visit you unless it's dark outside! I'm paranoid all the time. I can't even sleep without nightmares anymore."

He rubbed his eyes, then ran his hand through his hair, leaving it disheveled. I knew he had been tired lately; I knew he had been under more stress than usual, but I hadn't realized he was as bothered by things as he had been. I put my hand over his, and we sat there in silence.

"I'm afraid," he said. "And no matter what I do, I just can't shake this feeling. I feel anxious all the time. And the paranoia is valid even if there's no way to confirm it. I feel like they're watching me. I feel like every step I take is being recorded and catalogued, and I'm worried. I'm worried I'm putting you, and Ren, and even Aaron in danger. I keep hearing this voice in my head telling me to look around, to tread with caution, to not do certain things. It's messing with my head, but more than that, it's affecting my ability to do what needs to be done."

"And you think if you're just entirely off-grid, if you just disappear, that they won't be able to track your movements and then you'll be able to do what you need to do."

Finally, I could at least understand what was driving him. It wasn't about his dad at all; it was about his being able to focus on the next step in his vision—in being able to follow through with his plans for the prisons. He wasn't motivated by fear; it was a fear of failure, and all he wanted was to create the best-case scenario in which he could have the greatest odds of success.

"So, what can we do? How can we take some steps to weigh things out so you can make a fair assessment about what you should do? And what can you do to prepare for this in case you decide this is the best course of action to take?" I asked.

Ever logical, I pushed my feelings down, ignoring the breaking of my heart and the taste of bile in the back of my throat over the idea of losing him. My emotions would not help either of us in this situation—he needed to decide based on sound reasoning, not love or guilt. As much as I wanted to, I could not beg him to stay, to choose this life, to choose me.

"Well, I think I should talk with Ren, first. Probably before anything else. I could ask him about my father and grandfather. Find out what he knows—or as much as he knew back then. I never really asked him about that part of things. I don't even know if he wrote letters to Ren himself. And I could probably see what he knows from a professional standpoint. Do they actively still search for the political dissidents, and if so, how? How much do they invest into it as far as time and resources? I remember hearing they had full teams assigned to specific cases and people. I wonder if they still do, given how much time has passed without people speaking out like they used to."

I nodded—this was a good place to start.

"Yes! See, now this is how to do it. We need to find out as much information about these things as possible, even if the information is dated. And maybe he still has some of your dad's letters—or he can recall enough details to know where he was, or how much he moved around, or if he had a specific place he traveled to at certain times in the year like the nomadic tribes used to."

For the first time in a long while, Ben smiled, and I could see the relief wash over him.

"I don't want to go," he said. "But I don't want to die, either. I still have so many things I want to do."

I did my best to conceal my hurt, and tried to focus on what he was saying. The pressure of being caught had clearly been weighing him down, and his worries, no matter how unfounded they might currently be, were not outside of the realm of possibility.

"Maybe Ren can look into things—see where the PLS investigation is, see if they have any legitimate leads. See if there's anything behind your instincts." I offered.

"Yeah, that's fair. I'm pretty sure if he thought anything was amiss he would have reached out though. But it's possible they're just keeping things wrapped up tight, and since he's not an investigator, maybe it's just not out there. Maybe they're keeping a lid on things so tightly there aren't even any rumors."

"That's the paranoia again," I chided gently. "That's fear—not reason. You can't answer any of those types of questions—that's just your fear trying to convince you to worry."

He sighed. "Yeah, I know, but that's where my mind is."

"But you can't control certain things—you can't control the investigation, or the flow of information, or what the investigators are sharing with the news stations, or even what gossip might happen within the police departments or other agencies. All you can control is what you can verify, what you know to be true, and what you can factually find out from reliable sources. If you allow yourself to get into the headspace of second guessing every move you make based on your feelings of fear, you're going to drive yourself crazy—maybe even make mistakes that lead them to you."

"I know all this!" he blurted out, frustrated.

"Don't you think I can tell the difference between what's logical and what's fear-based? I'm a rational, thinking being. I know I'm losing my shit—but I can't help it! Everything is riding on our ability to succeed—and we can't succeed if I'm dead or rotting in a prison somewhere."

I didn't know what to say anymore. I didn't know how to help him. He'd never raised his voice before—I'd never seen him upset. And I knew, just as surely as we were both occupying the same space, that I didn't have the experience or skills to know how to navigate this level of emotion or psychological turmoil. I was no better equipped to handle conflict than I was to stand up for myself when being berated; there were simply some behaviors that not only had they had expected me to avoid, but would have likely been chastised or punished for demonstrating. I was well-trained to be submissive, obedient, and non-argumentative.

Everything I had become, all that I had developed into during the last year, had been because of him. Ben was my anchor—my link to a world that I desperately wanted to remain a part of, but that he alone had built. He was my only friend, and the man who had my heart, who had become my lover, and whom I yearned to please, always. It was difficult seeing him so out of sorts, but it was devastating and heart-wrenching to imagine him leaving me, too.

I couldn't fix any of this. I couldn't make him risk his life by staying, and I couldn't expect him to trust anything other than his own instincts. In a world where violence was commonplace and the value of human life was minimal, all he had was what he believed and could rely on—and for most of us, that was only ourselves. If his instincts were telling him to be afraid, to feel the level of situational-awareness that he was, to abandon the life he had built here and run, then I had to believe his instincts should be trusted. I knew I would trust my own.

At the end of the day, all we had was ourselves. Everything else was fleeting and unpredictable. People couldn't be counted on to tell the truth or to pull through for you. Betrayal was almost expected because self-preservation was often inevitable. Reality was unreliable because it could not be verified.

They provided all information to us to influence and control us. There was nothing any of us could legitimately trust except ourselves and what we could prove with our own instincts, experiences, and perceptions. It was all any of us had.

For now, all I could do was support his decision to speak with Officer Ren, and hope that he had some insight into Ben's father or the idea of going off-grid that would squelch Ben's plans. Hopefully, Officer Ren would also have enough intel regarding the PLS bombings to assuage Ben of his worries as well. Maybe it would be enough to convince him to stay here. Maybe he would find the reassurances that he needed, but I could not provide.

I sincerely hoped so, because a world without him was too incomprehensible to imagine, and for the first time since meeting him, I was now plagued with fear about events entirely beyond my control.

FIFTY-SIX ~ HARD TRUTHS

◆ ◆ ◆

The following weekend, at Ben's request, Officer Ren came to my dwelling unit shortly after midnight. He was out of uniform, wearing comfortable street clothes and a ball cap. Following Ben into the living room where I was sitting, Officer Ren tipped his cap in greeting to me and then sat on the chair opposite us. Ben settled in beside me, asking pleasantries about Officer Ren's family.

They talked for a few moments, and then Ben opened up about his concerns. Officer Ren listened patiently without expression. As Ben told him of his growing fears and paranoia, a look of compassion came over his face, and his eyes softened. It was only after Ben began discussing his father and grandfather, however, that Officer Ren finally interjected.

"Ok, I can't help much with the paranoia, but I'm going to advise you to listen to your instincts. A big part of my job requires me to stay on my toes, so I can't very well tell you to brush those feelings aside. I think if you're feeling something, there's probably a good reason for it. And since you said you never used to feel this way, I'd say there's something to it. Things have escalated lately, and there's good reason to feel paranoid or like you need to be extra vigilant. You should be—that's healthy—it could very well be what keeps you alive."

He looked at Ben as he spoke, maintaining strong eye-contact, and I was glad to see that Ben obviously respected his opinion. He was telling him the last thing I wanted him to hear, but hopefully he was going to bring some sort of silver lining to the conversation, too.

"That being said," he continued. "I haven't heard anything through the department. They have investigators assigned to the case, but as far as I know, it's closed out. They haven't found anything to tie anyone to it. The explosions were so big that they had little to go on—I'm assuming you've seen the wreckage. It's mostly cleared out now, but all the sites have craters in them. That's how big the explosions were. And I know they had some government agencies working on it—the FBI and ATF for sure —but as far as I know, it's all been a dead end. Not that the government is going to allow that to last—they're going to name someone at some point. They can't just have it unanswered. They'll either blame some old terrorist group that probably doesn't even exist anymore but still has some sway and people will remember, or they'll find or invent some new group they can assign credit to."

He studied Ben, trying to see if anything he said was sinking in.

"The important thing for the government isn't whether they find the party actually responsible, it's finding the right type of group to blame—and to see if they can do it without ever addressing the true nature of the attacks. The buildings getting blown up was a direct commentary against censorship and the extent of government control over all information and content created. Above all else, the leaders of this nation don't want that to be the headlining story. It was a slap in the face that twenty government buildings were destroyed, but the worst part of it was that it was an attack against one of the most benign targets conceivable. In the history of our nation, there's never been an attack against a library—let alone the places that manufacture the books. By nature, people are curious—libraries are supposed to be places of learning and intellectual growth. It makes little sense that anyone would ever target a library, and yet earlier this year, a group of people decided they would do their best to obliterate not just one library, but twenty of the buildings which produced every book published and put onto library shelves in the last twenty-five years. Now why would anyone do that?"

He raised his eyebrows and looked back and forth at each of us.

"I'm guessing it had something to do with the suppression of free speech, and the message the bombs sent is that even if we still have libraries, we don't really have the freedom to choose what we want to say or read as long as it's all being controlled and censored by the government. But that's the last thing our leaders want us to come to realize—which is why they're trying desperately to mask the true intent or purpose of why those buildings in particular were targeted. They'd rather people remain in the dark—completely transfixed on the superficial and banal—anything to keep them from thinking too much. Critical thinking is the death knoll for all tyrannical governance; as soon as the people recognize that they have always held the power to put an end to their own oppression, authoritarian leadership loses its power. This regime is already tottering on collapse; they know their absolute power will only survive as long as hate and fear fuels people. That's why they've allowed open discrimination against The Scourge. But with the crime and violence rates being what they are, with the criminal justice system crumbling because of poor policies, and with Law Enforcement jumping ship by the thousands, the last thing this government can risk is open rebellion."

"So you think they're going to pretend there's not an underground movement of dissidents on the rise even if they know we exist," I said flatly.

"Hell yeah, that's exactly what they'll do. Don't get me wrong— I have no idea if they know who's responsible for the bombings or not. I have seen nothing that shows they know anything. But what I believe is that even if they could confirm for certain that such a group existed—say, for example, they had acquired a pamphlet or two, or could verify that there were printing presses stolen from the buildings that were bombed—I doubt very much that the American people would ever hear a word about it. This government needs to create the illusion that they're being fully supported by the American People. They need to project that image both nationally as well as internationally, or the whole charade crumbles. And they can't do that if they admit there's a growing movement that has the audacity and gumption to go around destroying government buildings."

"So why do you think they're gonna try to pin it on some smaller, older group, or some new, fictitious group? What do you think they're going to say the reasoning was for it?" Ben asked him.

"Why do they really need a reason at all?" Officer Ren answered. "Right now they're just trying to downplay it. If you've seen the news, you know they only mention it in passing—it's not even a headlining story anymore, even though it's the biggest attack on US soil in years, and to date we've never had a domestic terror attack that's hit twenty separate targets all in one coordinated effort. The last time we saw an event of that magnitude was back in 2001 with the attacks on 9/11. But even considering just how enormous the PLS bombings were, you never hear them mention it. They never talk about how many people had to have been involved, either. They don't want people to figure out just how organized or widespread the group is."

That made sense. It's not like we ever had any reason to trust anything the government did anyhow—of course, they would create some sort of alternate version of events so it suited their purposes.

"So there you have it—so far, we can expect that the government is going to ignore the reasons behind the attacks and downplay that we did specifically it to government-sanctioned libraries. They're already downplaying the magnitude of twenty simultaneous attacks, all so it doesn't seem as well-organized or as big of a movement as it must be. And they're refusing to address entirely where the materials could have come from or how anyone could have learned how to make such extreme weapons—because if they discuss it, they'd have to admit that most of the people that had the knowledge to do so at one point had all been labeled as Scourge, rounded up, and either imprisoned or killed. Our government isn't prepared to have any of those conversations honestly with the American people —so yeah, everything we learn is going to be pure fabrication, intended to appease the public and create a false villain to take the blame."

"But wouldn't they still have to provide a decent explanation why either some old group or their fictitious new group would target the library services?" Ben asked.

Officer Ren nodded his head. "Well, yeah, I would imagine so. But what they're going to do is create whatever fiction they think will sell and create a story of victimhood designed to make everyone sympathetic. They'll also likely hype up the fear of future attacks—even though there wasn't a single person hurt by any of the explosions. Never underestimate the power of fear. They need two things to help them maintain control over this: an enemy and fear. All they have to do at that point is tell the American people no one is safe—that if there are terrorists out there who will bomb twenty government buildings, then they could bomb anything. Before you know it, they'll convince everyone that the terrorists could only perpetrate evil and are a threat to everyone's lives—and once they believe that, the fear will follow. They'll never stop to question why the buildings were bombed, and they won't even care that no one had actually been hurt. And that's what the government needs—blind sheep who are willing to fall in step with whatever is asked of them."

Thinking out loud, I said, "So really, what they need is probably some type of old Eco-Warrior group—some group they can pin this one on that no one would ever question. Then they can offer up some generic reason, no matter how ridiculous, so the People can understand the why behind their attack. It just needs to be something plausible enough to be widely accepted, such as books requiring trees to produce."

Both Ben and Officer Ren slowly nodded their heads at my

comment.

"That's smart," Officer Ren said. "You probably just nailed it. If they can blame some environmental group, pretty much everyone will just disregard the whole thing. They'll see it as a political statement rather than what it actually was. That's brilliant, actually. Good thinking."

He smiled at me, nodding his head in approval.

"So Ben, while I understand why you're feeling the pressure, it might just be you internalizing it a little. You have a lot to lose —you've built a life for yourself, at least as well as possible these days."

Officer Ren nodded at me, and I blushed furiously. But yes, I would hope he would have included me in his list of reasons to want to stay safe, maybe even as one of the things he feared losing.

Ben sighed.

"So you really don't think there's anyone keeping tabs on me? You think it's just stress I've built up?" he asked.

Officer Ren shook his head, disagreeing.

"No, that's not what I'm saying. I absolutely think you need to trust your instincts about this. All I can say is that as far as I know, and as much as I can deduce about the actions of our government, they have no reason to target you. I don't know for sure one way or another that they have any leads—and I'm not privy to anything that the FBI or ATF might have as far as their investigations. I can only say with certainty that I don't believe local Law Enforcement has any legitimate leads. I also don't believe that the government wants to find the truth about who was behind the attacks. I think they're working on burying it and they just want to move on. But that doesn't mean that you are wrong for feeling like you do. Have you noticed anyone or anything out of the ordinary?"

"No, never. Like I said, I'm just feeling paranoid. What about drones? What about trackers in the van? I mean, if they wanted to catch me doing illegal things, that's really all it would take. At some point, I'd get busted. If they know who I am, they could just monitor me so they could gather enough evidence to convict me based on my actions today—they wouldn't even need to link me to the bombings. If they're watching me, they're watching me, and it wouldn't take long before they found plenty to use against me."

Ben's words were a lament; he needed validation for his paranoia. He wanted for us to see his train of thought and at least understand how trapped he felt, even if we didn't feel it was merited.

It was then that I first understood that this would never be a fairy tale ending for me, or for us.

Eventually, at some point, no matter how careful we were, we were going to be placed into Harm's Way and would suffer the consequences.

Try as I might, I could not get back to the comfort I had originally felt thanks to Officer Ren's words and assessment. That familiar sense of foreboding and loss crept in again, reminding me that the only true friend I had ever known was loneliness.

As much as I wanted to, I realized at that moment that I could not trust or rely on Ben for my happiness or security. He was neither reliable nor trustworthy because everything fell apart at some point. It wasn't personal, and I knew he would never want for me to lose faith in him. But I understood then that there would be no happy ending with this love story, or probably the story of my life or his. We were alone, despite being near one another, and eventually, the blackness would swallow us all.

FIFTY-SEVEN ~ TWO FATHERS

◆ ◆ ◆

Officer Ren and Ben continued their discussion, speaking often of Aaron and then some others that I had neither met nor heard of. As I listened to them, I was surprised to hear the full extent of how much Officer Ren knew of Ben's nocturnal activities. He had told me that he had known Officer Ren since he was a child, but as they spoke, it became clear that Ben regarded him as something of a father figure, and Officer Ren seemed to embrace this role naturally. Ben asked his opinion on a variety of details, and Officer Ren was both knowledgeable as well as insightful with his responses. Above all else, Officer Ren both respected and loved Ben.

He had a tendency to reverse Ben's questions with questions of his own—intentionally designed to require Ben to think critically about his answers and consider all options. He seemed helpful and responsive to Ben's obvious desire for guidance, but he also believed Ben capable of forming his own conclusions with adequate critical thinking, and therefore didn't want to tell him what he should do. It was manipulation, to be sure, and I was certain Ben did not know that Officer Ren steered the conversation through this technique. But as confident as Ben seemed to be, it was easy to see that his respect for Officer Ren resulted in his submission to him, much like any child would to their elders. At any rate, I could see no harm in this, as Officer Ren clearly loved Ben and wanted what was best for him.

Eventually, the conversation circled back to the questions Ben and I had contemplated earlier regarding the men who had lived off-grid, including Ben's father. After asking Officer Ren about how much he had known of his father's transition into his nomadic, nameless lifestyle as a political outlaw, Officer Ren smiled grimly, but provided us with some much needed hard truths.

"I haven't heard from your father in well over a decade," he began. "Probably about fifteen years, actually."

"But how can that be? You read me the letters he wrote to us! He sent us money almost every month! Even if he didn't write messages, he still sent us money. It was the only way we survived during those years after my mother got sick!"

Ben's voice echoed his confusion. Officer Ren shook his head slowly, his eyes taking on a new sadness not there before.

"Your father only wrote a few times. He left the first letter in my mailbox the day after he left. On the first page was a note to me, and the second was for you and your mother. The note he wrote to me thanked me for always being a good friend to him. He asked me to remember our friendship, to set aside the differences between the men that we were through the changing eyes of society, and asked if I would please help look after you and your mother. The second note, if you recall, was his explanation to both you and your mother about why he had to go—why he was too great a risk to remain present, and why only by fleeing could he hope to keep both of you safe."

"I don't understand," Ben said.

"He sent several more letters after that—not regular, only a few, and only that first year. He never sent any money, and we never heard from him after that first year again—not through a letter for you or a letter to me personally. I tried to track him down through resources at work—I set up a notification system for him so it would inform me if he was ever arrested or detained anywhere in the US. But I never heard anything more from him or about him after that first year. I have no idea what happened to him or your grandfather."

"But you read me the letters. You gave us the money." Ben mumbled.

Officer Ren grimaced.

"Yes, I did. I read letters to you, told you that your father had sent them directly to me, and that he also sent funds to help keep you fed and clothed. I did what I could to help a grieving kid come to terms with an absentee father, and to help his sick mother get by. I hope you can forgive me for the years of deception, but I had to do what I thought was best. Your mother needed help. Your father was gone."

The room fell into silence as Ben tried to process all he had learned.

His father was most likely dead. All these years he had probably told himself that his father was out there somewhere, living off-grid, evading Law Enforcement, dedicated to his cause. But all of that was gone now.

Now, all that remained was only the slightest possibility of hope that he might still be out there, that he and others like him had survived being political dissidents simply by rebuking the changes in government and choosing to flee the constraints of modern society and its government restrictions. Now, the harsh reality existed that even if he were still alive, he had made no effort to maintain contact with his wife and son, that he truly had abandoned them all because he valued his political beliefs more than his family. Now, there was the actual possibility that our government had eradicated all those who had attempted to escape tyranny, and having gone off-grid or not, they had all been hunted down and systematically exterminated.

It did not bode well for Ben, should he choose to follow in his father's footsteps and attempt to live beneath the watchful eye of the government. Perhaps now, in these times, at this point in history, it was impossible for anyone to escape the attention of the government on every level—no matter how 'off-grid' they try to be. Anything that anyone would ever need to do would be documented and accounted for somewhere; one couldn't own land, travel, have a legal job, make purchases, or even seek medical attention without some form of authority knowing about it and keeping records. And all that was aside from the CCTV cameras that were prevalent in every major city and along every interstate, highway, and paved road. Even if one could avoid attracting unwanted attention through any of the million ways they could be tracked, they would still have to contend with nosy neighbors, observant do-gooders, and the brazenly militant turn-coats who derived a certain high-handed joy in shining a light on anyone they considered a 'threat to the greater good'.

Ben needed to know all of this—he needed to hear first-hand how things were likely stacked against him, that going off-radar was an almost delusional fantasy that had a brief shelf-life. Our government was too big, too vast, too all-knowing, and too encroaching to believe that anyone could escape recognition or accountability for long. If the government had cause to believe that someone was a threat to national security, that they were potential domestic terrorists, or that they held politically dangerous views—even if those views were only actually dangerous because they were contrary to the popular opinion and current government agenda—there was no rock on American soil that someone could safely hide under for long.

Going off-grid might actually be a greater reason for him to be found out. He had been doing things on his own so far with no one catching on. But abandoning his jobs, leaving his dwelling unit and all his possessions—those were things that might lead to something akin to an investigation, and once they began looking into his world a bit more closely, they might find more than anyone bargained for. Granted, because he was Scourge it was unlikely his absence would monopolize much attention from government officials. They'd probably chalk it up to an unsolved murder and forget about it. But on the off chance that they were able to discover even a bit of his political ideologies or nocturnal activities, the gates of hell would open wide and there would be agents from a multitude of agencies. And if that happened, not only would Ben's world be turned upside down, most of the people he had come into contact with would also be investigated—myself included.

Officer Ren and Ben continued talking, and though the conversation took on a lighter tone, Ben's mind seemed preoccupied with all that he had learned. He would now have to readjust his plans and expectations based on that information, and plan accordingly. Along with this, the absence of his father had now taken on a new meaning. Now, instead of feeling or hoping that his beloved father and grandfather were 'out there somewhere fighting against the government', he was forced to come to terms with the realities of their likely demise. No matter how long he had been absent from his life, Ben was still a son left to grieve for his father, and now he would be forced to grieve in an entirely new way—that of a son accepting the death of his father, not just his absence. Knowledge of death was the absence of hope, and for a little boy who had lost his father at a young age, perhaps the hope of his return had been something he carried with him to this day. All that was now changed.

Standing up, Officer Ren made ready to go. Ben stood and walked with him, hugging Officer Ren before opening the door. It was something Officer Ren probably appreciated, an affirmation that his good deeds had been understood and forgiven. Both men seemed grateful that they had the other, and their enduring bond seemed stronger than ever. It was good to take stock of Ben in this manner; he had accepted and processed both the lie held by Officer Ren over the years, and the truth of the matter, with great dignity and class. He hadn't reacted with anger or outrage over having been deceived, but appreciated the lengths that Officer Ren had gone to instead. It was remarkable and showed genuine maturity that I found very endearing and worth noting.

The two men exchanged a few more words, and then, with a tip of his hat in my direction, Officer Ren left silently through the door.

As Ben walked back toward me, shoulders drooping, I knew that his plans for going off-grid had been dashed. We would have to sort things out another way.

FIFTY-EIGHT ~ THE CORNERSTONE

◆ ◆ ◆

As much as Ben had decided to hand things off to their respective leaders and regions, he still held the reins for a few specific areas, and wanted the message to be the same from coast to coast. One of those requests was regarding my own publications. He openly advocated for the various regions to get their own printing presses and secure people who could write persuasive and relevant newsletters and pamphlets. But he also wanted my work to become the cornerstone of all publications —the ultimate voice of authority for our organization. This flattered me, of course, but I hoped it was for the content of my work rather than my personal relationship with him.

Having read through my last pile of messages, he reassured me that was not the case. He enjoyed writing, and it was not uncommon for him to edit my work before handing it over to Aaron. Aaron would type everything before he sent it off to the various liaisons and those in charge of the printing presses, but he would not make alterations or corrections to the original content. As my name was not listed on any of the pamphlets, and as our identities needed to remain confidential, both Ben and I were safe from any association with the pamphlets. There were messages being created throughout the states by various authors, but the ones produced by Ben, Aaron and myself were the only ones distributed nation-wide and which bore the same signature—a name we had come up with to demonstrate our role within society.

It was a good system, and allowed for Ben's message to continue to be shared with hundreds of thousands of people.

We were still doing high-risk activities, but there were so many other citizens nationwide doing the same thing now that we felt a little more secure in what we were doing. We were a movement of people who refused to be silenced. We were citizens who knew the risks for our actions, but we were willing to take such risks anyhow. Our message, along with the advancement of libraries and the networking of people, were all forms of rebellion against our government that only empowered us. And so we carried on, writing, publishing pamphlets, and spreading our message as best as we could throughout the country. On a non-violent level, we were building relationships and planting seeds of unity intending to overthrow our government.

The violent side was not an area I was directly associated with, but through Ben, I knew they were making gainful headway with their prison plans.

FIFTY-NINE ~ THE CALM
BEFORE THE STORM

◆ ◆ ◆

During the winter of 2043, everything fell into place. Ben had put leaving and trying to live off-grid out of his mind—or at least I believed he had, as he no longer mentioned it. He continued to work with James Dwayne and Aaron as they finalized their plans for the Washington State prisons. James Dwayne, the official 'face' of the prison guard union, had recruited hundreds of guardsmen throughout the state who were willing to work toward their common goal of mass destruction.

By the end of the year, they were ready. They had assembled all bombs that would be used, the leaders for each prison had been selected, all additional necessities had been accounted for and put in place, and the only thing left to be determined was the date on which the attacks would be carried out.

There would be no attacks until after the winter holidays—mostly because if there were any casualties, I knew Ben would not want it to happen directly ahead of them, leaving families to grieve.

And so we entered a phase of quiet waiting—the calm before the storm.

PART ~ THREE ~ 2044

SIXTY ~ THE PLAN IN MOTION

◆ ◆ ◆

It was now February in the Year of Our Lord, 2044.

22 February, 2044 was the date selected for the bombings of the Washington State prisons. It had been chosen because it was the recognized birthdate of our first President, George Washington. Ben was nothing if not a person who enjoyed a sense of irony.

He theorized that the government had no reason to believe that 'important dates' would have any significance, nor should they result in greater security measures within the U.S. He believed that the 4th of July might cause higher security measures from now on, but they had no reason to suspect that there would be further attacks. At any rate, as cautious as they might have been around the anniversaries of certain dates, there was no reason to believe they would be on high alert over a seemingly insignificant date such as our first President's birthday. It wasn't a date that most people even knew—other than it being one of the federal holidays on which they gave all government jobs the day off.

So he was confident in the date he had chosen, and even more confident in the buildings he had selected. No one would weep for dead criminals—at least, not anyone who had suffered at their hands or had a Loved One suffer because of them.

He expected, as did I, that our citizenry would find it difficult to muster any compassion or become genuinely enraged over what they were going to do. After all, it was because of such criminals that the crime and violence rates were so staggeringly high. It was because of the political climate and lack of support by government officials that it was impossible to retain enough Law Enforcement to help keep crime rates down, and it was because of sympathetic criminal justice policies that violent predators were all-too-frequently allowed back out on the streets where they continued to harm others without ever facing severe consequences.

If there was going to be public backlash for the destruction of the prisons—and the deaths of hundreds of thousands, if not millions—of convicted criminals, it would likely come from government officials and those who supported their tyrannical rule. Most others, even if they disapproved of the violence, would not be terribly concerned about dead predators.

And so, finally, the plan was set into motion.

SIXTY-ONE ~ THE MORNING OF 22 FEBRUARY

◆ ◆ ◆

The morning of 22 February, 2044 was a cold, cloudy day, but it was dry throughout the state—a rarity for February, especially on the western side of the Cascade Mountains.

Ben had visited the night before, leaving before dawn. He had shared with me he intended to drive to the Washington State Penitentiary with Aaron—despite the high risks involved. Although I felt strongly against it, and believed it to be too dangerous for several reasons, I had refrained from being critical. This was something that he and Aaron had worked on together and organized over a number of months. If they succeeded, and if even half of the prisons within the state were significantly destroyed, it would be the single greatest act of domestic terrorism ever committed on U.S. soil—far exceeding the bombings of the PLS buildings. This would also have actual casualties, albeit convicted prisoners.

Their plan was simply to observe, not take part directly. Neither Ben nor Aaron had any specific reason to visit the prison or enter the premises. Even as visitors, it would have been highly suspect if they had each arrived to visit inmates for the first time on the day of the bombings. The only legitimate way to be in the area was to observe from a distance, and hopefully from a position not covered by CCTV cameras. Given that the prison was there, it seemed unlikely they could find a suitable view of the area without being under surveillance themselves, but Ben did his best to reassure me before he left. He and Aaron had mapped out the surrounding areas and even identified routes they could take to escape from the area quickly in case things escalated. As I did not expect to be there, it was all I could do to pray they were as prepared and cautious as they would need to be.

The explosive devices selected to carry out this plan had two styles and largely depended on the assessments of the guardsmen for placement. Several locations would utilize bombs built into service vehicles that would gain entry at designated times, while others would be radio-controlled IEDs, activated through cell phones. The guardsmen in each prison had worked with James Dwayne to determine which method would be the most effective.

The usage of vehicles was easier, it seemed to me, because they could take more time with each bomb as it was incorporated into the backs of the trucks. They could also use larger explosives, and have multiple trucks per prison. The cell-phone triggered explosive devices, however, would need to be brought onto the prison grounds and then moved to various positions throughout the prison buildings. Activation would be carried out once the drivers had abandoned the vehicles, so they were not anticipating any loss of life, and none were 'suicide missions'.

The cell-phone devices would require careful handling and transport within the prisons themselves. They would need to be moved manually from the vehicles and then placed in their designated locations. It was unlikely that they would detonate prematurely, but given they would need to be carried by hand, the risk for loss of life was exponentially higher for the cell-phone devices.

There were countless dozens of guardsmen working within the prison system who were involved in this attack. They had all been carefully vetted, of course, but ultimately, it was through James Dwayne that each were screened and then assigned a role in the plan. Ben and Aaron had very little to do with the men selected for carrying out the attacks, and though this made it higher risk overall, it also helped them avoid direct responsibility. Nothing, save being at the locations of prisons during the times of the blasts, could directly incriminate them.

Despite this, Ben still intended to be present at the Supermax— even knowing the risks. Only time would tell if it was worth the chances he was willing to take.

SIXTY-TWO ~ AN UNEXPECTED JOURNEY

◆ ◆ ◆

Shortly before 8 a.m. there was a knock on my door. I never received guests, and the only people who ever visited never came during daylight hours. Panic immediately set in, and before I went to the door, I hastily looked around my compact unit to be certain there were no books or writing materials present.

I looked out through the only window in the kitchen and was surprised to see Ben standing there.

Opening the door, I asked him, "What are you doing here?"

He hadn't told me what time he was planning on being at the Washington State Penitentiary, but it was a drive which would take several hours.

"I want you to come with me," he blurted out.

I opened the door wide enough so he could pass through and looked down the stairs. He had driven the black van straight here, parking in the designated parking slot below. He had never done that before—and he had never been here in the daylight.

I stepped away from the entrance and shut the door behind me, taking the extra second to lock it.

"I don't understand—what's changed? You didn't even mention this last night or before." I was confused; he was usually well-organized and liked to plan everything down to the most miniscule detail.

He pulled me close to him, kissing me, and then held me tightly against him. I felt him sigh deeply, and then kiss my forehead as it rested against his chest.

"I don't know. I just had this feeling that I needed you to be there. I wanted you to be there. Maybe it's just nerves. Maybe I just want you to be there as part of it all—it's the biggest thing we've ever done, and you've been a part of this on a level that sets you apart from everyone else except Aaron and myself. I just wanted you to at least have the choice, and I realized I never even asked you."

I pulled away from him enough to look up into his face. He stared down at me and gave a weak smile.

"Are you afraid something will happen? Do you know something I don't?" I asked him, my fears growing.

"No, no! Of course not. Everything should be fine. We're prepared and organized. It should all be fine. I just realized I didn't want to do this without you. I want you to be there."

"I have to work, you know that." I told him.

"But you've never missed a day as long as I've known you. Surely you can call in sick."

I shook my head. "You're right. I rarely miss any work. It's probably not that big of a deal—everyone misses work at some point. And since there will not be a delivery by the Services For The Deceased, it's probably not that big of a deal. But don't you think that will raise suspicions if I miss the very day of a major event?"

He shook his head, staring at me.

"Why would it? One librarian page missing a day of work at a library almost four hours away from the event? And a female, at that? I seriously doubt anyone would think twice about you even if they inventoried every single Scourge who missed work today."

By that logic, it seemed reasonable.

"Everything will happen at 1 p.m., so if you want to go, we need to get on the road. Will you do it? Will you come with me?"

I started walking toward the living room area, grabbing my handbag and coat. Meeting him back near the door, I slipped my feet into my plain, black sneakers, and smiled at him.

"I'll need to stop at the payphone on the corner so I can phone the library and let the librarian know I won't be in this afternoon. Luckily, she's not there yet, so I should be able to just leave a message. I'll tell her I have some type of stomach flu. She won't want me there if I'm contagious and having stomach issues."

Smiling at me, Ben opened the door and motioned for me to exit ahead of him.

What we were doing was crazy—what I was doing was crazy. But I couldn't honestly say I wasn't glad to be going or to have been invited. This was my war too, and I wanted to be involved on every level. I wasn't worried about the violence of it—and I certainly would not lose any sleep over the thought of dead violent predators. We were going to the Supermax—the one location that housed the worst of the worst—men and women who had committed the most evil, brutal acts of violence that had ever been committed against our fellow citizens. If our criminal justice system was worth anything, they would have all been sentenced to death already, not just handed life imprisonment sentences because our weak government had abolished the death penalty. I was glad to go, and glad I would be there. It was a message that the world needed to hear, and I was glad to take part in sharing it.

America needed this wake-up call, and my fellow citizens needed to see that there were people out there who were willing to fight back against our government and the policies that cost so many people everything.

We were about to make history, and change the future direction of our country. I was grateful to be invited.

SIXTY-THREE ~
TIMESTAMP 1 P.M.

◆ ◆ ◆

The ride down to the Walla Walla area was pleasant, and unremarkable other than it being the longest drive Ben and I had been able to enjoy together. It was also the furthest away from home that I'd ever been, and I was surprised to see how much the landscape changed from Western to Central and then to Eastern Washington. We passed through desert regions and finally into farmland, a drastic contrast from the greenery and rainforest quality climate I had always known.

Aaron intended to meet us there, and had made plans to drive separately. It wasn't a matter of convenience, as he did not live too far away from either of us. We could not have picked him up along the way. It was, instead, a matter of security. If Ben were pulled over, he would already have to explain why he was on a road trip so far away from his home with a librarian page in a van owned by the Services For The Deceased. This issue would have only been magnified if Aaron had been with us as well. Neither of them could justify my presence, but at least Ben and I worked in the library sector and could fabricate a suitable reason we were together. Aaron had no connection to either of us professionally, and they would only find one between Ben and Aaron if they investigated them in greater depth.

It was a lovely ride. I enjoyed every moment I could spend with Ben, always, and it was so rare that we could meet during the daytime or even outside of my dwelling unit. We filled the time with conversations about our favorite authors and the content of their books. Even though he had not been around his father since his childhood, his memories of him had still influenced how he processed reading and employed critical thinking about everything he read, fiction and non-fiction alike. Conversations with him were never dull; he always had new questions to ask, or would volunteer a new perspective I had not noted or considered. I enjoyed our talks, and I loved how he challenged my mind. But I also adored listening to him; he was a wonderful communicator and was both knowledgeable and impassioned about all that he read and believed in. Our drive to the prison was over much too quickly.

I learned how Ben had been to the Washington State Penitentiary once before, doing a reconnaissance mission where he met up with Aaron and James Dwayne. Because the Supermax would be the largest target, and because they wanted to ensure the explosion was adequate enough to destroy the entire compound to rubble, they had worked collectively together on the plan. It would not be easy to pull off, and there was a fairly high chance that there would be at least one casualty among the guardsmen or staff who were innocent.

Another factor that would need to be considered was regarding explanations for why only inmates were killed. The only viable solution, according to James Dwayne, was to create a mandatory union meeting for the time frame when the bombs were expected to go off, thus isolating all guardsmen in one centralized location and ensuring they were not in the blast zones. This would, and could, save a lot of lives, but it still seemed an inevitability that the follow-up investigations would cause government officials to target the guardsmen afterward. Ultimately, they all entered this with an expectation of one day being caught, and so they faced it head on, accepting whatever fate befell them.

It was entirely possible that the explosions would be so vast that all evidence was obliterated, as it had been with the PLS bombings. This would be ideal, but no one was going to count on it.

There would be thorough investigations made of every prison that was hit—and probably even the ones that failed to detonate or which claimed the lives of guardsmen during the act itself.

I was saddened by the possibilities—good men being sacrificed unnecessarily or things going wrong. There should not be any casualties on our side if they could avoid it. I hated the notion that we would lose men who believed in our cause just because we couldn't guarantee their safety or because they would need to be sacrificed.

But I reminded myself, as I did at every turn when people took action, that they were involved by choice, that they were aware of potential risks, and they believed in what they were doing enough to move forward despite the loss of freedom or loss of life they might face if they were ever apprehended or in danger. We were soldiers. This was war. We were doing dangerous things for reasons we believed to be significant enough to be worth the risks. It wasn't my place to decide what people were willing to put on the line, just as it wasn't my place to ask anyone to do anything they weren't prepared to do.

Before long, we pulled into a parking lot with an assortment of small businesses. Ben drove toward the back end of the parking area and slowed down almost to a complete stop. Ahead of us, Aaron emerged from a large metal building, and a rolling garage door slowly opened next to him. Ben circled around and then backed into the empty stall next to another work vehicle—the Department of Ecology truck Aaron typically drove. Once we were safely inside, the garage door closed behind us, blocking out more and more daylight as it lowered. Aaron stepped back inside through the adjacent door, locking it behind him. There were long halogen lights hanging overhead, and windows lined the back of the building.

Ben and I exited the van and greeted Aaron warmly. He nodded to the stairs, telling us we could see parts of the prison through the windows from the second floor.

The timestamp signaled it was about a half an hour before 1 p.m.

SIXTY-FOUR ~ NO-SHOW

◆ ◆ ◆

We followed Aaron up the stairs to the landing above. It wasn't much of a second story—it was little more than a catwalk along the back wall of the building with one enclosed room at the far end—an office of sorts, with a window overlooking the shop and a closed door. But the elevated position gave us ample room to view the high walls of the penitentiary across the street from us. From this angle, we could see the tops of buildings over the edges of the cement walls and the barbed wire protruding along the top. We couldn't risk using a drone to see over the penitentiary walls because they were shot down and investigated if it happened. Drones had long since been commissioned by convicts to fly in drugs and other contraband, and prison air space was restricted. I imagined that if we were expecting a sizeable explosion, the walls surrounding the prison wouldn't be much of a barrier, as we would likely see a more vertical blast.

Just as we reached the landing, there was a hard knock on the external door previously used by Aaron. Ben and I looked sharply at one another, and I was certain I appeared panicked.

Aaron held up his hand, putting a finger to his mouth, motioning for us to be silent.

"It's probably just James," he said, and began walking down the stairs and then toward the door.

I looked furtively around, but there was nowhere to go, and nothing to hide behind. We were visible from the door and had absolutely no cover. Ben took a step toward me and took my hand in his. The look on his face was calm, and I know he intended for his touch to be reassuring. But the moment of panic had taken hold already, and I began feeling a deep sense of foreboding.

Maybe this was too dangerous. Maybe this wasn't the right way to go about things. Maybe the risks were too high, or they weren't in our favor. Nothing had been in our favor for many years.

All of these dark thoughts flashed through my mind in the moment it took Aaron to walk from the stairs to the doorway, and then open the door. My fight-or-flight response was almost a physical reaction at that second, and I was certain I would have tried to flee or hide had Ben not been holding my hand.

But my fears were unmerited as I watched Aaron step aside, allowing James Dwayne to enter. Aaron locked the door once again, and we could hear the two men engaging in a lively discussion, but couldn't hear their words.

Ben, taking an interest, began walking back down the stairs. My hand still resting in his, I followed him.

Something wasn't right.

"What's going on?" Ben asked, directing his question to James Dwayne.

"One of the guys didn't show up. No reason, no notice. No one has heard from him and no one can reach him by phone. He just no-showed for his shift." James Dwayne responded, clearly concerned.

"And this is out of character for him?" Ben asked.

James Dwayne nodded his head. "He's always been reliable. He wouldn't just no-show—not for work and not today."

"What do you think happened to him?" Ben asked. His tone was level, but his grip had tightened considerably as he held my hand.

James Dwayne shrugged his shoulders and Aaron held up his hands as if to say, "Don't ask me; I don't know what's going on". It wasn't looking good.

With a grimace, James Dwayne started talking again. "I don't know what's going on, but something isn't right. He wouldn't just disappear. He wouldn't miss work, and he knows we needed him today."

"So he knows about the plan and was involved. This wasn't just some guardsman; he had an active role in things?" Ben questioned.

Both men nodded.

"What was he supposed to do? Can you proceed without him?"

Ben looked down at the watch on his wrist.

"What did he need to do? We've got fifteen minutes."

"He was designated to drive one of the trucks to the far end of the compound. Even if I rearrange drivers, I'm still short one man."

Ben let go of my hand and sighed.

"OK, let's go."

"Ben, no!" I gasped. Aaron began to respond, but Ben held up his hand and stopped him.

"We don't have time to discuss this. Either you go or I go," he said.

Aaron nodded once, agreeing with Ben without another word. He made no effort to take his place and instead took a step backward so the two men could leave.

James Dwayne made his way to the door, and Ben turned toward me. He took my face into his hands and kissed my lips softly. Slowly. Staring into my eyes, he told me not to worry. Then, with a kiss on my forehead, he turned and left the building without another word.

For a long moment, I stood there, staring at the locked door. There hadn't been time to argue, there hadn't been time to convince him not to go, and neither of the other men had offered an alternative. Would it have really been so awful if they just didn't have one area covered by explosives? Most of the inmates would still be dead. If the whole point was to deliver the message, it would be done after the bombings, regardless of how effective they were.

With a heavy step, I followed Aaron silently back up the stairs and toward the windows.

SIXTY-FIVE ~ CONTINGENCY

◆ ◆ ◆

We did not speak as we stood there. We just waited.

I thought of all the reasons a guardsman would not show up for work on the day when he was most needed. My paranoia immediately went to the bleakest thought possible—that he had been compromised. I thought of how they could have caught him—how any of them could have been caught. They could have been on the radar from clear back during the months when everyone was acquiring the ingredients for the bombs. After the PLS bombings, surely they had assessed how they had been made and would have investigated all the ways such materials could have been acquired. If that were the case, then every single guardsman involved throughout the state who had been involved in their acquisition could have potentially been compromised.

There could have been guardsman missing from every one of the prisons today—but because there had been no time devoted to investigate this, and assuming everyone responded in the same hurried manner that James Dwayne had, we would never know until it was too late.

I couldn't help but feel they had proceeded too quickly instead of pausing everything and reassessing the way things stood. They should have postponed. They could have called it all off, rescheduled for another day, coordinated things with the other guardsmen and other prisons. Looked for patterns. Discovered if there were other missing guardsmen who had no-showed. They could have simply waited.

But the one thing I couldn't ever recall hearing Ben, Aaron, or James Dwayne discuss was a contingency plan. They hadn't faced obstacles before that would have resulted in a disruption to their plans; Ben and Aaron had pulled off the PLS bombings with no issues.

But this was decidedly different, and without question, more dangerous. There were hundreds of moving parts that had needed to be arranged, including working with the guardsman. More people meant more risk, more chance of being found out, more possibilities for betrayal. It was decidedly different to recruit guardsmen than it was to have volunteers from the movement. The guardsmen were oath-takers; they had an obligation to our Constitution and citizenry that required they be men of honor. Blowing up government property and killing thousands of criminals was hardly something they should readily embrace. The fact that they could not be Scourges was also worth weighing out; they were men who were employed by the same government that we Scourges were asking them to destroy. We could have been set up by James Dwayne, or turned in by a hundred guardsmen. Trusting any of them may have been our worst mistake, and yet we had eagerly moved forward with the opportunity when it presented itself.

Had they spent just a little of their time working on a suitable contingency plan—a plan they were dedicated to following at the slightest sign of problems or unforeseen variances—then Ben wouldn't have ran off so hastily to step into the missing guardsman's shoes just to ensure that everything continued on.

I was worried. Far more worried than Aaron seemed to be, or at least more so than he was letting on.

A contingency plan. That was all they had needed, and it was the one thing they hadn't planned for.

Deep inside, the feeling of dread continued to grow.

SIXTY-SIX ~ BLAST ZONE

◆ ◆ ◆

The explosion rocked the entire building, rattling the windows and shaking the ground beneath our feet. In a single instant, we were met with a deafening blast and a plume of smoke that filled the air as far as the eye could see. A series of echoes sounded in the distance—the series of blasts set off by each of the individual trucks. The sky filled with grey dust which began falling back toward the ground and covering everything in sight.

It was tremendous to watch, and was the single greatest event I'd ever experienced, even with a partially obstructed view as I looked onward through the buildings and over the prison fence line. For a long moment, the two of us just stood there, awed by the magnitude of the blast.

The silence that followed did not last, however, as the sound of sirens filled the air. The response time seemed almost instantaneous.

How could first responders have already arrived? How had they received any calls or reports and arrived all within moments of the blast occurring? It didn't make any sense.

No one had attempted to gauge the response times for Law Enforcement, to my knowledge, because it shouldn't have mattered. As soon as the explosives were put into place, the men responsible for placing them were supposed to leave the prison grounds immediately, whether they had been the ones driving vehicles into specific areas surrounding the prisons or the ones responsible for putting the devices into designated locations within the walls of the prisons. This was partially why so many men had been necessary—men had needed to have access to the prison to gain entry and had therefore required other guardsmen to be on duty to give them access.

As such, none of the men who had actually touched the bombs or took part in the blasts should have been on the grounds. The only people who should have been there were those who had been assigned to work that day, whose absences would have been noted during the investigations which were to follow.

The sirens were almost upon us.

Where was Ben? Why wasn't he back yet? He should have left the area before the blast even happened.

I could hear the sirens approaching closer and closer, and within seconds, vehicles and flashing lights could be seen through the buildings that stood between us and the now decimated walls surrounding the prison yard. Blurry figures quickly emerged from the vehicles, yelling loudly over the sirens.

I turned from the window, intent on leaving—running toward them, just to get close enough to see what they were doing, why they were yelling.

Aaron grabbed my wrist, his eyes pleading with me not to go, to just wait and see.

I knew then, looking at him, that he, too, feared exactly what I feared—that Ben was compromised, that he had somehow got caught still on the prison grounds, and that he and other men were the reason the police were yelling.

Pulling myself away from Aaron, I ran toward the stairs and the door, fear and blind panic leading the way.

SIXTY-SEVEN ~ THE UNKNOWN

◆ ◆ ◆

I struggled, trying desperately to unlock the door, unable to control the shaking of my hands as I twisted the lock. Finally, it gave way, and I yanked the door open. I looked around quickly, scanning the parking lot area for any signs of Ben or even police vehicles, but the entire area was vacant. I heard Aaron clamoring down the stairs behind me. I ran from the garage before he could catch me or tell me not to go.

I ran straight across the parking lot to the edge of the next building, allowing me time to collect my thoughts and think about what to do. I needed to get to the backside of the garage—closer to the two buildings behind it that I had looked between.

There were several vehicles parked alongside the building, so I kept low and traveled in a zig-zag fashion between them until I was finally at the back end of the garage. The two buildings were straight ahead, and each had several cars and trucks parked along their brick walls.

The sirens of the police cars filled the air, but there was another siren off in the distance that wailed louder than all of them. I thought it must have belonged to the prison—an alert system, perhaps, designed to issue warnings.

Smoke and grey ash filled the sky, covering everything in a layer of grey dust and making it difficult to breathe. As I crouched down between vehicles, I tried to catch my breath, using my forearm to cover my mouth and nose.

I was only about thirty feet from the closest police vehicle—a car, its driver's side door left open, no police officer visible. I could see parts of other vehicles as they crowded the roadway between the buildings where I hid and the mountains of rubble that once served as a barrier between the prison and the outside world.

I could hear dozens of voices shouting—all men, and echoing throughout the buildings, making it difficult to visualize where they were. The further into the distance I looked, the harder it was to see; there was so much debris and dust within the prison perimeter that it was impossible to tell how much wreckage there was or if any of the voices were coming from within. I was close enough now I could see the flicker of flames in various areas where fires raged. Black smoke billowed into the sky.

I had to get closer.

There were still a few cars toward the edge of the buildings, so I used them as cover, and crept along the inside space between the wall of the building next to me and the cars. Whatever the police were doing, they weren't right in this area. It seemed like they were trying to get past the rubble of the fence line and into the prison area, but unless I could get closer so I could have better visuals, I couldn't be certain.

I was careful as I maneuvered not to touch anything or leave any fingerprints. I pulled my sleeves down over my hands and kept them balled up tightly just to help remember. By now, there was enough dust covering everything that even resting my hand on the top of a bumper or the trunk of a car would leave a definable handprint. Any fingerprints would be impossible to explain—I would immediately be incriminated simply for being in this area today. There would be no other explanation for why I was so far away from home.

I crept closer and wedged down small and tight between a car and the edge of the building. I could see dozens of police vehicles, including several large S.W.A.T. trucks, black and armored. Off in the distance, near the area where the high fence used to be, heavily armed police officers hid behind vehicles, handguns and rifles all pointed toward the prison. A S.W.A.T. team of six men lined the backside of one of their trucks, wearing tactical gear, weapons drawn.

I could not see what they were all shouting at; there were too many vehicles, too much smoke, and mountains of rock and chunks of cement rubble everywhere.

I heard a noise behind me and felt something brush against the back of my jacket. Turning, Aaron was there, crouched down alongside me, finger to his lips, reminding me to be quiet. I had not heard him until he was right behind me—a dangerous thing to realize when I could have easily been discovered by one of the police officers.

I turned my head toward the road again. Something caught my eye as I scanned the roadway—it was the members of the S.W.A.T. team signaling one another as they broke formation and move toward the prison.

We stayed there, crouched down, waiting, watching. The police who had arrived so quickly were now doing nothing except hiding behind the doors of their vehicles, guns drawn, lights on, some with their sirens still going.

Within a few moments, we heard heavy shouting, and then gunshots—dozens of shots all fired off in quick succession. It sounded like a battlefield.

Almost against my will, I tried to stand, a scream caught in my throat.

Aaron pulled me back down, and I struggled against him.

"We have to go!" he whispered angrily behind me.

"No! We have to find him! We have to wait for him!"

"We have to go now! If we don't leave now, they're going to lock this entire area down and they'll search every building. We have to leave now!"

"I can't. We can't leave him!" I pleaded.

I looked at Aaron and realized he was almost a complete stranger to me. I didn't know him. I didn't trust him. I needed Ben.

"We need to go. We need to be ready to leave. Maybe he's made his way back to the shop by now. We can check and wait for him there. But we can't stay here. It's too dangerous."

Tears in my eyes, I nodded. I knew he was right. I felt bile rise in the back of my throat. Turning around, I followed Aaron as he crept along between the cars and the wall. I wanted to tell him to be careful not to leave any fingerprints, but no words came out.

As if on auto-pilot, I followed Aaron back to the shop. He crouched, I crouched. He paused, I paused. He ran, I ran.

And then we were back at the shop, through the door, resting in the darkened room. I coughed into my sleeve for several moments, the dust in the air outside having made it difficult to breathe.

"Where is he?" I asked desperately. I could hear the hysteria rising in my voice.

We had no contingency plan. We had made no plans to meet later—he had left so suddenly we had not even discussed how or when he would return. We didn't know if he was leaving the area with James Dwayne, if he was stuck on the prison grounds with all the rest of the guardsmen and any survivors from the blast, or if he had fled the area in one of the vehicles that had been in the prison parking lots. We had no way to contact him, and he had no way to contact us.

"We can't stay here. We have to leave. You have to come with me."

"I can't just leave him! We don't know where he is! He could need our help!"

"And what are we going to do?" Aaron asked. "Think about it! We're sitting ducks here! They're going to close off this entire area and we're going to be trapped in here until they find us! And they will find us, eventually! They will search these buildings and lock down this entire area. We're going to be gone, or we're going to be trapped in here right alongside the van Ben drove down here."

I covered my mouth with my hands, my throat tightening as I tried not to cry.

"Look," Aaron said, more calmly. "He has his vehicle here. He has his keys. If he's safe—if he left the area in another vehicle, or if he managed to get out of the prison through another exit, he'll be able to come back here and get his vehicle. Or he can hot-wire a car—he's a smart guy—he knows how to survive. But I'm telling you, we can't stay here. He wouldn't want you to stay here and risk getting caught, and he wouldn't want me to let you. You need to come with me. We need to leave now."

Tears spilled out of my eyes, and I nodded my head. He was right. We needed to go.

Trying hard not to cry, I allowed Aaron to lead me to the passenger side of his Department of Ecology truck. He motioned for me to climb onto the sidestep, and then shut the door behind me once I was safely inside.

I was numb. My mind was racing, but my heart was breaking. Every worst fear I had was happening, and I could do nothing to control any of it.

I watched Aaron through the side mirror as he went to the door, opened it, and the peeked around. I could only assume he was checking to see if there were any police vehicles around, or perhaps he was hoping to see Ben coming. But then he shut and locked the door once again, and made his way to the driver's side.

Once he was sitting, he used a button on a small plastic square to open the rolling garage door behind us. We waited for the door to open wide, and then he backed us out slowly.

"You should keep your head down," he told me.

Without even questioning him, I leaned over sideways, my head resting in the middle of the long bench seat.

I listened to the sounds of the sirens as they faded, heard the ticking of the blinker as Aaron changed lanes and turned down streets, and listened to the rumble of the V8 engine as he drove.

The more distance he put between us and the prison, the heavier my heart got, and the more tears I cried.

Beside me, I could hear Aaron occasionally sigh deeply, and once, just for a second, I felt his hand gently touch my head.

Neither of us spoke, each lost in our own thoughts and drowning in the possibilities of grief.

SXTY-EIGHT ~ AFTERMATH

◆ ◆ ◆

At precisely 1 p.m. on 22 February, 2044, the ground shook throughout the state of Washington as twelve prisons were reduced to rubble. More than a half of a million inmates, convicted of all manner of crimes, died that day.

Among the casualties were eleven Washington State guardsmen, including their state union leader, James Dwayne, who had been shot dead while trying to flee the scene after the Washington State Penitentiary bombing. Alongside him in the passenger seat, a scientist named Benjamin Granger was also shot and killed. Trapped within the prison parking lot after the explosion and police arrived, James Dwayne had attempted to drive a service truck through the rubble, only to be stopped by the surrounding S.W.A.T. team and dozens of other members of Law Enforcement who had all arrived within moments of the blast.

James Dwayne decided for both himself and his passenger that he would rather die than go to prison himself or face the death penalty.

The government wasted no time denouncing both James Dwayne and Benjamin Granger as domestic terrorists, and hailed the other deceased guardsmen as innocent victims caught in the blast. They could have died in all the gunfire we heard, but no one would ever know the truth of the matter. There was only one story being told, and the government was narrating it. Anyone who knew what had actually occurred that day was dead, had disappeared, or was never known to have been there.

James Dwayne and Benjamin Granger would live on in infamy, given full credit for orchestrating and carrying out each of the prison attacks.

For reasons we could only assume to be political, and driven by the desire to downplay the magnitude of the attacks, the guardsmen who had worked at each of the prisons the day of the explosions were all cleared of any wrong-doing. They determined that James Dwayne, having had access to each of the prisons because of his position within their union, had successfully worked with Benjamin Granger and planted explosive devices throughout each of the prisons over a period of months, and then detonated them all remotely in one synchronized attack.

It was explained to the American People that there were so few casualties among the guardsmen on duty that day because James Dwayne had scheduled a meeting for all personnel. And so, at 1 p.m. on 22 February, 2044, the prisons had been cleared of all guardsmen as they all convened in designated areas far away from the zones where inmates were housed. The eleven who died at the Supermax could not attend the meeting because of protocol, and James Dwayne had apparently considered this an acceptable range for collateral damage. I believed Law Enforcement shot the guardsmen while they tried to escape, but it would never be verifiable, and no one could contradict the lies set forth by the investigators except Aaron and myself—neither of which could ever admit to being in the area.

They demonized Benjamin Granger in the press. They branded him a domestic terrorist, used his education in science to explain how he knew how to build explosives, and painted him to be an anti-American with sociopathic tendencies. As ugly as they were, they never linked him to the underground movement he had created, nor did they link him publicly to the PLS bombings.

Throughout all of this, Aaron and I kept to ourselves, and kept quiet. We did not speak for many weeks after the bombing, and I was left to grieve alone. No one knew what I had lost—who I had lost. No one knew my heart had been ripped out of my chest, that I had lost my only friend and the lover I had given my heart to. I suffered in silence, mourning the loss of someone that I had both known intimately yet did not know at all in the eyes of the world.

In the weeks that followed, I struggled to keep my emotions under control, especially at work. The day after the attacks, when I arrived at work, the head librarian had said I still seemed very ill, and as she did not want me around anyone if I were contagious with a stomach bug, sent me home. I called in sick the next day, and she told me to stay home for the rest of the week. I did not argue.

There was only one night which broke the monotony of the hell I was trapped in. There was a light tapping on my door well after midnight, almost two full weeks after the attacks. For one heartbeat, I imagined it could be Ben—that the news and government investigators had gotten it all wrong, and he was safe. But I knew this was not possible—how else could they have learned his name unless they had recovered his body? Even I had not known his last name.

With the recklessness of grief, I opened the door without even bothering to see who it was. It didn't matter—it could have been the police, or government agents, coming to take me away, taking me to disappear. Nothing they would have done could have been worse than what I was already suffering through. At least if it were them, my suffering would have an end.

I had assumed it would be Aaron, who had learned where I lived when he had dropped me off after that endless drive back home. But it was not him, either.

Instead, I found Officer Ren standing at my door, in uniform. His vehicle was parked down below. I opened the door wide, allowing him to enter.

He stood there for a moment, simply staring at me. I dared not look at him for fear of crying. I was always crying now. I couldn't sleep, I wasn't eating. I knew I looked exhausted, and I could not stop myself from crying from one moment to the next. Grief was a terrible companion, made even worse when no one knew one was suffering.

I closed the door behind him, and pulling my sweater tightly around me, tried my best to look at him without breaking down.

His eyes said everything he as a stranger could not. We had one link between us, and now he was gone. He and I had nothing else to connect us, just as I had nothing to connect me to Aaron anymore.

Officer Ren sighed heavily, and then pulled me into his arms, holding me close against him and stroking my hair as if I were a child.

I cried.

I wept with the suffering of one who had never been loved and knew I would never be loved again.

I wept for the lost future we might have shared, the plans we had made, and the promises we had whispered to one another in the quiet of the night. I wept for the one who had kissed me tenderly, stared into my eyes, who had whispered sweet words into my ears, and who, with just a wink and his precious smile, had filled my heart with joy. I wept for all that we had lost, and all that we could never be.

And through it all, Officer Ren held me, saying nothing, but sharing in my grief. He, too, had lost someone, and between us, we were shattered.

SIXTY-NINE ~ THE HARSH REALITY

◆ ◆ ◆

I spent a lot of time alone during those first few months following Ben's death. I worked, shopped when necessary, and stayed home. Spring arrived, and the days grew longer and warmer, but I barely noticed. I seldom left my small dwelling unit. I understood I was grieving, but I was also coming to terms with the sickening reality that there was no one in the world who cared about me or even knew I existed. I was alone —far more alone than I had ever felt before Ben had entered my life. Now, something was missing. Someone was missing. Now, every night was filled with never-ending cycles of exhausted sleep and the nightmares which inevitably followed. My days were long and painfully slow. I went days at a time—sometimes even a week or more—without talking to anyone. I was a shell of a person, living an empty, meaningless, and valueless life. No one cared if I was alive or dead. Ben was gone, and there was no one else. I was nothing more than a carcass—a piece of meat waiting to die and rot back into nothingness.

He was never coming back to me.

He was gone.

It was during the quiet of the night that I could not help but think of him, and it was then that the darkness seemed endless. There was nothing with which to soothe my aching heart— no words, no book, no song, no well-meaning friend, no poetic verse. He was lost to me, and I was bereft. His time had been cut short, and all that remained was an empty space beside me and deep within—a space that I was certain would always remain empty and reserved just for him. It was then, in the quiet, in the dark, that I wept with an anguish that had no words, a pain so deep that only God could understand.

He was gone.

He was never coming back to me.

I would never hear his soft voice again, never feel his hand over mine, never feel him bring my fingertips to his lips to kiss them, and never see him smile and wink at me. He would do none of those things because he was dead.

He was dead because he had chosen to leave me to go do something without taking the time to think things through, dead because he had not chosen to delay everything, to wait until he knew all of the facts. He was dead because he had blindly put his faith and trust into James Dwayne, and never considered that the reason the guardsman who no-showed would have done so because he had been compromised. He could never have imagined the reason, never could have known it was because the guardsman had been reported to Law Enforcement by someone who overheard him bragging when he was drunk about what he was going to do, and once he was arrested, he had confessed everything he knew. Ben was dead because some loudmouth drunk couldn't keep a secret, and for that reason, the police knew what was going to happen, and thus had been waiting on standby for the attack.

None of the lies mattered. All the lies they told only reaffirmed that nothing reported by the investigators or government officials could be trusted, and all information stemming from the various government agencies was nothing more than pieces of fiction designed to placate and distract the American People.

They reported nothing with honesty, including what they said about Ben. They said such awful, terrible things about him. As much as I couldn't stand to hear what they said, I could not help but watch and listen. Ironically, their constant analyzation of who he was as a man was comforting to me. They showed photographs of him—just a few, and none with him smiling or looking happy. But they showed his university ID photograph and the picture from his work pass, and to me, being able to see his face and hear his name was better than nothing. At least people remembered him. At least they knew he had existed.

I was drowning in darkness and self-pity.

I saw nothing ahead of me but years of stifling work under the heel of those who believed themselves to be my betters, with nothing changing except the seasons and the lines on my face.

I had no hope anymore. I was suffocating under the weight of my memories and negative thinking.

SEVENTY ~ LEGACY

◆ ◆ ◆

It was not until June 2044 that I had contact with Aaron again. I did not have the means to contact him other than to visit his cabin, and as I did not drive, it was impossible. If he had a phone, I did not know the number, and I did not have one in my dwelling unit, so he would have needed to visit if he were to attempt to contact me.

But eventually that was exactly what happened, and I was rather surprised by it. He simply showed up one night—well after ten in the evening, since the days were now getting longer and it wasn't getting dark until after 9 p.m. I was not expecting anyone. The last visitor that had been to my home had been Officer Ren. He had stopped by several times since that first night just to check in on me, but he did not stay long and he always arrived near midnight, and only on nights he worked. The last time he had visited, he had brought me copies of the two photographs of Ben that had been used by the media in their reports. He told me that all the police departments had copies of them; he just wanted to make sure I could have something to remember him by.

I could have told him I saw his face every time I closed my eyes, that I was haunted by the look on his face as he prepared to leave me that day, or that I could see him lying next to me as we fell asleep side by side, but all of that was too painful. And so I had smiled and thanked him for his efforts. I knew he was grief-stricken as well, and his visits were more than just checking up on my well-being—he was searching for a connection to someone who had known and loved the boy he had all but raised as well.

But this time, when there was a knock on my door, I knew it was different from how Officer Ren knocked, and I was immediately on guard. I wondered if it was Law Enforcement or government agents finally there to take me away, having connected me to Ben at long last.

But it wasn't. It was only Aaron.

Aaron, who had let his best friend and partner walk out the door without a single discussion. Aaron, who had allowed his best friend to travel into an unknown situation with a man Ben had barely known, to go drive a vehicle that countless other guardsmen on site could have stepped up to do. Aaron, who had been responsible for introducing James Dwayne to Ben, and whom he clearly did not know was a complete psychopath who had thought Suicide By Cop was the best way to handle things when backed into a corner.

Such were the dark thoughts in my moments of silent rage, fueled by my heartache and never-ending self-pity.

I knew I was being unfair. I knew I could not blame Aaron for choices that Ben himself had decided to make. I knew, ultimately, that it was Ben I was most angry with. Ben and Aaron had both determined that their lives were too invaluable as leaders to take unnecessary chances with the bombings, and yet Ben had chosen to go instantly toward the danger when presented with the need.

Aaron had been Ben's best friend, and Ben had been an adult who had made his own decisions. I was angry—especially at Aaron—but I was also rational enough to understand that even though Aaron had not volunteered to go himself, Ben had not given the slightest indication that he would have preferred it be Aaron rather than himself. I knew that Aaron had not spoken up because Aaron was not the true leader of the pair—he took his lead from Ben, and when Ben made decisions, Aaron did not question them. As much as I wanted to, Aaron was not to be blamed. Ben had done exactly what Ben felt he needed to do, and he would probably never have changed the events as they occurred if he had known to do so would have endangered Aaron or claimed his life. Ben alone was responsible for the decision to go, and I could not hate Aaron for it. I couldn't even hate Ben, even though it had cost him everything.

We were at war, and war had casualties.

Still, Aaron was here, and Ben was not. That alone made it difficult to see him.

But I invited him in, and we sat in my small living room—me on my sofa and he in the chair that Officer Ren had last occupied months earlier.

He seemed different; more subdued. Neither of us made much eye contact. I imagined seeing me was no easier today than the last time. There was much left unsaid between us, but I don't think either of us was willing to open the channels of communication regarding Ben. I wondered, for the first time, if Aaron felt any guilt or personal blame for Ben's death, and if he had avoided me because seeing me suffering compounded his guilt.

"You've been following the news?" he asked.

I nodded. I had a small television in the corner.

"You know they've pinned everything on Dwayne and Ben? They've basically denied that any other guardsmen were involved, despite how ludicrous and improbable it seems."

I nodded again.

"They're blaming him for building all the bombs himself. They said he must have worked on them for a year before the attacks, and said James Dwayne planted all of them. Twelve different prisons, hundreds of miles between some of them, but they've convinced the people that just two guys pulled it off. It's garbage reporting!" He spit out the words, full of disgust.

"What would you have them do? Report that there were dozens of guardsmen involved at each location? Public hangings in the town square?" I asked. Surely it was better that so many guardsmen had their lives spared rather than being found out and punished.

He shook his head and ran his hand through his hair, exhaling deeply.

"No, of course not. But it's a level of propaganda that only proves just how manipulative and false our government is. You know as well as I do he built none of the bombs used in these attacks. He wasn't even directly responsible for any of the PLS attacks. I mean, yeah, sure, he was trained just like I was initially, but he wasn't the one doing the work after we trained that first group of zone leaders. Man, that seems like forever ago now..."

I stared at him, too exhausted to argue, too sad to hash out why our government had used Ben as their scapegoat.

"They're all trying to say he learned how to do this because they educated him in the sciences and because he held a PH.D. But anyone who's studied the same program knows it's not true —he would never have learned how to make explosives that way. People know this, but because it's being reported, we're all supposed to accept it as gospel. No one is supposed to question any of it. We're all just supposed to buy this story they're narrating, no matter how fictitious it presents."

Well, that was certainly true, but nothing would change whether we believed the stories—regardless of what we knew ourselves to be true. It was also likely, I knew, that they would use this as a steppingstone to implement more restrictions on The Scourge. They would say that 'in order to ensure public safety and reduce the threat of domestic terrorism, no Scourges should be allowed to work or get educated in the sciences, or hold PH.Ds, or work in fields that allowed access to any potential bomb-making materials. I did not doubt in the least that the government would use this 'national tragedy' to impose more restrictions and openly create further bigotry and discrimination against Scourges; it was what they had always done.

Never let a tragedy go to waste.

Our nation had a lengthy history of this very Cause/Consequence routine, and they never missed an opportunity to create more laws that further reduced the rights of the citizens. This would be no different.

"Anyhow," he continued. "It's time to get busy again. That's why I'm here. I need your help."

I laughed, a little more hysteria rising than I had expected.

"Are you kidding me? What could you possibly want to do? What's left?" I asked.

"Well, you've heard all the narratives being put forth by the news—but do you know what the people think? Have you been listening? Have you been able to talk to anyone?"

I shook my head, sorrow overwhelming me once again. I sat on the sofa, little more than a rack of bones. I had dark rings under my eyes, and I was incessantly on the brink of tears. I wasn't out there having conversations with anyone; I didn't know anyone. The only person I had known had been gunned down by a squad of militarized "Peacekeepers".

"Well, the people aren't buying any of it. They're asking questions that no one has answers to. We need to share everything with them that we can. We need for them to know that they're right to be suspicious and distrustful of the narrative."

"Like what? And how do you know?"

"Because they're all talking—everyone, everywhere. No one is buying the stories anymore. Everyone has questions that aren't being answered. They want to know how two men managed to pull it off. The math isn't adding up, and neither are the other details.

"They're trying to figure out how Ben could have accessed all the components he would have needed for the devices—how he could have acquired some of the ingredients that would have needed to be regulated by the government. They're saying that it would have been impossible to get materials, especially after the PLS bombings, when everything should have been under much tighter security.

"They're questioning how Ben could have managed to find the time to build all the bombs, travel all over the state, and then plant the bombs. Supposedly, he did all that while still working a full-time job in a lab, and doing part-time work for the Services For The Deceased. And all without ever missing a shift.

"And that doesn't even cover the questions about how Ben could have pulled it off when he didn't even have a valid reason or right to access any of the prisons. Even if he gained access to the prisons with the help of James Dwayne, they still would have needed to coordinate a lot of different trips to meet up at each of the prisons. If the two of them really had planted all the bombs together, then there would be plenty of evidence to show they were both together.

"The people are wondering where all the proof is to show that Ben accessed the prisons. They're looking at photographs of the prisons and questioning how many bombs would have needed to have been planted in each prison in order to create the damage they did. Some prisons had four to six different bombs planted. They're wondering how two random men could have planted sixty-plus bombs all over the state.

"People are even saying that the government knew he was a terrorist, but they let him do it. They think there wasn't a downside to blowing up the prisons, and the government just let it happen."

"Well, that part's probably true enough," I said bitterly. "It seems pretty clear they had the missing guardsman ahead of time and just let it happen. They were on scene far too quickly afterward to not have been tipped off."

Aaron nodded in agreement. "Exactly. And yet they allowed the attacks to happen. Even if they only knew about the Supermax, they still let it happen. Why, though? Maybe they really just don't care about human life. Maybe they didn't care about protecting the lives of violent predators enough to stop it from happening. Maybe they just let Ben and James take the fall, but they were happy enough to let them do their dirty work."

"Well, even if that's the case, there's not much that can be done about any of it. We can't clear Ben's name without incriminating dozens of other people. We can't even say we were there, or that the other guardsmen probably died by gunfire rather than in the blast like they're trying to say happened."

"True enough," he replied. "But we can still get the messages out there. We can still write about it. We can get the same statements out there and spread the truth from coast to coast. We can give the people a reason to question their government and fight back."

I laughed—a short, angry burst of noise that revealed all too plainly that I had no faith in anything, least of all in the people rising against our government.

"Look, I know where you're coming from," he told me. "But I need you. The people need you. Ben's people. People that you were writing for. We all need you. Just because Ben's no longer here doesn't mean the movement is gone. It's gained more support since the bombings than ever before. It's no longer ours. It's no longer a secret."

"What do you mean?" I asked. How could it not be a secret anymore?

"The people are rising. Not against the government, per se, but against the system. People are defending Ben. They're defending James Dwayne. They're supporting what they did. The news isn't allowing it to be covered, but people are talking. They're vandalizing buildings in every major city—tagging Ben's name. Calling him a hero. Calling him a martyr. Saying he took action against the crime and violence throughout our nation that everyone else was afraid to tackle. People are speaking out—they're demanding change."

"Change how?" I asked. It was too crazy to believe. Everything on the news painted Ben and James Dwayne out to be evil, violent, sociopathic.

"Changes to our current system. They're rallying behind what Ben and James did because they're saying that our government has failed to protect the people. They talk about how our Law Enforcement numbers have tanked in the last couple of decades, and about how violent crime has sky-rocketed. They talk about how women aren't safe on the streets, how they can't go anywhere alone, how they can't go out at night without being raped and killed. They talk about how women and girls are disappearing every day, how the abduction, rape and murder rates have become a national crisis. They talk about the lack of response by Law Enforcement and the criminal justice system for rape and domestic violence cases."

I stared at him in disbelief. Could it really be true? Could Ben's death really have started this chain reaction?

"They're not just talking about how the cities aren't safe anymore, or how there's never any Law Enforcement around to respond to calls. They're talking about how the criminal justice system is releasing too many predators and repeat offenders back out onto the streets—about how they're just going back out and committing more violent crimes. They're demanding Sentence Reform. They're saying that Ben was a hero for blowing up the buildings—that killing all the violent offenders and career criminals was the best thing to happen to America in decades."

For the first time in months, I felt something stir within me. It was faint, but it was the slightest ember of hope holding on. I had thought I had lost everything, that there was nothing left to live for, that the years ahead of me were all going to be long, empty, and meaningless. But this was something. This was new. It was the possibility of purpose. The chance to still create change. A means of giving value to the sacrifice Ben made and the price he paid. Something to make it all worthwhile—to give light to the movement he began years ago, and share his vision of the world he wanted to live in.

"The people care. They're speaking out. For the first time in decades, people are speaking openly and freely about the state of the union—about the discrimination, the bigotry, the hate directed at The Scourge. They're defending Ben for rising against the government and the broken criminal justice system that was protecting criminals more than victims. It's hard to imagine because the news is still doing their best to pretend this movement doesn't exist and it isn't spreading like wildfire, but it's true. People everywhere are speaking out. They've had rallies and marches demanding Sentence Reform. They're carrying posters with pictures of Ben. They're refuting that he was a domestic terrorist, and saying the Founding Fathers would have been proud of him for standing up against the tyranny we've all been living under."

It was too much—it was all too much to comprehend.

"But how do you know all this? None of this has been mentioned on the news."

"Well, it wouldn't be, would it? If they want him to be an enemy of the state, they've got to control the narrative. But people are rising up everywhere—there are websites put up and then taken down by the government censors every day. They're tagging his name in graffiti everywhere. We've got people in every major city now, and they're all reporting the same thing. And these aren't just our people—they aren't even Scourges talking—it's everyone. Everyday citizens from every background imaginable. Different zone leaders are giving me updates non-stop from every single state."

He looked at me, gauging my response, seeing how receptive I was to all of this new information.

"Look, I know you're still grieving, but I need your help. I'm overwhelmed. I'm getting reports every day—almost on the hour—from coast to coast, and they're looking for new information. They want a firm statement from us—they've been recycling your old messages, reprinting, and redistributing. They said the flyers are everywhere—completely out in the open now. They're finding them on benches, in grocery stores, even pinned to poles on street corners. They can't keep up with the demand for more information, for more messages. Zone leaders want something new—something that can affirm that our movement is backing Ben's actions—even if no one knows that Ben was our original leader. I need your help. I need some new material."

I nodded my head, feeling part of me coming back to life, feeling Ben encouraging me to do once more what he had always wanted me to do—to get involved, to spread his message, to fight.

I didn't know what else to do but try. At least by writing, by putting his message into words for the whole world to see, they could know what sort of man he truly was. And maybe I wouldn't be able to share with anyone that the two men were one and the same. Maybe they would never get to know that the leader of the underground movement of libraries and the founder of our national uprising was the same man they had branded a domestic terrorist. But I would know. And maybe someday I could share this with the world, and they would begin to understand just what a tremendous human being he had been. Maybe by writing and carrying on with his mission, we could create the changes within our own government and society that he had been so passionately driven by. At the very least, by writing for him and sharing his vision, I would be keeping his memory alive, and I could help others feel the connection to him that I had been so fortunate to experience.

Maybe it was time for action. The only way we could ever truly know if the people were ready to rise was to show them it was possible, that there were citizens out there willing to lead the way and stand with them. We couldn't hope to create change without taking a stand, and we couldn't hope to reform our nation unless we all stood together and fought for the changes we needed. No one was going to do it for us. Our government had proven that they didn't value human life through every national mandate, discriminatory law, lax criminal justice policy, and their mistreatment and devaluation of our Law Enforcement and military. Maybe We The People really did have enough power to make a difference if we all rose against it and stood together.

Looking at Aaron, and for the first time in months feeling as though I had something worth fighting for, I nodded my head.

I thought of Ben, the man that he was, the man that he could have become, and the world he had been fighting for. I thought about all that he had done during his brief time here before death took him. I thought of the dedication to freedom, to knowledge, and to the country that he loved so much he was willing to die trying to restore it.

I considered all that he had blessed me with, how he had given me not only the gift of my own free thought, but the blessings that came with being brave and selfless. I thought of the legacy that he had left behind, the lives he had impacted through his desire to share the written word of our ancestors, and how he had wanted nothing more than to see all Americans free once again—free to choose their own path.

I thought of the baby he had left growing inside of me, and the world that he or she would be inheriting from us if we did nothing to change things. And I was reminded of the words of Thomas Paine—words that were invaluable, and never more relevant: "I prefer peace. But if trouble must come, let it come in my time, so that my children can live in peace."

I would honor his legacy and pick up his fallen torch. Not only for our child, but for all children to come.

SEVENTY-ONE ~ THE CROSSROADS SPEECH

◆ ◆ ◆

Fellow Americans,

We come to you today with heavy hearts. Although we wish for it to be very different than it is, there is little point in denying the current state of the nation or the unbearable weight of the problems contained within.

We are no longer at a point where we can speak of matters as we 'wish' for them to be; we have passed that window of time and must now make the concerted effort to either create the changes that we long to see in our country, or we must accept the state of the nation as it is, and henceforth submit to every abysmal, immeasurable dysfunction and misdeed.

When the writing is on the wall, only those who are willfully ignorant and intentionally in denial refuse to admit it. It has now reached the point of necessity when all good, law-abiding Citizens must take a full and careful measure of the state of the nation in which they are living. We must engage in a fully-comprehensive evaluation of all relevant social issues, the Criminal Justice system, and its heavy toll on our society. We must address the persistent, undeniable social decline of our Citizenry through the degradation of our moral and ethical standards.

This evaluation must be done with the same level of candid thoroughness one should use when contemplating whom to choose from among us to represent the American People through our election process, and should be done without bias or ill-will. Every Citizen should spend time in thoughtful contemplation and with a sincere heart, weighing all evidence one considers to be relevant for their evaluation. It will only be through such inward self-reflection that the truth of the matter will be manifested to each of us with each conclusion being entirely subjective and uniquely our own. There are no right or wrong answers to these questions. We ask only that Citizens address these issues to the best of their ability and with their own personal beliefs, standards, and desires in mind.

Is this the America that our Founding Fathers dreamed of, and imagined would exist in the future? Is the America we are living in today the best version of America that we can achieve? And is this the America that we wish to pass on to our Children and our future generations?

Is this truly "the Greatest Nation on Earth" anymore? Or has America deteriorated into such a cesspool of Savagery, Violence, and Lawlessness that we can no longer distinguish ourselves from other 3rd world nations?

America has no room for Citizens who believe in the principles currently being promoted by our lawless government. Every Citizen is at risk because of the policies set forth by the current regime, and those who support this administration are betraying the American People and the very foundations upon which this nation was built. All those who stand on the side of the Savage Predators, the Sex Offenders, the Career Criminals, and the Illegal Invaders have made the choice to stand against their own Countrymen, and the security of their nation. They have chosen to defend the worst among us at the expense of our Children and our most Vulnerable Citizens. We must ask ourselves if they are the types of neighbors and Citizens we are willing to continue sharing our nation with.

America is standing at the crossroads. How we proceed will determine the trajectory of our future, and the state of the nation that we will leave for our Children and future generations.

No matter how we choose to present these facts and circumstances, there are several truths which will remain undeniable and unavoidable. If Americans are going to prevail, we can no longer be a nation of pacifists, naysayers, or truth-deniers; we must come to terms with the reality in which we live.

If we choose to take the path of conscious denial, we risk everything. The restoration of our faith and values is already predicted to be a brutal upward battle because we have taken the path of least resistance for too long already. Continuing to deny the existence of our problems and their sources will only hurt us further, and hinder our ability to self-correct before it's too late.

Whether we choose to act or not, we are making a choice. Apathy, inaction, avoidance, or denial, by hell or highwater, all will still create and produce results, and those results will create change.

Inaction is a choice, and no one that chooses to remain silent today should have any illusions or expectations regarding what sort of reaction their apathetic indifference will cause tomorrow.

We must acknowledge that we are no longer safe among our own Fellow Man. The bitter reality is that we never were. But we are no longer living in a time where we can afford to live with naivety, optimism, and delusional denial about this subject.

There is no middle-ground anymore, and no one can choose neutrality. Failing to choose to fight for one's nation and future is choosing to submit to tyranny and die.

It is the slow hemorrhage as one watches first his neighbors bleed out, then his family, and then finally, himself.

The Wolf is at the door.

Those who make deals with criminals and corrupt politicians

will reap the costs soon enough. But is it fair to expect equal consequences by those that are loyal to our Constitution, the Rule of Law, and our Heavenly Father?

Those who wish to dismantle the foundation of our nation have worked diligently for decades doing everything within their power to deconstruct all that our Founding Fathers and our Framers envisioned and created. Their agenda is the antithesis of what America was intended to be. Our Founding Fathers created this nation not only for themselves, or based on what type of world they themselves wished to live in, but for The People, and for every American that would follow after them, reaping the endless bounty and protections that their hard work and determination brought to fruition.

We have endured years of Civil Unrest and the intentional disruption of peace throughout our country by those who intend only to destroy all that we are. For too long, the American People have quietly watched as violent predators tore apart our nation, murdered our Innocent, and targeted our Law Enforcement. We have watched as they clogged our Criminal Justice system with perpetual criminality and recidivism at our expense. We have sacrificed our privacy and freedom in order to establish extreme laws to curb such lawlessness and destruction. These laws are only necessary because of those who cannot, and will not, abide by the Rule of Law and the social rules of civility upon which every civilized nation and People exist.

It has never been the intention, nor the Will of the People—the rightful Patriots and ancestors of this great nation that adhere to the principles of our Founding Fathers—to evoke political strife, disharmony, or a Second Civil War. The People of These United States have demonstrated long-standing positions of patience, tolerance, and self-control regarding the continuous, unyielding deterioration of the nation they hold so dear.

Only through the unified rising of our individual voices will we begin to implement the changes necessary for our nation to prevail against these dark forces which seek to destroy us from within. Every voice counts, including the Victims who have been silenced forever due to the Violence inflicted upon them by their Fellow Citizen.

The time for apathy is no more. The time for action, accountability, and justice is upon us. Let no man ever find cause to reflect upon his time granted here on earth and second-guess his own indecisiveness or lack of action. God has not only provided each of us with the unalienable right to self-protection, He has commanded that we Love our Neighbor as Ourselves. This means we have a duty to Protect and Defend the Sanctity of Human Life.

We have an inherent obligation to protect those who cannot protect themselves.

We are Mortal Beings with a Divine Purpose. Let no man squander the Time and Gifts he has been granted only by the Grace of God. Take up arms, my Fellow Citizens. The time to reclaim our nation is upon us.

The Watchers On The Wall

On this date, the Fourth of July
In the Year of our Lord, 2044

MARA O'REILLY

EPILOGUE ~ FOR BEN

◆ ◆ ◆

Invictus

Out of the night that covers me,
    Black as the pit from pole to pole,
I thank whatever gods may be
    For my unconquerable soul.
In the fell clutch of circumstance
    I have not winced nor cried aloud.
Under the bludgeoning's of chance
    My head is bloody, but unbowed.
Beyond this place of wrath and tears
    Looms but the Horror of the shade,
And yet the menace of the years
    Finds, and shall find me, unafraid.
It matters not how strait the gate,
    How charged with punishments the scroll,
I am the master of my fate,
    I am the captain of my soul.

~William Ernest Henley

BOOKS IN THIS SERIES

THE WATCHERS ON THE WALL

The Scourge Of The Earth

RELEASE DATE: 2022

The Last Stand

COMING SOON IN 2023

The Great Reformation

COMING SOON IN 2023

BOOKS BY THIS AUTHOR

The Scourge Of The Earth

BOOK ONE
OF
THE WATCHERS ON THE WALL
SERIES

The Measure Of A Man

BOOK ONE
OF
THE SANCTITY OF LIFE
SERIES